INTRODUCT

1. GENERAL

1. THE book now presented to English readers has never been translated before: not only is this so, but the very existence of it has remained unknown to the great mass of students for over three hundred years, although it was printed no less than five times in the course of the sixteenth century.

What is it, and why is it worth reviving after so long a period of oblivion? It is a Bible history, reaching, in its present imperfect form, from Adam to the death of Saul. It has come to us only in a Latin translation (made from Greek, and that again from a Hebrew original), and by an accident the name of the great Jewish philosopher of the first century, Philo, has been attached to it. Let me say at once that the attribution of it to him is wholly unfounded, and quite ridiculous: nevertheless I shall use his name in italics (*Philo*) as a convenient short title.

Its importance lies in this, that it is a genuine and unadulterated Jewish book of the first century--a product of the same school as the *Fourth Book of Esdras* and the *Apocalypse of Baruch*, and written, like them, in the years which followed the destruction of Jerusalem in A.D. 70. It is thus contemporary with some of the New Testament writings, and throws light upon them as well as upon the religious thought of the Jews of its time.

2. HISTORY OF THE BOOK

2. (*a*) The HISTORY OF THE BOOK, as known to us, can be shortly told. It was printed by Adam Petri in 1527, at Basle, in a small folio volume, along with the genuine Philo's *Quaestiones et Solutiones in Genesim* and a fragment of the *De Vita contemplativa* (called *De Essaeis*). These were followed by the *Onomasticon* (*de Nominibus Hebraicis*) ascribed in Philo, in Jerome's version, and a Latin rendering of the *De Mundo* by Guillaume Budé. The whole volume is in Latin, and was edited by Joannes Sichardus: for the first three tracts he used two manuscripts, from Fulda and Lorsch, of which more hereafter. In 1538 Henricus Petri (son of Adam) reprinted this collection in a quarto volume, which I have not seen, and in 1550 included it all in a larger collection of patristic writings called *Micropresbyticon*. In 1552 our book (without the accompanying tracts) was printed from Sichardus' text in a small volume issued by Gryphius at Lyons, under the title *Antiquitatum diversi auctores*, and in 1599 in a similar collection *Historia antiqua*, by Commelin, at Heidelberg, edited by Juda Bonutius.

During the sixteenth and seventeenth centuries Philo was read and occasionally quoted, *e.g.* by Sixtus Senensis in the *Bibliotheca Sancta*, and by Pineda in his treatise on Solomon: but the greatest critics and scholars of the eighteenth and nineteenth centuries seem never to have seen it. J. A. Fabricius would certainly have accorded it a place in his *Codex pseudepigraphus Veteris Testamenti* if he had read it: and very little escaped his notice. He does speak of it in his *Bibliotheca Graeca* (ed. Harles, IV. 743, 746), but only from the point of view of the editions. It is not too much to say that the chance which kept it from him has kept it also from the flock of scholars who have followed him like sheep for two hundred years. The first investigator to pay any attention to it seems to have been Cardinal J. B. Pitra. In the *Spicilegium Solesmense* (1855, II. 345 note, III. 335 note, etc.) there are allusions to it: in the later *Analecta Sacra* (II. 321; 1884) he printed the Lament of Jephthah's daughter from a Vatican MS. of it, treating it as a known work, and referring to the printed edition.

In 1893 I came upon four detached fragments in a manuscript at Cheltenham, in the Phillipps collection, and printed them as a new discovery in a volume of *Apocrypha Anecdota* (1st series, Texts and Studies, II. 3). No one who reviewed the book in England or abroad recognized that they were taken from a text already in print. At length, in 1898, the late Dr. L. Cohn, who was engaged for many years upon an edition of Philo's works, published in the *Jewish Quarterly Review* an article in which the source of my fragments was pointed out and a very full account given of the whole book, with copious quotations. This article of Dr. Cohn's is at present our standard source of information. Nothing to supersede it has, so far as I know, appeared since. A few scholars, but on the whole surprisingly few, have used *Philo* in recent years, notably Mr. H. St. John Thackeray in his book, *The Relation of St. Paul to Contemporary Jewish Thought*.

(*b*) Can we trace the history of *Philo* further back than the printed edition of 1527 by means of quotations or allusions to it? The whole body of evidence is remarkably small. At the very end of the fifteenth century Joannes Trithemius, Abbot of Sponheim, writes a book, *De Scriptoribus ecclesiasticis*, printed at Paris in 1512. On f. 18*b* is a notice of *Philo*, derived principally from Jerome, and a list of his writings. Among these he includes *De generationum successu*, lib. I. (which is our book), and adds the opening words: *Adam genuit tres filios*, which shows that he had seen the text. It is the *only* item so distinguished in all his list. Then, going back and setting aside certain extracts from the text (of which we shall speak under the head of authorities), we find, in the twelfth century, Petrus Comestor of Troyes, in his *Historia Scholastica* (one of the famous text-books of the Middle Ages), making a single incorrect quotation from our book (V. 8). He calls his source 'Philo the Jew, or, as some say, a heathen philosopher, in his book of questions upon Genesis': the words show that he was quoting a manuscript which contained that work as well as our text. His quotation is borrowed by several later mediaeval chroniclers.

In the catalogues of monastic libraries *Philo* is of rare occurrence. The Fulda catalogue of the sixteenth century has "Repertorii noni ordo primus, liber Philonis antiquitatum 36." The number 36 is the older library number, perhaps as old as the thirteenth century, which was written on the cover of the volume. This was one of the two manuscripts used by Sichardus: we shall return to it.

In the twelfth century a monk writes to the Abbot of Tegernsee for the loan of the "liber Philonis." In 831 the abbey of St. Riquier, near Abbeville, has in its catalogue "liber Philonis Judaei unum volumen." Both these references may be found in Becker's *Catalogi*.

One possible hint, and one only, of the existence of *Philo* in the Eastern Church is known to me. The *Taktikon* of Nicon, cap. 13, in the Slavonic version, as quoted by Berendts (*Zacharias-Apokrypken*, p. 5, note 3), reckons among the canonical books of the Old Testament "the *Palaea* (the Eastern text-book of Bible history comparable to the *Historia Scholastica* in the West) and *Philo*."

The *Decretum Gelasianum* of the fifth or sixth century condemns, among many other apocryphal books, "liber de filiabus Adae Leptogeneseos." The natural and usual interpretation of the words is that they refer to the *Book of Jubilees*, which the Greeks called ἡ λεπτὴ γένεσισ, but it is worth noting that *Philo* mentions the daughters of Adam in the first few lines, whereas in *Jubilees* they do not occur before the fourth chapter.

I know of nothing in earlier centuries which looks like an allusion to *Philo*, unless it be a passage in Origen on John (Tom. VI. 14.) in which he says: "I know not what is the motive of the Jewish tradition that Phinees the son of Eleazar, who admittedly lived through the days of many of the Judges, is the same as Elias, and that immortality was promised to him in Numbers (XXV. 12)," with more to the same effect.

He refers to no book, but to a tradition which is, in fact, preserved in several Midrashim. The identification is found in *Philo*, c. XLVIII. See the note *in loc*.

3. AUTHORITIES FOR THE TEXT

3. The next business is to describe the AUTHORITIES FOR THE TEXT of *Philo*.
(*a*) We will take the printed edition of 1527 first (of which the four others of 1538-50-53-99 are mere reprints). Its symbol shall be **A**. In his preface, addressed to the monks of Fulda, Sichardus, like many editors of the Renaissance period, tells us but little of the manuscripts he used. The substance of what he says is as follows. At one time he had hoped to be able to remedy the many corruptions of the manuscripts, of which he had two; but he gradually came to despair of doing so, and resolved to give the text as he found it. His two manuscripts were as like each other as two eggs, so that he could not doubt that one was a copy of the other, though they were preserved in libraries far apart. He employed the Fulda copy, and had previously obtained the use of one from Lorsch Abbey, which was very old, and had expected that these would provide the materials for a satisfactory edition; moreover, he had got wind of the existence of another copy. But his manuscripts proved disappointing, and he is well aware that the present edition is inadequate. In preparing it he has aimed at following his manuscripts as closely as possible, and in issuing it now has judged that the evils of delay are greater than those of haste; especially as he looks forward to putting forth a greatly improved text in the future.

(*b*) We have seen that the Fulda MS. is traceable in the library catalogues late in the sixteenth century. Until lately it was thought to have been lost, along with the bulk of the Fulda MSS.: but it has been identified, first by Dr. Cohn, and then, independently, by Dr. P. Lehmann, with a MS. at Cassel (*Theol.* 4° 3) of the eleventh century. The Lorsch MS. still remains undiscovered.

The identity of the Cassel MS. with that used by Sichardus is not doubtful. In its cover is an inscription by him stating that he had it rebound in 1527. It also retains the old label, of the fourteenth century, with the title *Liber Philonis Antiquitatum*, and the old Fulda press-mark.

The book which furnishes this information is a special study, published by, Dr. Lehmann in 1912, of the libraries and manuscripts used by Sichardus for the purpose of his various editions of ancient authors. Dr. Lehmann has collected, *à propos* of Sichardus's *Philo*, notices of all the MSS. of the Latin *Philo* known to exist, and has succeeded in increasing the number, from three which were known to Dr. Cohn in 1898, to sixteen, eleven of which contain the text of the Antiquities. They are as follows-

Admont (an abbey in Austria) 359, Of cent. xi., containing *Ant.* and *Quaest. in Gen.*
Cassel, theol. 4° 3, of cent. xi. (the Fulda MS.), containing *Ant.* and *Quaest.*
Cheltenham) Phillipps 461, of cent. xii, from Trèves, containing *Ant.*
Cues (near Trèves), 16 (or H. II), Of 1451, paper, containing *Ant.* and *Quaest.*
Munich, lat. 4569, of cent. xii., from Benedictbeuren, containing *Ant.* and *Quaest.*
Munich, lat. 17,133, of cent. xii., from Schäftlarn, containing *Ant.* and *Quaest.*
Munich, lat. 18,481, of cent. xi., from Tegernsee, containing *Ant.* and *Quaest.*
Rome, Vatican, lat. 488, of cent. xv., containing *Ant.* and *Quaest.*
Vienna, lat. 446, of cent. xiii., containing *Ant.*
Würzburg, M. ch. f. 210, of cent. xv. (paper), containing *Ant.*
Würzburg, M. ch. f 276, of cent. xv. (paper), containing *Ant.* and *Quaest.*

Besides these, there are at Augsburg, Florence, Rome, Trèves, MSS. containing *Quaest.* only, and at Coblenz one of which no particulars were forthcoming.

For the purposes of the present volume only four of the above authorities have been employed, namely, the Fulda-Cassel MS. as represented by Sichardus's edition (and with it we must allow for some use of the lost MS. from Lorsch), the Cheltenham, Vatican, and Vienna MSS. The fact that Dr. Cohn was known to have in contemplation a full critical edition precluded others from trying to cover the whole ground, and, even had it been otherwise desirable to do so, the investigation would have been very difficult for anyone outside Germany. There are, for instance, no printed catalogues of the Admont, Cassel, or Würzburg libraries.

However, the paucity of authorities here brought to bear is of little importance. What Dr. Lehmann tells us is sufficient to show that none of the MSS. present a completer text than we already know. All must go back to an ancestor which was already mutilated when our first transcripts of it were made. Upon this point more will be said. At present we will take account of what Dr. Lehmann has to say of Sichardus's MSS., and proceed to the description of the MSS. actually used, and of some subsidiary authorities.

Of the Fulda MS. we now learn that it is the work of more than one scribe, of the eleventh century. The *Antiquities* occupy ff. 1-65*a*, and have a title in a late medieval hand: *Libri Philonis Iudei de initio mundi*, which, or the like, is "usual in the MSS." The *Quaestiones*, entitled (in the original hand): *Filonis Questionum in genisi et solutionum*, follow on ff. 65*a*-89*a*, and in them is a noteworthy feature. On f. 86, in the middle of the page the MS. omits, without any sign of a break, a long passage containing the end of the Quaestiones and the beginning of the *De Essaeis*, and corresponding to pp. 82, l. 40-84, l. 16 of Sichardus's edition. At this point Sichardus has a marginal note: "Here the copies differed, but we have followed that of Lorsch, as being the older." Now this same gap is found in most, if not in all, of the other MSS., and not all of these are copied directly from the Fulda MS. We may say, therefore, that all MSS. showing this gap are independent of the Lorsch MS., but not necessarily dependent on the Fulda MS.

It is clear from what has been said that Sichardus was wrong in regarding the Fulda MS. as a copy of that of Lorsch, and that the latter represented an old and valuable tradition: and, further, that he exaggerates greatly when he says that the two MSS. were as alike as two eggs. Dr. Lehmann's final remark is that the disappearance of the Lorsch MS. is very much to be deplored, for, judged by the Greek fragments and the Armenian version of the *Quaestiones*, it represented a better tradition than all the extant Latin MSS.

Of the other MSS. in the list given above, it may be observed that the Cues MS. (written at Gottweih in 1451) and the two Würzburg MSS. are not likely to be of very much value: and that, of the three Munich MSS., that from Tegernsee (18481) is to all appearance the parent of the other two. Probably the monk who wrote to Tegernsee to borrow a Philo (see p. 10) was a member of Benedictbeuren or Schäftlarn. The Schäftlarn copy (17133) was written between 1160 and 1164.

I now proceed to give a detailed account of the three complete MSS. which I have been able to use, and of certain subsidiary authorities. The three MSS. are those mentioned by Dr. Cohn in his article, and I have been led to examine them during recent years by my interest in the text, and without serious thought of using them for the purposes of an edition. They are the copies preserved at Cheltenham, Vienna, and Rome.

P. The Phillipps MS. 461 is a small vellum book (6 5/8 x 4 3/4 in.) of 124 leaves, with 20 lines to a page; a few leaves palimpsest, over not much older writing. It is of cent. XII., clearly written: on f. 1*a* the provenance is stated, in this inscription: Codex SX (?) *Sci. Eucharii primi Trevirorum archiepi. siquis eum abstulerit anathema sit. Amen.* A hand of cent. XV. adds the word *Mathie*. Then follows the title, of cent. XV.: *Philo iudeus de successione generacionis veteris Testamenti*. On f. 1*b* is Jerome's account of Philo (*de virr. illustr.* c. XI.): the text of the book begins on 3*a*: *Adam genuit*, and ends on 119*b* without colophon. It is followed by a few pieces of medieval Latin verse, of no great interest. The first begins; *Carnis in ardore flagrans monialis amore*. Another is on Chess: *Qui cupit egregium scacorum noscere ludum Audiat. ut potui carmine composui*.

V. Vindobonensis lat. 446, a small folio of 53 leaves, with 31 lines to a page, in a tall, narrow, rather sloping hand, doubtless German, by more than one scribe: of cent. XII. late or XIII. early. There is an old press-mark of cent. XVI.: XI°. 68. The text is preceded by *Jeronimus de Phylone in catalogo uirorum illustrium*. It begins *Incip. Genesis*. INITIUM MUNDI. *Adam genuit*, and ends on 53*a* without colophon, occupying the whole volume.

R. Vaticanus lat. 488, of cent. XV., in a very pretty Roman hand, in double columns of 35 lines. The first 8*c*, leaves contain tracts of Augustine, Prosper and Jerome. Our book, to which is prefixed the extract from Jerome, begins on f. 81. It is headed: *Genesis*, and begins: *Inicium mundi. Adam Genuit*. The colophon is: *Explicit ystoria philonis ab initio mundi usque ad David regent*. It is followed by the *Quaestiones et Solutiones in Genesim*, which occupy ff. 129-148 (end). The arms of Paul V. and of Cardinal Scipione Borghese the librarian are on the binding: there is no other mark of provenance.

P is thus the only one of the three manuscripts whose old home can be definitely fixed. It belonged to the abbey of St. Eucharius, otherwise called of St. Matthias (whose body lies there), just outside Trèves.

(*c*) Next come certain manuscripts which contain extracts from the text.

Ph. The Phillipps MS. 391, Of 92 ff., of cent. XII. early, contains principally tracts of Jerome, notably *Quaestiones Hebraicae*. On ff. 87-8 it has the four extracts which I printed in 1893 (see above). It belonged to Leander van Ess, and has an old press-mark C I or C 7.

T. No. 117 in the Town Library at Trèves. A paper MS., dated 1459. It contains five of the same tracts as Ph and two of the extracts from *Philo*. It retains its old press-mark, B II, and an inscription showing that it belonged to the abbey of S. Maria ad Martyres at Trèves. The contents of the book and the text of the extracts make it clear that T is a copy of Ph or of a sister-book, while the form of the press-mark shows that Ph and T belonged to the same library. Thus T is only important as helping to "place" Ph.

F. MS. McClean 31 in the Fitzwilliam Museum, Cambridge (fully described in my catalogue of the McClean MSS.), is a remarkable copy of the *Aurora*, or versified Bible, of Petrus de Riga. It is of cent. XIII., and is copiously annotated. Among the *marginalia* are many extracts (a complete list will be found at the beginning of the Appendix on various Readings) from *Philo*, uniformly introduced under that name, and for the most part abridged. The manuscript may have been written in the Rhine Provinces, or in Eastern France.

J. The Hebrew *Chronicle of Jerahmeel*, edited in an English translation by Dr. M. Gaster (*Oriental Translation Fund, New series* IV., 1899), was compiled early in cent. XIV. somewhere in the Rhineland. It contains large portions of Philo, some *in extenso*, some abridged. A list is given in the Appendix. Dr. Gaster will have it that the Hebrew is the original text; but Hebraists do not agree with him, and it is, in fact, possible to show that the Hebrew writer was translating from Latin, and from a manuscript which contained misreadings common to those we now have. See the Appendix of Readings on III. 10, VII. 3.

(*d*) Glancing back over the list, we see that for all but one of the items a German origin is established. The Vatican MS. is the exception, and even this presents certain indications of German origin. Near the beginning of the book (III. 3) is a speech beginning *Deleam*. R reads *Vel eam*. Now it is a habit with German scribes of the twelfth and thirteenth centuries to write their capital D's with a sharply-pointed base, making the letter very like the outline of the conventional harp, and also very like a capital V; nor do I know any other script in which the likeness between D and V is so striking. My guess is that the scribe of R, encountering the puzzling letter near the beginning of his work, made the mistake, which he does not repeat; and I regard it as an indication that his archetype was a German book of the same age as V (and, I may say by anticipation, presenting a remarkably similar text to that of V).

Thus the geographical distribution of the authorities combines with the evidence of the literature to show that in the Middle Ages *Philo* was circulated within very narrow limits, and practically confines those limits to Germany and Northern France.

(e) Of these authorities I have transcribed A, collated P (on the spot), and R (from a photograph) in full; have examined and partially collated V (on the spot), and have transcribed Ph, T, and F: J is in print, and I have collated that also.

The complete copies which are known to us are all ultimately derived from a single imperfect ancestor. All exhibit the same *lacunae*. The text, as we have it, ends abruptly in the midst of Saul's last dying speech: "Say to David: Thus saith Saul: Be not mindful of my hatred nor of my unrighteousness." How much further the story went we shall discuss later on. That it is imperfect is clear, and all our copies agree in the imperfection. Two other obvious *lacunae* occur about two-thirds of the way through the book, in the story of Abimelech. After the death of Gideon (XXXVII. 1) we read that "he had a son by a concubine who slew all his brethren, desiring to be ruler over the people. Then came together all the trees of the field to the fig-tree, and said: Come reign over us." Thus we pass from the first entry of Abimelech to a point somewhere in the Parable of Jotham. I think we must assume that at this place a leaf was missing in the ancestor of all our copies. None of them make any attempt to fill the gap. At the end of the story of Abimelech is another bad place (XXXVIII. 1): "After these things Abimelech ruled over the people for one year and six months, and died (under a certain tower) when a woman let fall half a millstone upon him. (Then Jair judged Israel twenty and two years.) He built a sanctuary to Baal," etc. The words in parentheses represent the supplements of P. The text as read in A would imply that Abimelech built a sanctuary to Baal; but it was in fact Jair who did so. Here, then, is another gap, the extent of which is uncertain. The immediate successor of Abimelech in the Bible is Tola. Our historian may or may not have noticed him: he does, later on, omit one of the minor judges, Ibzan. At most, another leaf is wanting at this point: at least, a few lines have been lost by casual damage.

There are, further, indications that the imperfect archetype was an uncial MS. with undivided words. In the early pages of the book much space is occupied by lists of names, which, being invented by the author, could not be corrected by recourse to the Bible. The many disagreements as to the divisions of the names (*e.g.* Sifatecia Sifa. Tecia, Lodo. Otim Lodoothim, filii aram filiarum, etc.) point to a stage at which the scribe had no guidance in this matter. So do such variants as memoraret artari for memorare tartari, in chaoma tonata for in chaomate nata. Again, in XIX 15 certain unintelligible words (istic mel apex magnus) are written in capitals in V, which I interpret as an attempt on the part of the scribe to represent exactly the *ductus litterarum* of an ancestor.

A minuscule stage is evidenced by frequent confusions (in proper names) of *f* and *s*, of *c* and *z*, of *ch* and *di*, and an occasional *r* for *n* or the converse. This last error, were it more frequent, might point to an "insular" ancestor somewhere in the pedigree. There is an a priori likelihood that a rare text current in the Rhenish district would have attracted the notice of Irish monks and have been preserved by them. A closer study of the variants may perhaps confirm this notion.

External and internal evidence combined lead me to the conclusion that our text was preserved in a single imperfect copy written in uncials, and containing the *Antiquities*, the *Quaestiones in Genesim*, and *De Essaeis*, which had survived at some centre of ancient culture in the Rhenish district, most likely in or near Trèves.

(*f*) The authorities used in this book fall into three groups: (1) Lorsch and Fulda, represented by the printed text, which I call A; (2) The Trèves group P, Ph, T; (3) VRFJ. This is a rough division. Sichardus gives us no means of distinguishing readings peculiar to either of his MSS. and, as we have seen, is probably wrong in saying that they were very closely allied. The Trèves MSS. are in more frequent agreement with A than VR. V and R, if not parent and child (and probably they are not) are at least uncle and nephew. Generally speaking I am of opinion that, though manifestly wrong in a number of small points, A is preferable to any one of the complete MSS. that I have seen.

It will be readily understood that, in an edition like this, a complete exposition of the evidence for the text is impossible: but by way of illustration we will take a short passage for which all our authorities except J are available, and in which the grouping is (if imperfectly) shown. The Song of David before Saul (LX. 2 *sqq.*) runs thus in APPhTVRF. A is taken as the basis.

Tenebrae et silentium erant (erat RF) antequam fieret seculum, et locutum est silentium et apparuerunt tenebrae.

Et factum est tunc (*om.* tunc RF) nomen tuum in compaginatione extensionis quod appellatum (+ est VRFPhT) superius coelum, inferius vocatum (invocatum. V) est terra.

Et praeceptum est superiori ut plueret secundum tempus eius (suum F) et inferiori praeceptum est (praec. est inf. F: *om.* praec. est R) ut crearet escam omnibus quae facta sunt (homini qui factus est VRF).

Et post haec facta est tribus spiritum uestrorum (nostrorum F).

Et nunc molesta, esse noli tanquam secunda creatura (factura VRF).

Si comminus memoraret artari in quo ambulas A.

Si comminus memorarer artare, etc. PPhT (artare rather obscure in T).

Si quominus memorare tartari (tractari R) in quo ambulabas VRF.

Aut non audire tibi sufficit quoniam per ea quae consonant in conspectu tuo multis (in multis VRF) psallo?

Aut immemor es quoniam de resultatione in chaoma tonata (in chaomate nata VRF) est uestra creatura?

Arguet autem tempora noua (te metra noua VRF) unde natus sum, de quo nascitur (de qua nascetur VRF) post tempus de lateribus meis qui uos donauit (domauit P, domabit PhTVRF).

VRF here show themselves the best in some important readings. The first (*homini* for *omnibus*) is the least obvious: but it will be quickly seen that the point of the invective is that evil spirits are a secondary creation, and particularly that they are inferior to man. If not actually created after man, at least they came into being after the earth, which was to supply food to him. Moreover, a similar variant occurs early in the book (III. 2), non diiudicabit spiritus meus in omnibus (AVR: hominibus P) istis, The LXX of Gen. 6, ἐν τοῖσ ἀνθρώποισ τούτοισ, shows that P is right.

But VR (F is rarely available) are not uniformly successful. They sometimes shirk difficulties. In IX. 13 Moses "natus est in testamento dei et in testamento carnis eius" (*i.e.* was born circumcised). Here VR read "in testamentum carnis, which makes nonsense: and a few lines later, where it is said of Pharaoh's daughter: "et dum uidisset in Zaticon (sc. διαθήκην) hoc est in testamento carnis," the whole clause is omitted by VIZ.

In III. 10, we have "et reddet infernus debitum suum, et perditio restituet *paralecem suam.*" This is the obviously right reading of AP: VR read *partem suam*, and J betrays itself not only as a version from Latin, but as dependent on a Latin MS. allied to VR, by saying "and Abaddon shall return its portion."

When Pharaoh has determined to destroy the Hebrew children, the people say (IX. 2): "ὠμοτοκείαν (ometocean cett.) passa sunt viscera mulierum nostrarum." All the authorities, including F, keep the strange word, but V writes "Ometocean id est passa sunt," showing that at some stage there was an intention to insert a Latin equivalent. Still, the word has survived.

The shirking of difficulties is not confined to VR. The priestly vestments, *epomis* (XI. 15) and *cidaris* (XIII. 1), become *ebdomas* and *cithara* in AP, but not in VR. In a list of the plagues of Egypt (X. 1), one, *pammixia*, is omitted by AP and retained by VR. This word *pammixia* (panimixia in the MSS.) deserves a passing note, for it does not seem to have made its way into dictionaries or concordances. It is intended to mean the plague of all manner of flies, for which the LXX and Vulgate equivalent is κυνομυια, *coenomyia*. Jerome, writing on this, says it ought to be κοινομυια, signifying a mixture of all manner of flies, and adds that Aquila's word for it was παμμικτον. Older editors read παμμυιαν for παμμικτον, but Field, or some one before him, corrected it, and our text confirms the correction.

VR do not always go together: R, as being later, has corruptions of its own. *Psalphinga*, a trumpet, is a favourite word with our author: R at first writes this as *psalmigraphus*; later, when he has realised that this is nonsense, he reproduces *psalphinga* as he should.

We have not yet cited examples in which the Trèves MSS. stand apart. I will give two specimens, one of a few words, the other longer, in which this is the case.

i. XXII1. 4. Una petra erat unde effodi patrem uestrum. et genuit *uir scopuli illius* duos uiros A. P has: incisco petre illius, which is nearly right: VRF have "incisio petre illius," which is quite right.

ii. In the *Lament of Jephthah's Daughter* (XL. 6 seq.) all our authorities are available except F. J is very loose and paraphrastic, and its evidence will be given after the rest.

The first clause has no important variants. After that, taking A as the basis, we have-

(*a*) Ego autem non sum saturata thalamo meo, nec repleta sum coronis nuptiarum mearum.
(*b*) Non enim uestita sum splendore sedens in genua mea.
   Non enim uestita sum splendore sedens in uirginitate mea P.
   Non enim uestita sum splendore sedens in ingenuitate mea PhT.
   Non enim uestita sum splendore secundum ingenuam meam VR.
(c) Non sum usa Mosi odoris mei.
   " "   preciosi odoramenti mei PPhT.
   " "   moysi odoris mei VR (*om.* usa R).
(Sichardus conjectured Moscho for Mosi: Pitra prints non sunt thymia odoris.)
(*d*) Nec froniuit (fronduit V) anima mea oleo unctionis quod (quibus R) praeparatum est mihi AVR.
Nec froniuit animam meam oleum unctionis quod praeparatum est mihi PPhT.
(e) O mater, in uano (uanum V) peperisti unigenitam, tuam AVR.
   O mater, in uano peperisti unigenitam tuam et genuisti eam super terram PPhT (see below, (*g*)).
(*f*) Quoniam, factus est infernus thalamus meus.
(*g*) et genuam meam super terram A.
   et genua mea super terram. VR (*om.* mea R).
    P PhT have the equivalent above in (*e*).
(*h*) et confectio omnis olei quod praeparasti mihi effundatur.
   (*om.* et) confectio omnis olei quam preparauit mihi mater mea eff. PPhT.
   et confectio omnis olei quam preparasti mihi effundetur VR.
(*i*) et alba quam neuit mater mea tinea comedat eam.
   et albam (alba Ph) quam neuit tinea comedat PPhT.
     et albam quam neuit mater mea tinea comedet eam VR.
(*k*) et corona quam intexuit nutrix mea in tempore marcescat.
   et corona quam intexuit mea nutrix in tempore marcescat PPhT.
   et flores corone quam intexuit nutrix mea in tempore marcescant (marcescet R) VR.
(*l*) et stratoria quae texuit in genuam meam de Hyacinthino. et purpura uermis ca corrumpet.
   et stratoria quae texuit mihi de iacincto et purpura uermis ea corrumpat PPhT (corrumpet P).
   et stratoria quae texuit ingenium meum de iacinctino et purpuram meam uermes corrumpant V.
   et stratoriam quae texuit ingenium meum de iacinctino et purpuram meam uermis corrumpat R.
(*m*) et referentes de me conuirgines meae in gemitu per dies plangant me.

et referentes de me conuirgines meae cum gemitu per dies plangant me PPhT.
et referentes me conuirgines meae in gemitum per dies plangant me VR.

  The passage reads thus in J, p. 178 (*a*): "I have not beheld my bridal canopy, nor has the crown of my betrothal been completed. (*b*) I have not been decked with the lovely ornaments of the bride who sits in her virginity. (*c*) nor have I been perfumed with the myrrh and the sweet smelling aloe.
(*d*) I have not been anointed with the oil of anointment that was prepared for me.
(*e*) Alas, O my mother, it was in vain that thou didst give me birth.
Behold thine only one (*f*) is destined for the bridal chamber of the grave.
(*g*) Thou hast wearied thyself for me to no purpose.
(*h*) The oil with which I was anointed will be wasted.
(*i*) And the white garments with which I was clothed the moths will eat.
(*k*) The garlands of my crown with which thou hast exalted me will wither and dry up.
(*l*) And my garments of fine needlework in blue and purple the worm shall destroy.
(*m*) And now my friends will lament all the days of my mourning."

  It will be seen that J has some equivalent for every clause (though in (*g*) he has wandered far from the text).

  In (*b*) he read *sedens in uirginitate* or *ingenuitate* with the Trèves MSS.: in (*k*) "garlands of my crown" seems nearer to *flores corone* of VR. For the rest he is too paraphrastic to be followed closely.

  It is very odd that three times over in this short passage the words *in genua mea, genuam meam, in genuam meam* should occur in one of the groups, each time disturbing the sense, while another group somehow avoids the difficulty. It looks suspicious for the group which does so. But the evidence of the Trèves group is not to be lightly dismissed. It would justify a theory that where the words first occur they are corrupt for *ingenuitate*, that on the second occasion an obscurity of a few letters genu . . . eam, present in the ancestor of the other MSS., was not in that of the Trèves group: and that in the third case the words are merely intrusive--perhaps wrongly inserted from a margin. Another blurring of a few letters would account for the differences between *moysi* and *preciosi*, and between *odoris* and *odoramenti*. But I do not regard this as a really satisfactory explanation.

4. TITLE, AND ATTRIBUTION TO PHILO

4. The TITLE of the book is somewhat of a puzzle. Sichardus calls it *Philonis Judaei antiquitatum Biblicarum liber*, the Fulda catalogue (and the label on the Fulda MS.) *Philonis antiquitatum liber*; a late title in the same MS. is: *libri Philonis iudei de initio mundi*; P has a title of cent. XV.: *Philo iudeus de successione generationum veteris testamenti*; R, in the colophon: "*ystoria Philonis ab initio mundi usque ad David regem*" (so also two at least of the Munich MSS.); Trithemius has *De generationis successu*. Sixtus Senensis has two notices of the book: in the first, which is drawn from Sichardus., he calls it *Biblicarum antiquitatum liber*; in the second, which depends on some MS., his words are: "In Gen. Cap. 5 *de successione generis humani* liber unus, continens enarrationem genealogiae seu posteritatis Adae. Liber incipit: Ἀδὰμ ἐγέννησε *Adam genuit tres filios*." The two Greek words I take to be no more than a re-translation from Latin. The MS. V has no title at all.

Thus we have authority for three names. The first, *Biblicarum antiquitatum*, I think, must be in part due to Sichardus; the epithet "Biblicarum" savours to my mind of the Renaissance, and has no certain MS. attestation. "Antiquitatum" (which is as old as cent. XIV.) is probably due to a recollection of Josephus's great work, the *Jewish Antiquities*. The other name, *de successione generationum* or the like, has rather better attestation, and: *Historia ab initio mundi*, etc. (if original in the Munich MSS.) the oldest of all. I can hardly believe, however, that any of them are original; it seems more probable that some Biblical name was prefixed to the book when it was first issued. Rather out of respect to the first editor than for any better reason I have retained the title *Biblical Antiquities*, under which the text was introduced to the modern world.

The ATTRIBUTION TO PHILO I regard as due to the accident that the text was transmitted in company with genuine Philonic writings. Certainly, if the *Antiquities* had come down to us by themselves, no one in his senses could have thought of connecting them with Philo; unless, indeed, knowing of but two Jewish authors, Philo and Josephus, he assumed that, since one had written a history of the Jews, the other must needs have followed suit.

5. ORIGINAL LANGUAGE

5. The ORIGINAL LANGUAGE of the book, its date, its form and its purpose, must now be discussed.

Original Language.--The Latin version, in which alone we possess the work, is quite obviously a translation from Greek. The forms of proper names, the occurrence of Greek words which puzzled the translator, *ometocea, pammixia, epomis*, etc., make this abundantly clear. It is hardly less plain that the Greek was a translation from Hebrew. As Dr. Cohn has pointed out, the whole complexion, and especially the connecting links of the narrative, are strongly Hebraic, and there is a marked absence of the Greek use of particles, or of any attempt to link sentences together save by the bald "et," which occurs an incredible number of times.

Some statistics may be given: *Et factum est* occurs at least 33 times; *Et tum* (usually of the past) 37; *Tunc* 25; *Et nunc* (of present or future) 85; *In tempore illo* 18; *In diebus illis* (and the like) 10; *Et post haec*, or *postea* 30; *Ecce* 105; *Ecce nunc* 47; *Et ideo* 27; *Et erit cum*, or *si* 24. Other common links which I have not counted are *Et ut* (*uidit*, etc.), *Et cum, His dictis, Propterea*.

The leading Hebraisms are present: *adiicere*, or *apponere* with another verb, meaning "he did so yet again," 9 times at least; the intensive participle and verb (*Illuminans illuminaui*) 15 times. We have *Si* introducing a question 4 times; *a uiro usque ad mulierem* and the like (XXX. 4; XLVII. 10); ad uictoriam, in uictoria (= למנצח, "Utterly"); IX. 3; XII. 6; XLIX. 6.

Hebraists, among whom I cannot reckon myself, may probably detect the presence of plays upon words, passages written in poetical form (some of which are indeed obvious), and mistranslations.

From what has just been said it will be rightly gathered that the literary style of *Philo* is not its strong point. Indeed, it is exceedingly monotonous, full of repetitions and catchwords. The author's one device for obtaining an "effect" is to string together a number of high-sounding clauses, as he does, for example, in his repeated descriptions of the giving of the Law. As a narrator, he has another trick. An incident is often compared to another in the past (or future) history of Israel, and many times is an episode from that history related in a speech or prayer.

Some of the recurrent phrases are: *I spake of old saying* about 25 times; *in vain*, or *not in vain* 14; *it is better for us to do* this *than . . .* 7; *not for our sakes, but for . . .* about 5 times; *who knoweth whether* 4; *dost thou not remember* 3; *To thy seed will I give this land* (or the like) 7-9; *the covenant which he made* 5-8; *I know that the people will sin* 8-9; *God's anger will not endure for ever* 10; *The Gentiles will say* 4-8; *I call heaven and earth to witness* 4-5; *in the last days* 4; *make straight your ways* 5-6; *corrupt* (your ways, etc.) 18; *remember or visit the world* 6; *be for a testimony* 10. Of single words *accipere* occurs 88 times in the first half of the text; *habitare, inhabitare* about 80 times in the whole text; *iniquitas* 33; *disponere* 37; *testamentum* 47; *ambulare* 21; *uia, uiae* 25; *adducere* 19; *sed ucere* 21; *saeculum* 27; *sempiternus* 15; *constituere* 20; *expugnare* 27; *zelari* 14; *illuminare* 12 ; *renunciare* 15.

Other lists are given in Appendix II.

6. DATE

6. As to the DATE of the book, a positive indication of a *terminus a quo* has been detected in the text by Dr. Colin. He draws attention to a speech of God to Moses (XIX. 7): "I will show thee the place wherein the people shall serve me 850 (MSS. 740) years, and thereafter it shall be delivered into the hands of the enemies, and they shall destroy it, and strangers shall compass it about; and it shall be on that day like as it was in the day when I brake the tables of the covenant which I made with thee in Horeb: and when they sinned, that which was written thereon vanished away. Now that day was the 17th day of the 4th month." Dr. Cohn's comment is: "These words are meant to signify that Jerusalem was taken on the 17th of Tamuz, on the same day on which the Tables of the Law were broken by Moses. The capture of Jerusalem by the Babylonians, however, took place on the 9th of Tamuz (Jer. 52; Cf. 2 Kings 25). The . . . 17th of Tamuz can relate only to the second temple (*read* capture) as it is expressly mentioned in the Talmud (Taanith IV. 6, cf. *Seder Olam Rabbah*, cap. 6 and 30) that on that date the Tables of the Law were destroyed and Jerusalem was taken by Titus. Thus the author betrays himself by giving as the date of the capture of Jerusalem by the Babylonians what is really the date of the capture by Titus."

The point is so important that I have felt it only right to present the evidence in some detail. The Mishnah of *Taanith* IV. 6 says "Five calamities befell our fathers on the 17th of Tamuz and five on the 9th of Ab. On the 17th Tamuz the Tables of the Law were broken: the daily sacrifice ceased to be offered: the city of Jerusalem was broken into: Apostomos burnt the Law and set up an idol in the sanctuary. On the 9th of Ab our fathers were told that they should not enter the holy land (Num. xiv.). The first and the second temple were destroyed; Bethar was taken, and the plough passed over the soil of Jerusalem."

It must be borne in mind that the capture of Jerusalem, and not the destruction of the Temple, is the event of which the date is important. To establish Dr. Cohn's argument, it is necessary that the capture of the city by Titus, and not the capture by Nebuchadnezzar, should be assigned to the 17th Tamuz.

The Gemara of the Jerusalem Talmud on the Mishnah quoted above attempts to show that there is a confusion in the chronology, and that probably both captures took place on the 17th Tamuz. But that of the Babylonian Talmud, which Mr. I. Abrahams has kindly translated for me, makes the requisite distinction between the dates, in these terms--

The city was broken up on the 17th. Was it indeed so? Is it not written "in the 4th month, on the 9th of the month, the famine was sore" (Jer. 52): and is it not written in the following verse: "then the city was broken up"? Raba replied: There is no difficulty: for the one refers to the first, the other to the second Temple. For there is a *baraitha* (teaching) which teaches: "On the first occasion the city was broken into on the 9th of Tamuz, and on the second occasion on the 17th."

This clearly justifies Dr. Cohn in taking the 17th of Tamuz as the date primarily associated with the capture by Titus. The attempt of the Jerusalem Talmud to place the Babylonian capture on the same date is of a later complexion, and is made, it seems, in the interests of a factitious symmetry. The *baraitha* quoted in the Babylonian Talmud is of the same age as the Mishnah (*i.e.* before A.D. 200).

Thus *Philo* is indeed referring to the capture by Titus, and is therefore writing at a date later than A.D. 70. But, apart from this piece of positive evidence, the general complexion of the book strongly supports Dr. Cohn when he holds that it was written after the destruction of the second Temple. There is a singular absence of interest in the Temple services and in the ceremonial Law, whereas the moral Law, and especially the Decalogue, is dwelt upon again and again. Of course we read of sacrifices and the like, and it was impossible for the author to avoid all mention of the Tabernacle and its vessels, and of the yearly feasts. But the space devoted to them is strikingly small. The Passover is twice mentioned by name, and its institution is once referred to, together with that of the Feasts of Weeks, of Trumpets, and of Tabernacles, but no stress is laid upon it. The prescriptions for the observance of the Sabbath mention only synagogal services. When we compare *Philo* with *Jubilees* (second cent. B.C.), where the constant effort is to antedate the ceremonial Law in every part, we feel that we are in a wholly different stage of Judaism. Further, the evidence derivable from the resemblances between *Philo* and other books certainly written after A.D. 70, which will be found collected in another part of this Introduction, points unequivocally in the same direction.

In the portion of the book which we have (and it is important to remember that it is but a fragment) the writer's anticipations of a restoration and his allusions to the desolation of Jerusalem are equally faint and dim. It is probable that as occasion served--*e.g.* when he came to treat of Solomon's temple--he would have spoken more plainly than he could well do when dealing with the earlier history. If an opinion based upon what we possess of his work is demanded, my own is that an appreciable interval must be placed between the destruction of the city and our author's time. I should assign him to the closing years of the first Christian century.

7. FORM

7. As to the FORM, I suggest that the chief model which the author set before himself was the Biblical *Book of Chronicles*. He begins abruptly, as that does, with genealogies and with Adam: he introduces from time to time short pieces of narrative, which rapidly increase in importance until they occupy the whole field: he devotes much space to speeches and prayers, and is fond of statements of numbers. His aim is to supplement existing narratives, and he wholly passes over large tracts of the history, occasionally referring to the Biblical books in which further details are to be found: and it is to be noted that he seems to place his own work on a level with them. "Are not these things written in the book of" the Judges, or the Kings, is his formula, and it is that of the Bible also. In all these respects he follows the Chronicler: only, as has been said, we miss in him the liturgical and priestly interest of that writer. Like the Chronicler, too, he is, and I believe was from the first, anonymous; I can find no trace of an attempt to personate any individual prophet, priest or scribe.

8. PURPOSE

8. The PURPOSE of the author I read thus. He wishes to supplement existing narratives, as has been said; and this he does by means of his fabulous genealogies (which, especially in the corrupt state in which we have them, arouse but a faint interest) and also by his paraphrases of Bible stories, (for example, those of Korah, Balaam, Jael, Micah) and by his fresh inventions, especially that of Kenaz, the first judge, which is on the whole his most successful effort. In this side of his work he seeks to interest rather than to instruct. On the religious side I detect a wish to infuse a more religious tone into certain episodes of the history, particularly into the period of the judges, and to emphasize certain great truths, foremost among which I should place the indestructibility of Israel, and the duty of faithfulness to the one God. Lapse into idolatry and union with Gentiles are the dangers he most dreads for his people. I have collected the passages in which his positive teaching, is most clear and prominent, and purpose in this place to digest them under several heads, usually in the order in which they occur in the text.

The Future State of Souls and the End of the World.

III. 10. When the years of the world (or age) are fulfilled, God will quicken the dead, and raise up from the earth them that sleep: Sheol will restore its debt, and Abaddon its deposit, and every man will be rewarded according to his works. There will be an end of death, Sheol will shut its mouth, the earth will be universally fertile. No one who is "justified in God" shall be defiled. There will be a new heaven and a new earth, an everlasting habitation.

XIX. 4. God will reveal the end of the world.

XIX. 7. Moses is not to enter into the promised land "in this age."

12. He is to be made to sleep with the fathers, and have rest, until God visits the earth, and raises him and the fathers from the earth in which they sleep, and they come together and dwell in an immortal habitation.

13. This heaven will pass away like a cloud, and the times and seasons be shortened when the end draws near, for God will hasten to raise up them that sleep, and all who are able to live will dwell in the holy place which he has shown to Moses.

XXI. 9. God told the fathers in the secret places of souls, how he had fulfilled his promises: cf. XXIV. 6; XXXII. 13.

XXIII. 6. He showed Abraham the place of fire in which evil deeds will be expiated, and the torches which will enlighten the righteous who have believed.

13. The lot of the righteous Israelites will be in eternal life: their souls will be taken and laid up in peace, until the time of the world is fulfilled, and God restores them, to the fathers, and the fathers to them.

XXVI. 12. The precious stones of the temple will be hidden away until God remembers the world, and then will be brought out with others from the place which eye hath not seen nor ear heard, etc. The righteous will not need the light of the sun or moon, for these stones will give them light.

XXVIII. 10. The rest (*requies*) of the righteous when they are dead.

XXXII. 17. The renewal of the creation (cf. XVI. 3).

XXXIII. 2-5. There is no room for repentance after death, nor can the fathers after their death intercede for Israel.

XXXVIII. 4. Jair's victims are quickened with "living fire" and are delivered. (This, however, does not seem strictly to apply to the future state: see the passage.)

XLVIII. 1. When God remembers the world Phinehas will taste of death. Until then he will dwell with those who have been "taken up" before him.

LI. 5. God quickens the righteous, but shuts up the wicked in darkness. When the bad die they perish: when the righteous sleep they are delivered.

LXII. 9. Jonathan is sure that souls will recognize each other after death.

The Lot of the Wicked.

XVI. 3. Korah and his company: their dwelling will be in darkness and perdition, and they will pine away until God remembers the world, and then they will die and not live, and their remembrance will perish like that of the Egyptians in the Red Sea and the men who perished in the Flood. 6. Korah and his company, when they were swallowed up, "sighed until the firmament should be restored to the earth."

XVIII. 12. Balaam will gnash his teeth because of his sins.

XXXI. 7. Sisera is to go and tell his father in hell that he has fallen by the hand of a woman.

XXXVIII. 4. Jair will have his dwelling-place in fire: so also Doeg, LXIII. 4.

XLIV. 10. Micah and his mother will die in torments, punished by the idols he has made. And this will be the rule for all men, that they shall suffer in such fashion as they have sinned.

Punishment, long deferred, for past sins, is much in our author's mind.

VI. 11. Abram says "I may be burned to death on account of my (former) sins. God's will be done."

XXVII. 7. If Kenaz falls in battle it will be because of his sins.

15. Certain men were punished, not for their present offence, but for a former one.

XLII. 2. Manoah's wife is barren because of sins.

XLV. 3. The Levite's concubine had sinned years before and is now punished.

XLIX. 5. Elkanah says: If my sins have overtaken me, I had better kill myself.

The greatness of Israel and of the Law.

VII. 4. The Holy Land was not touched by the Flood.

IX. 3. The world will come to naught sooner than Israel can be destroyed.

4. When Israel was not yet in being, God spoke of it.

XII. 9. If God destroys Israel there will be none left to glorify him.

XVIII. 13. Israel can only be defeated if it sins.

XXXII. 9, 14. The heavenly bodies are ministers to Israel, and will intercede with God if Israel is in a strait.

15. Israel was born of the rib of Adam.

XXXIX. 7. The habitable places of the world were made for Israel.

IX. 8. God thought of the Law in ancient days.

XI. 1. It is a light to Israel but a punishment to the wicked.

2. It is an everlasting Law by which God will judge the world. Men shall not be able to say "we have not heard."

5. It is an eternal commandment which shall not pass away.

XXXII. 7. It was prepared from the birth of the world.

Of Union with Gentiles.

IX. 1. The worst feature of the Egyptian oppression was the proposal that the Hebrew girls should marry Egyptians.

5. Tamar sinned with Judah rather than mingle with Gentiles, and was justified.

XVIII. 13. The union with the daughters of Moab and Midian would be fatal to Israel.

XLIII. 5. Samson mingled with Gentiles, and was therefore punished. He was unlike Joseph.

Angelology.

The service of angels is fairly prominent, and several are named.

XI. 12. "Bear not false witness, lest thy guardians do so of thee." This, I think, refers to angels.

XV. 5. The angels will not intercede for the people if they sin. The angel of God's wrath will smite the people.

"I put angels under their feet." (Also XXX. 5.)

XVIII. 5. "I said to the angels that work subtilly (?)."

6. Jacob wrestled with the angel that is over the praises.

XIX. 16. The angels lament for Moses.

XXVII. 10. Gethel or Ingethel is the angel of hidden things; Zeruel the angel of strength. (Also LXI. 5.)

XXXII. 1, 2. The angels were jealous of Abraham,

XXXIV. 3. Certain angels were judged: those who were condemned had powers which were not given to others after them. They still assist men in sorceries.

XXXVIII. Nathaniel the angel of fire.

XLII. 10. The angel Phadahel.

LXIV. 6. When Samuel is raised up by the witch, two angels appear leading him.

Demons and Idols.

Of evil spirits hardly anything is said, but some space is devoted to descriptions of idols.

XIII. 8. Adam's wife was deceived by the serpent.

XXV. 9. "The demons of the idols."

9 *seq.* The idols and precious stones of the Amorites are dwelt upon.

XLIV. 5 *seq.* Micah's idols are described in terms which remind one slightly of the images in a sanctuary of Mithras. (See the note.)

XLV. 6. "The Lord said to the Adversary" (*anticiminus*, ὁ ἀντικείμενος). He is quite suddenly introduced, and without any explanation.

LIII. 3, 4. Eli wonders if an unclean spirit has deceived Samuel. If one hears two calls at night, it will be an evil spirit that is calling: three will mean an angel.

LXI. An evil spirit oppresses Saul.

Evil spirits were created after heaven and earth (on the Second Day) and are a secondary creation. They sprang from an echo in chaos: their abode was in "Tartarus."

A *holy spirit* is mentioned occasionally, but in rather vague terms.

XVIII. 3. Balaam says that the spirit (of prophecy) is given "for a time."

11. "Little is left of that holy spirit which is in me."

XXVIII. 6. The holy spirit leapt upon Kenaz.

XXXII. 14. (Deborah addressing herself.) "Let the grace of the holy spirit in thee awake."

The character of God and His dealings with men are, naturally, illustrated in many passages, in some of which there is a strange lack of perception of what is worthy and befitting.

XII. 9. Moses says, "Thou art all light."

XXII. 3. "Light dwells with him."

XVI. 5. The sons of Korah say that God, not Korah, is their true father: if they walk in his ways, they will be his sons.

XVIII. 4. God knew what was in the world before he made it.

XXI. 2. He knows the mind of all generations before they are born (cf. L. 4).

XXVIII. 4. He willed that the world should be made and that they who should inhabit it should glorify him.

XXX. 6. God is life.

XXXV. 3. He will have mercy on Israel "not for your sakes, but because of them that sleep" (cf. XXXIX. 11 *end*).

5. Men look on glory and fame, God on uprightness of heart.

XXXVI. 4. God will not punish Gideon in this life, lest men should say "It is Baal who punishes him": he will chastise him after death.

XXXIX. 4. (LXII. 6.) If God forgives, why should not mortal man?

God, being God, has time to cast away his anger.

11. He is angry with Jephthah for his vow. "If a dog were the first to meet him, should a dog be offered to me? It shall fall upon his only child."

XLV. 6. Israel took no notice of Micah's idols; but is horrified at the Benjamite outrage: therefore God will allow Benjamin to defeat them, and will deceive them (cf. LXIII. 3).

XLVI. He deceives Israel, telling them to attack Benjamin.

XLVII. 3. If God had not sworn an oath to Phinehas, he would not hear him now.

LII. 4. He will not allow Eli's sons to repent, because aforetime they had said "When we grow old we will repent."

LXIV. 1. Saul put away the wizards in order to gain renown: so he shall be driven to resort to them.

Man, especially in relation to sin.

XIII. 8. Man lost Paradise by sin.

XIX. 9. What man hath not sinned? Who will be born without sin? Thou wilt correct us for a time, and not in wrath.

XXXII. 5. Esau was hated because of his deeds.

XXXVI. 1. The Midianites say, "Our sins are fulfilled, as our gods told us, and we believed them not."

LII. 3. Eli says to his sons: "Those whom you have wronged will pray for you if you reform."

LXIV. 8. Saul thinks that perhaps his fall may be an atonement for his sins.

The Messiah.

Dr. Cohn speaks of the Messianic hope of the writer, but I am myself unable to find any anticipation of a Messiah in our text. It is always God, and no subordinate agency, that is to "visit the world" and put all things right.

The word *Christus* occurs in two chapters: in LI. 6, and LIX. 1, 4, which refer to Saul or David.

There are two other puzzling passages, of which one inclines at first to say that the meaning is Messianic.

XXI. 6. Joshua says: "O Lord, lo, the days shall come when the house of Israel shall be likened to a brooding dove which setteth her young in the nest, and will not leave them or forget her place, like as also these, turning (*conuersi*) from their acts, shall fight against (*or* overcome) the salvation which shall be born of them (*or* is born to them)."

LI. 5. Hannah says: "But so doth all judgement endure, until he be revealed who holdeth *it (qui tenet)*." As, a few lines later, she says: "And these things remain so until they give a horn to his (*or* their) Anointed," which certainly refers to Saul; it is probable that Saul or David is meant in the present passage also. Nevertheless the resemblance between *qui tenet* and ὁ κατέχων of St. Paul (2 Thess. ii. 6, 7) is noteworthy.

9. UNITY. CONTENTS

9. I have not raised the question of the UNITY of the book. No one has as yet suggested that it is composite, and I am content to wait until, a theory is broached. That there are inconsistencies in it I do not deny (for instance, the story of Korah is told in two ways in XVI. and in LVII.), but they are not of a kind that suggest a plurality of writers. It may be that their presence here will furnish an argument against dissection of other books based on the existence of similar discrepancies.

As to the INTEGRITY of the text: We know that it is imperfect, and this matter will be discussed at a later stage.

The CONTENTS will be found summarized in a synopsis at the end of the Introduction.

10. RELATION TO OTHER LITERATURE

10. THE RELATION OF PHILO TO OTHER BOOKS now comes up for consideration. The author's knowledge of the Old Testament literature is apparent on every page. There are obvious borrowings from all the books to the end of 2 Kings; of Chronicles he seems to be a definite imitator. He knows the story of job, and quotes a Psalm; he draws from Isaiah, Jeremiah, Ezekiel, Daniel. With the Wisdom literature he has not much in common, and traces of the use of the Minor Prophets, of Ezra, Nehemiah, or Tobit, are hard to find, though I will not deny their presence. If he lived, as I believe he did, near the end of the first century, we should naturally credit him with a knowledge of the whole Jewish canon.

It is more important to determine his relation to the apocryphal books--the literature to which he was himself a contributor. Four of these, *Enoch, Jubilees*, the *Syriac Apocalypse of Baruch*, and the *Fourth Book of Esdras*, afford interesting material.

(*a*) Certain affinities with the *Book of Enoch* are traceable in *Philo*. It is true that Enoch is not one of his heroes; in fact, he tells us no more of him than is found in Genesis, but I believe that the Book was known to him, though it is only in the first part of it that I find any striking parallels.

In the first place, his view of the stars and other heavenly bodies is like that of *Enoch*. They are sentient beings, who receive commands from God and move about to execute them. See the story of Sisera, and the hymn of Deborah, and compare in *Enoch* 6, etc., the punishment of the errant stars.

Again, a passage in Enoch (14) seems to be the model of some in Philo. "Behold, clouds called me in my vision, and mists cried to me, and runnings of stars and lightnings hastened me, and in the vision winds gave me wings and lifted me up." Compare *Philo* XI. 5: "The heavens were folded up, and the clouds drew up water . . . and the thunders and lightnings were multiplied, and the winds and tempests sounded; the stars were gathered together, and the angels ran before " (XIII. 7); "the winds shall sound and the lightnings run on," etc. (XV. 2); "the lightnings of the stars shone, and the thunders followed, sounding with them" (XXXII. 7); "the lightnings hasted to their courses, and the winds gave a sound out of their storehouses," etc. The phrase in *Enoch* 14 , , is διαδρομαὶ ἀστέρων καὶ ἀστραπαί. In 16 we have ὁ αἰὼν ὁ μέγασ, which may be the source of the *immensurabilis mundus* (*seculum tempus*) of Philo IX. 3, XXXII. 3, XXXIV. 2.

In Enoch 17, τόξον πυρὸσ καὶ βέλη. Philo XIX. 16, *praecedebant eum fulgura et lampades et sagittae omnes unanimes*.

Enoch 18, Εἶ᾽δον τοὺσ θησαυροὺσ τῶν ἀνέμων; cf. Philo XXXII. 7, above. The winds gave a sound out of their storehouses (*promptuariis*).

In Enoch 18 *seq*. we hear something of precious stones which reminds us of those of Kenaz in *Philo* XXVI. *seq*.

The words of 21: "I saw neither heaven above nor earth founded, but a place imperfect and terrible" recall the vision of Kenaz in *Philo* XXVIII. 6 *seq*.

So also the description of the sweet plants of Paradise in *Enoch* 24 may have suggested the words of Moses in *Philo* XII. 9.

In Enoch 25 "to Visit the earth" has more than one parallel in *Philo*, e. g. XIX. 12, 13, *visitare seculum, orbem*: and Enoch 25 (Then I blessed the God of glory . . . who hath prepared such things for righteous men, etc.) is like *Philo* XXVI. 6: Blessed be God who hath wrought such signs for the sons of men, and 14: Lo, how great good things God hath wrought for men.

(*b*) The *Book of Jubilees* is perhaps most nearly comparable to *Philo*, in that it follows the form of a chronicle of Bible history. Its spirit and plan are, to be sure, wholly different; it is regulated by a strict system of chronology, and its chief interest is in the ceremonial law. It is also far earlier in date, belonging to the last years of the second century B.C.

Our author has read *Jubilees*, and to a certain extent supplements it in the portions which are common to both books. Thus *Jubilees* supplies us with the names of the wives of the early patriarchs: *Philo* omits these, but gives the names of their sons and daughters. It is true that he gives other names for the daughters of Adam, and that in the one case in which he supplies the name of a wife he also differs from *Jubilees*: with him Cain's wife is Themech, in *Jubilees* it is Awân (daughter of Adam and sister of Cain, which *Philo* may have wished to disguise). In the same way *Philo* devotes much space to the names and number of the grandsons of Noah and their families, which are wanting in *Jubilees*; and whereas *Jubilees* gives full geographical details of the provinces which fell to Shem, Ham and Japhet, *Philo* indulges only in a series of bare names of places, now for the most part hopelessly corrupt. There is a small and seemingly intentional contradiction of *Jubilees* in this part of his history: *Jubilees* , says that Serug taught Nahor to divine, and worshipped idols. *Philo* agrees that divination began in the days of Terah and Nahor, but adds that Serug and his sons did *not* join in it, or in idolatry.

Then, whereas the bulk of *Jubilees* is occupied with the lives of Abraham, Isaac and Jacob, *Philo* tells in detail one episode--the rescue of Abram from the fire--which *Jubilees* omits, and passes over the rest of the period in a single page. Anything else that he has to say about Abraham and the rest is introduced into the speeches of later personages (Joshua, Deborah, etc.) by way of illustration. The two books agree in giving the names of the seventy souls who went down into Egypt.

All this seems to me to show a consciousness of *Jubilees*, and an intentional avoidance, in the main, of the ground traversed by that book. Very rarely is there any coincidence of thought, but two possible examples can be cited. *Philo* has surprisingly little to say about Satan or evil spirits, as we have seen: but suddenly (in XLV. 6) he says: *Et dixit Dominus ad anticiminum*: And the Lord said to the Adversary. This must surely be the equivalent of the "prince Mastema" whom we meet so frequently in *Jubilees*. There is also a difficult passage (XIII. 8) which may go back to *Jubilees*. God is speaking to Moses, and says: "And the nights shall yield their dew, as I spake after the flood of the earth, at that time when I commanded him (or Then he commanded him) concerning the year of the life of Noah, and said to him: These are the years which I ordained," etc. The words, which may be corrupt, at least remind me of the stress laid in *Jubilees* 6, upon the yearly feast that is to be kept by Noah after the Flood.

Upon the whole *Philo's* knowledge of *Jubilees* is to be inferred rather from what he does not say than from what he does.

(*c*) The Syriac APOCALYPSE OF BARUCH has, as I have elsewhere shown (JTS 1915, 403), certain very marked resemblances to *Philo*. It will be right to repeat and expand the list of them here. We will take the passages in the order in which they appear in the Apocalypse, in Dr. R. H. Charles's last translation (*Pseudepigrapha of O.T.*).

Bar. IV. 3. The building now built in your midst is not that which is revealed with Me, that which was prepared beforehand here from the time when I took counsel to make Paradise and shewed it to Adam before he	*Ph*. XIII. 8. And he said: This is the place which I showed the first-made man, saying: If thou transgress not that which I have commanded thee, all things shall be subject unto thee. But he transgressed my ways. . . . And the

sinned, but when he transgressed the commandment it was removed from him, as also Paradise.

Lord further shewed him (Moses) the ways of Paradise, and said to him: These are the ways which men have lost because they walked not in them.

XXVI. 6. Kenaz says: Blessed be God who hath wrought such marvels for the sons of men, and made the protoplast Adam and shewed him all things, that when Adam had sinned therein, then, he should deprive him of all things . . .

IV. 4. And after these things I shewed it to my servant Abraham by night among the portions of the victims.

XXIII. 6. (of Abraham) And sent a sleep upon him and compassed him about with fear, and set before him the place of fire wherein the deeds of them that work wickedness against me shall be expiated, etc.

IV. 5. And again also I shewed it to Moses on Mount Sinai when I shewed to him the likeness of the tabernacle and all its vessels.

XI. 15. (on Sinai) He charged him concerning the tabernacle and the ark . . . and the candlesticks and the laver and the base, and the breastplate and the oracle and the precious stones, and shewed him the likeness of them.

XIX. 10. (on Pisgah) He shewed him the place whence the manna rained upon the people, even up to the paths of paradise; and he shewed him the manner of the sanctuary and the number of the offerings ... (See also XIII. 8 above.)

V. 5. Jabish, an unknown person, summoned with others by Baruch.

XXVIII. 1. Kenaz summons the prophets Jabis and Phinees.

VI. 7. The forty-eight precious stones.

See below, p. 64.

X. Baruch's lamentation generally resembles that of Jephthah's daughter.	XL. 5.
X. 11. And do ye, O heavens, withhold your dew and open not the treasures of rain.	XLIV. 10. I will command the heaven, and it shall deny them rain. XI. 9. I will command the heaven, and it shall give its rain. XIII. 7. The nights shall yield their dew. XXIII. 12. I will command the rain and the dew. XXXII. 7. the storehouses of the wind. XV. 5. the treasuries of darkness.
XI. 4. The righteous sleep in the earth in tranquillity.	III. 10. I will raise up them that sleep from the earth.
XXI. 24. Abraham, etc., who sleep in the earth.	XI. 6. I will recompense the sins of them that sleep. XIX. 12. I will raise up thee and thy fathers from the earth (of Egypt *intrusive*) wherein ye shall sleep. XXXV. 3. because of them that are fallen asleep. LI. 5. when the righteous shall fall asleep, then shall they be delivered.
XI. 6, 7. That ye might go and announce in Sheol and say to the dead: Blessed are ye more than we who live.	XXIV. 6. Who shall go and tell the righteous Moses (that Joshua is dead)? XXXI. 7. (To Sisera) Go and boast thyself to thy father in hell. XXXII. 13. Go, ye angels, tell the fathers in the treasuries of souls. LXI. 6. (To Goliath) then shall ye tell your mother (after death).

XV. 5. Unless he had accepted my law.	Emphasized in XLIV. 6 *seq*. (Cf. XI. 2).
XVII. 4. brought the law to the seed of Jacob and lighted a lamp for the nation of Israel (cf. LIX.).	IX. 8. I will light for (Moses) my lamp. XV. 6. I came down to light a lamp for my people.
LIX. 2. the lamp of the eternal law.	XIX. 4. kindling among you an eternal lamp. Besides repeated references to the Law as a light.
XIX. 1. (Moses) called heaven and earth to witness against them; also LXXXIV. 2.	Occurs 4 times, of Moses (twice), Joshua, Jonathan.
XX. 1. The times shall hasten more than the former, and the seasons shall speed on . . . the years shall pass more quickly. LIV. 1. Thou dost hasten the beginnings of the times. LXXXIII. 1. The most High will assuredly hasten his times and . . . bring on his hours.	XIX. 13. When I shall draw near to visit the world, I will command the times and they shall be shortened, and the stars shall be hastened, and the light of the sun shall make haste to set, etc.
XX. 2. That I may the more speedily visit the world in its season.	XIX. 12. Until I visit the world. (See also III. 10, XXVI. 12, XLVIII. 1.)
XXI. 23. Let Sheol be sealed, so that from this time forward it may not receive the dead, and let the treasuries p. 50 of souls restore those which are enclosed in them (Cf. XXX. 2).	III. 10. Hell shall pay its debt and destruction restore its deposit . . . hell shall shut its mouth. p. 50 XXXIII. 3. Death is now sealed up.
XLII. 7, 8. the dust shall be called, and there shall be said to it: Give back that which is not thine, and raise up all that thou hast kept until this time (cf. L. 2).	Hell will not restore its deposit unless it be required of him who gave it.

XXI. 9. our fathers in the hidden places of souls.
XXXII. 13. the fathers in the treasuries of their souls.

XXV. 4. The Mighty one doth no longer remember the earth.
XXVIII. 2. The measure and reckoning of that time are two parts a week of seven weeks.

XXVI. 13. until I remember the world.
The phrase occurs at least five times.
(See the Note on *Ph.* XIX. 15.)

XXIX. 8. the treasury of manna shall again descend from on high.

XIX. 10. the place whence the manna rained upon the people.

XXX. 4. the souls of the wicked . . . shall then waste away the more.

XVI. 3. Korah shall pine away until I remember the world.
XLIV. Micah's mother is to waste away in his sight. So also Doeg LXIII. 4.

XLIV. 15. the dwelling of the rest who are many shall be in the fire.

XXXVIII. 4. (of Jair) in the fire wherein thou shalt die, therein shalt thou have thy dwelling-place.

LXIV. 7. (Manasseh) finally his abode was in the fire.

LXIII. 4. (of Doeg) his dwelling shall be with Jair in unquenchable fire for ever.

L. 3, 4. it will be necessary to show to the living that the dead have come to life again . . . and . . . when they have severally recognized those whom they now know.

XXIII. 1. until I restore you to the fathers and the fathers to you.
LXII. 9. (Jonathan) Even if death part us, I know that our souls will recognize each other.

LI. 11. the armies of the

militiae, of angels, occurs

angels.

LIV. 1. the inhabitants of the earth.

5. thou breakest up the enclosure (of the ignorant).

9. What am I amongst men?

11. I will not be silent in praising.

LV. 3. Ramiel who presides over true visions.

LVI. 6. The list of disasters that followed the Fall is much in *Philo's* manner.

LIX. 2. The law which announced to them that believe the promise of their reward, and to them that deny, the torment of fire which is reserved for them.

3. but also the heavens at that time were shaken from their place.

five times.

one of *Philo's* most frequent catchwords.

XXXIII. 6. Deborah closed up the hedge of her generation.

Cf. Gideon XXXV. 5, Saul LVI. 6.

Cf. Deborah and Hannah.

XVIII. 6. the angel who was over the praises.
XXVII, 10. Gethel set over hidden things. Zeruel, over strength (LXI. 5).
XXXIV. 2. angels are sorcerers.
XXXVIII. 3. Nathaniel who is over fire.

XXIII. 6. I set before (Abraham) the place of fire wherein the deeds of them that work wickedness against me shall be expiated, and showed him the torches of fire whereby the righteous that have believed in me shall be enlightened.

XI. 5. at Sinai. The heavens were folded up. I bared the heavens (XV. 6), XXIII. 10. I stopped the courses of the stars, etc. There are several lists of the portents which accompanied the

	giving of the law.
4-11. He showed him the pattern of Zion and its measures, "the measures of the fire, the number of the drops of rain," etc., c. p. 52 4-11. The greatness of Paradise . . . the number of the offerings.	XIX. 10. He showed him the place whence the clouds draw up water, the place whence the river takes its watering the place p. 52 whence the manna rained . . . up to the paths of Paradise . . . the measures of the sanctuary and the number of the offerings.
The splendour of the lightnings.	Very frequent in *Philo*.
LX. 1. The works which the Amorites wrought and the spells of the incantations which they wrought, and the wickedness of their mysteries.	XXV. 10. *seq*. The Amorites figure as great idolaters in the story of Kenaz the first judge: their idols are called the holy Nymphs. The episode of Kenaz is almost the longest in *Philo*. XXXIV. A wizard Aod came from Midian who sacrificed to fallen angels, and made the sun appear at night and seduced Israel.
2. But even Israel was then polluted by sins in the days of the Judges, though they saw many signs which were from Him who made them.	
LXVI. 2. Josiah removed the magicians and enchanters and necromancers from the land.	LXIV. 1. Saul said: I will surely remove the wizards out of the land of Israel (though for unworthy motives).
LXXI. 1. The holy land will . . . protect its inhabitants at that time.	Compare the statement (VII. 4) that the holy land was not touched by the Flood.
LXXVI. 2. Baruch is to be taken up (cf. XIII. 3; XXV. 1) and is to go up into a certain mountain, and the whole world will	XLVIII. Phinehas is to go and live in a named mountain till be has fulfilled his destiny in the person of Elijah and then is to be

be shown to him. (See on LIX.)

taken up into the place where those before him have p. 53 been taken up. These "*priores tui*" are the "others like thee" who are mentioned in *Bar.* II. 1; XIII. 5; (LVII.; LIX. 1); XXI. 24; LXVI. 7.

LXXVII. 6. if ye direct your ways.

At least five times.

13. shepherds of Israel.

XIX. 3. Of Moses.

20. he sends a letter by an eagle.

XLVIII. An eagle is to feed Phinehas.

25. Solomon's mastery over birds.

LX. 3. David predicts Solomon's mastery over evil spirits.

LXXXII. 3-5. The Gentiles will be like a vapour ... like a drop . . . as spittle.

VII. 3; XII. 4. like a drop and like spittle.

9. as a passing cloud.

XIX. 13. like a running cloud.

LXXXIV. 4. after Moses' death ye cast them (the precepts) away from you.

XXX. 5. Moses (and others) commanded you . . . while they lived ye shewed yourselves servants of God; but when they died, your heart died also.

7. (let this epistle) be for a testimony between me and you.

At least nine times.

10. that he may not reckon the multitude of your sins, but remember the rectitude of your fathers.

XXXV. 3. God will have mercy, not for your sakes, but because of those that have fallen asleep (cf. XXXIX. 11).

11. for if He judge us not according to the multitude of His mercies, woe unto all us who are

XIX. 9. What man hath not sinned against thee? How shall thine heritage be stablished if thou

born.

have not compassion, etc.

XXVIII. 5. Is it not he that shall spare us according to the abundance of His mercy (cf. XXXIX. 7; LV. 2).

LXXXV. 9. That we may rest with our fathers.

XXVIII. 10. The rest of the righteous after they are dead.

12. There will be no place . . . for prayer . . . nor intercessions of the fathers, nor prayer of the prophets, nor help of the righteous.

XXXIII. 5. While a man yet liveth he can pray for himself and for his sons, but after the end he will not be able to pray . . . Put not your trust therefore in your fathers.

It will be seen that these resemblances (not all of which, of course, are supposed by me to be equally strong) are scattered over the whole text of *Baruch*. To me they seem to constitute one among a good many weighty arguments against the hypothesis that *Baruch* is a composite work but this is not the place to discuss that matter.

(*d*) We will examine 4 ESDRAS in the same fashion, only here it will be better to cite the Latin of both texts. We must keep in mind the difference between coincidences of vocabulary and parallels in matter. The versions of the two books are extraordinarily alike in their Latinity. One is tempted to say that they are by the same hand; but it will be safer to regard them as products of the same school and age.

4 *Esdr*. III. 13. Et factum est cum iniquitatem facerent coram te, elegisti ex his unum (Abraham) . . . et demonstrasti ei temporum finem solo secrete noctu et disposuisti ei testamentum aeternum et dixisti et ut non unquam derelinqueres semen eius.

Philo XXIII. 5. Et cum seducerentur habitantes terram singuli quique post praesumptiones suas credidit Abraham mihi . . . et dixi ei in uisu dicens: semini tuo dabo terram hanc.

VII. 4. Et ante onmes hos eligam puerum meum Abram . . . et disponam testamentum meum cum eo, etc.

17. Et adduxisti eos super montem Sina.

XV. 3. et adduxi eos sub montem Sina.

p. 55 XXIII. 10. et adduxi eos in conspectu meo usque ad montem Sina.

XXXII. 7. et duxit in

montem Sina.

18. et inclinasti coelos.	XV. 3; XXIII. 10. et inclinaui coelos.
et statuisti terram et commouisti orbem et tremere fecisti abyssos et conturbasti saeculum.	XXIII. 10. mouebantur in descensu meo omnia . . . obturaui uenas abyssi. XXXII. 7. terra mota est de firmamento suo et tremuerunt montes et rupes, etc.
22. permanens. 24. oblationes. 27. tradidisti ciuitatem.	All very common words in *Philo*.
34. pondera in statera.	XL. 1. quis dabit cor meum in statera et animam meam in pondere.
momentum puncti.	XIX. 14. momenti plenitudo.
IV. 7. quantae uenae sunt in principio abyssi.	uena five to six times; abyssus nine times.
exitus paradisi.	uiae, semitae paradisi XIII. 9; XIX. 10.
12. (and elsewhere) melius erat nos . . . quam.	At least seven times.
16. factus est in uano.	Fourteen times.
18. incipiebas (iustificare) = μέλλειν.	Three times at least.
35. animae iustorum in promptuariis suis.	XXXII. 13. patribus in promptuariis animarum eorum.

42. festinant reddere ea quae commendata sunt.	III. 10. reddet infernus debitum suum et perditio restituet paratecem suam. XXXIII. 3. mensura et tempus et anni reddiderunt depositum tuum infernus accipiens sibi deposita non restituet nisi reposcetur ab eo qui deposuit ei.
44. si possibile est et si idoneus sum.	LIII. 7. si possibilis sum.
si plus quam praeteriit habet uenire, etc.	XIX. 14. quanta quantitas temporis transiit, etc.? . . .
IV. 50. superhabundauit quae transiuit mensura; superauerunt autem guttae et fumus.	cyathi guttum, et omnia compleuit tempus. Quatuor enim semis transierunt et duae semis supersunt.
V. 4. relucescet sol noctu.	XXXIV. Nunquid aliquando uidistis solem noctu? . . . ostendit populus solem noctu.
12. non dirigentur uiae eorum.	Frequent.
16. quare uultus tuus tristis.	L. 3. quare tristis es, etc.
18. pastor.	XIX. 3. of Moses.
23. elegisti uineam unam (also IX. 21).	Israel as vine or vineyard occurs six times.
26. columbam.	Israel as dove thrice.
29. sponsionibus.	Seven times.
42. adsimilabo.	Very common.

VI. 2. coruscuum.	Six times in varying forms (coruscus -atio -ans).
3. militiae (angelorum).	Five times.
8-10. manus Jacob tenebat calcaneum Esau, etc.	XIX. 13. apex ma(g)nus remains.
16. finem eorum oportet commutari.	XXVIII. 9. cum completum fuerit tempus . . . pausabit uena et sic mutabuntur.
VI. 18. quando adpropinquare incipio ut uisitem habitantes in terra.	XIX. 13. cum appropinquauero uisitare orbem.
IX 2. uisitare saeculum.	12. donec uisitem seculum. XXVI. 13. et uisitabo habitantes terram.
VI. 26. qui recepti sunt homines qui mortem non gustauerunt.	XLVIII. eleuaberis . . . ubi eleuati sunt priores tui . . . et adducam uos et gustabitis quod est mortis.
39. tenebrae circumferebantur et silentium.	LX. 2. Tenebrae et silentium erant antequam fieret seculum.
41. ut pars quidem sursum recederet, pars uero deorsum maneret.	Both the song of David and the vision of Kenaz (XX VIII.) dwell on the division of the firmaments.
42. imperasti aquis congregari, etc.	XV. 6. nihil simile factum est uerbo huic ex qua die dixi congregentur aquae sub caelo, etc.
56. gentes saliuae	VII. 3. et tanquam

adsimilatae sunt, et sicut stillicidium de urceo.	stillicidium arbitrabor eos et in scuto (sputo) approximabo eos. XII. 4. erit mihi hominum genus tanquam stillicidium urcei et tanquam sputum aestimabitur.
VII. 32. terra reddet qui in ea dormiunt.	III. 10. erigam dormientes de terra. XIX. 12. excitabo te et patres tuos de terra [Aegypti] in qua dormietis, etc.
74. non propter eos, sed.	About five times.
75. creaturam renouare.	XVI. 3. ero innouans terram (cf. III. 10). XXXII. 17. ut in innouatione creaturae.
87. detabescent . . . marcescent.	XVI. Korah, etc., tabescent. XLIV. Micah's mother, erit marcescens.
92. cum eis plasmatum cogitamentum malum.	XXXIII. 3. plasmatio iniqua perdet potestatem suam.
102. etc. Si iusti impios excusare poterint, etc.	5. Adhuc uiuens homo potest orare . . . post finem autem non poterit, etc.
VIII. 15. tu magis scis.	tu plus scis, tu prae omnibus scis two or three times.
53. Radix signata est a uobis.	XXXIII. 3. signata est iam mors.
IX. 22. cum multo labore perfeci haec.	XXVIII. 4. tu uidisti . . . quantum laborauerim populo meo: also XIX. 5.

XII. 20. anni citati.	XIX. 13. iubebo annis . . . et breuiabuntur.
XIII. 26. liberabit creaturam suam.	LI. 5. cum dormierint iusti tunc liberabuntur.
52. scire quid sit in profundo maris.	XXI. 2. tu scis . . . quid agat cor maris (cf. XXIX. 4)
53. inluminatus es.	Twelve times in this sense.
XIV. 3. Reuelans reuelatus sum super rubum.	LIII. 8. Illuminans illuminaui domum Israel.
et locutus sum Moysi.	et elegi tunc mihi prophetam Mosen.
et adduxi eum super montem Sina.	See above on III. 17.
et detinui eum apud me . . . et enarraui ei mirabilia et ostendi ei temporum finem.	Cf. XIII. and XIX. quoted above on *Bar.* LIX. 4.
9. Tu enim recipieris ab hominibus et conuerteris . . . cum similibus tuis.	XLVIII. non descendes iam ad homines . . . eleuaberis in locum ubi eleuati sunt priores tui.

In the later chapters of *Esdras*, which are taken up with visions, we--perhaps naturally--find fewer parallels than in the earlier.

Other instances of words and phrases common to the two books, which are stylistic rather than anything else, are--

Ecce dies uenient, qui inhabitant terram, sensus, delere orbis, sustinere, adinuentio, renuntiare, in nouissimis temporibus, odoramentum, in nihilum deputare, requietio, aeramentum, corruptibilis, plasmare, uiuificare, mortificare, conturbare, exterminare, humiliare, fructus uentris, apponere or *adicere* (*loqui*, etc.), *oblato, pessimus* in the positive sense, *a minimo usque ad maximum, expugnare, scintilla*.

With the *Assumption of Moses* I find no community of ideas. Moses' intercession for the people and Joshua's lament are rather like those of the people over Joshua and Deborah. But *Philo* discards the story of the Assumption proper. Nor do I find illustrative matter in the *Testaments of the XII. Patriarchs*.

My general conclusion is that *Philo* is a product of the circle from which both *Baruch* and 4 *Esdras* emanated: and it seems to me clear that the writer of *Baruch* at least was acquainted with *Philo*. Let it be noted once more that a feature common to all three books is a remarkable want of interest in the subject of Satan and evil spirits: *Esdras* never mentions them, *Baruch* very seldom, *Philo* rather oftener, but not often, and always vaguely.

(*e*) What points of contact are there, it will be asked, between *Philo* and the NEW TESTAMENT?

My answer is that there are not many direct resemblances. There are a few coincidences of language, and one or two illustrations of beliefs. That the author, living at the date to which I assign him, was conscious of the existence of Christianity, I do not doubt: whether he allows his consciousness to find expression in his book, I do doubt. He is not a speculative theologian or a controversialist; he sticks very close to the language of the Old Testament, and steers clear of disputed questions. I see no veiled polemic in his stories of the idolatry under Kenaz, or of Aod the Magician and Micah. The persecution under Jair may very well be an imitation of the Maccabæan martyrdoms, or of the story of the Three Children. The stress laid on the eternity of the Law may as well be a prophylactic against heathenism as against Christianity. Paganism is, I think, a more formidable adversary in his eyes than heresy.

The tradition of the "rock that followed them" (X. 7, XI. 15: see the notes) and of the identity of Phinehas with Elijah (XLVIII.) are the chief that bear on New Testament thought. With reference to the latter it should be noted that the words of St. Mark (ix. 13), "as it is written of him," are specially interesting, as showing that Elijah upon his return to earth was to suffer death (in which *Philo* agrees), and that there was written teaching to that effect.

Among coincidences of language I reckon: new heavens and earth, III. 10; they that sleep, *ibid.* and elsewhere; justified, *ibid.*; fiat uoluntas dei, VI. ii; that which shall be born of thee, IX. 10; I will judge all the world, XI. 2; the law shall not pass away, XI. 5; Thou art all light, XII. 9; we shall be the sons of God, XVI. 5; gnashing of teeth, XVIII. 12; the end of the world, XIX. 4, etc.; uerbum (dei) uiuum, XXI. 4; God which knowest before the hearts of all men, XXII. 7 (Acts i. 24); eye hath not seen, etc., XXVI. 13; the righteous have no need of the light of the sun, etc., XXVI. 13; qui tenet (cf. ὁ κατέχων, 2 Thess. ii. 6, 7), LI. 5; lumen genti huic, LI. 6.

11. EXTENT OF THE COMPLETE BOOK: THE LOST CONCLUSION DISCUSSED

11. A question remains to be discussed, for answered it can hardly be unless fresh manuscript evidence comes to hand. It is this: How far did *Philo* carry on his narrative, and are there any traces of the lost conclusion?

There are certain anticipations in our text which, it is reasonable to suppose, were fulfilled. We can predict with confidence that Edab the son of Agag, who appears in the last few lines as the slayer of Saul, will be killed (as in 2 Sam. 1.), with appropriate denunciation. Again, there is a sensational story of the slaying of Ishbi-benob by David and Abishai (Talmud, Tract *Sanhedr.*, f. 45, ap. Eisenmenger, I. 413), in which Abishai kills Orpah the mother of the giant, and eventually David says to Ishbi, "Go, seek thy mother in the grave," whereat he falls. Now, in *Philo* (LXI. 6) David reminds Goliath that Orpah was his mother, and says to him, "After thy death thy three brethren also will fall into my hands, and then shall ye say unto your mother: He that was born of thy sister (Ruth) did not spare us." I see a foreshadowing here of another tale of giants slain by David. Further, David in his song before Saul (LX.) predicts the mastery over evil spirits that will be attained by Solomon; and elsewhere the writer, in his own person, names Solomon, and speaks of his building the Temple (XXII. 9). The allusion to Solomon and the demons, though unmistakable, is veiled, and, if I may judge from *Philo's* usual practice, would have received an explanation, accompanied by a reference back to David's song: *Nonne haec sunt uerba quae locutus est pater tuus*, etc. Another possible instance of foreshadowing is this: Phinehas (XLVIII.), when he has reached the term of 120 years, is commanded to go up into the Mount Danaben and dwell there. In years to come the heavens will be shut at his prayer, and opened again, and then he will be "taken up," and in a yet more remote future will taste of death. In other words, he will be Elijah. I do not think this obscure prediction would have been left hanging in the air: in some form it would have received interpretation. I imagine, therefore, that the story of Elijah (and Elisha) was told in the book. I hardly know if one can fairly adduce here the fact that in an old treatise called *Inuentiones Nominum* (printed by me in JTS, 1903) some names are given of personages belonging to that period who are anonymous in the Bible. Thus, Abisaac is the 'little maid" of 2 Kings v., Meneria is the Shunamite, and Phua the woman who devoured her child in the siege of Samaria. I lay no stress on this suggestion, for other names are given in the same document which disagree with those in *Philo*. Still, those I have cited did come from some written source of similar character.

Here is another curious phenomenon. In the *Apostolic Constitutions* (II. 22, 23) the whole story of Manasseh is quoted in a text avowedly compounded from 2 Kings and 2 Chronicles, with the addition of the Prayer and deliverance of Manasseh, which are non-Biblical, and after a short interval the story of Amon is given, with a spurious insertion to this effect: "Amon said, 'My father did very wickedly from his youth, and repented in his old age. Now therefore I will walk as my soul listeth, and afterward I will return to the Lord.'" just so, in *Philo* LII. 4, when Eli said to Hophni and Phinehas, "Repent of your wicked ways," they said, "When we are grown old we will repent": and therefore God would not grant them repentance. The resemblance is arresting. The consideration of it suggests the question whether this of Amon and the Prayer of Manasseh and the story of his deliverance can be excerpts from *Philo*. So far as the Prayer is concerned I cannot think it likely, for that composition is not in our author's manner, and is not believed to be a translation from Hebrew. And, if the Prayer is not from *Philo*, we need not unnecessarily multiply the authorities used by *Const. Ap*.

For all that, the story of Manasseh and his deliverance may have been told in *Philo*: the form of it which appears in the *Apocalypse of Baruch* (64) rather suggests to me that it was. The Apocalyptist uses Philonic language when he says of Manasseh that "his abode was in the fire"; and, further, he does not account Manasseh's repentance to have been genuine or final, and in this--if I read my author rightly--he writes in the Philonic spirit: for *Philo*, if he is willing to dwell on the repentance and reform of Israel as a whole, seems to take pleasure in recording the apostasies and transgressions of individuals who do not repent--the sinners under Kenaz, Jair, Gideon, Micah, Doeg.

When Saul protests to Samuel that he is too obscure to be made King, Samuel says (LVI. 6): "Your words will be like those of a prophet yet to come who will be called Jeremiah." This odd prediction is modelled, I suppose, upon the mention of Josiah in 1 Kings 13, and is comparable to Hannah's quotation of a psalm by Asaph (LI. 6). That the fulfilment of it was mentioned is likely enough, but by no means necessary.

Lastly, a phrase in the story of Kenaz demands notice. When God gives him the new set of twelve precious stones to replace certain others that had been destroyed, He says (XXVI. 12) that they are to be placed in the ark, and to be there "until Jahel shall arise to build an house in my name, and then he shall set them before me upon the two cherubim . . . and when the sins of my people are fulfilled, and their enemies begin to prevail over their house, I will take those stones and the former ones (*i.e.* those already in the priest's breastplate) and put them back in the place whence they were brought, and there shall they be until I remember the world and visit them that dwell on the earth. . . . And Kenaz placed them in the ark . . . and they are there unto this day."

Apart from the mention of Jahel (by whom Solomon is meant, but why so called I know not) this is rather a perplexing passage. Taken as it stands, it ought to mean that the temple, or at least the ark, was extant at the supposed date of the writer, *i.e.* that the story was not carried down as far as the destruction of Jerusalem by Nebuchadnezzar; which, on general grounds, one would select as a likely point for the conclusion. We must however, remember the legend that the ark and its contents were preserved and hidden by Jeremiah or by an angel (2 *Macc.* 2. *Apoc. Bar.* 64) . Besides, *Philo* elsewhere says (XXII. 9) that in the new sanctuary which was at Gilgal, "Joshua appointed unto this day (*usque in hodiernum diem*)" the yearly sacrifices of Israel, and that until the temple was built sacrifice at the other place was lawful. We cannot, then, press his use of the phrase "unto this day"; yet if it be insisted upon, there is a detail in *Baruch* (6) which may throw some light on *Philo's* meaning. *Baruch* says that the angel took, among other things, "the forty-eight precious stones wherewith the priest was adorned" and committed them to the guardianship of the earth. No one offers any reason for the mention of forty-eight (instead of twelve) stones, and though only twelve more figure in the story of Kenaz, I think it not unreasonable to suggest that here as elsewhere the Apocalyptist has our text in his mind, and that a belief in the legend of the hidden ark was common to both.

The sketch of Israel's history contained in *Apoc. Bar.* 56-67 (a section which shows many resemblances to *Philo*), with its alternations of righteousness and sin, gives, to my mind, a very fair idea of what *Philo* may have comprised when it was complete. We begin with the sin of Adam and of the angels: both are alluded to more than once in *Philo*. Then we have Abraham (important in *Philo*), the wickedness of the Gentiles, and especially of the Egyptians (not emphasized in *Philo*), the ages of Moses and Joshua (treated at length), the sorceries of the Amorites under the Judges (dwelt on at great length), the age of David and Solomon (*Philo* breaks off in David), the times of Jeroboam and Jezebel and the captivity of the nine and a half tribes, the reign of Hezekiah, the wickedness of Manasseh, the reforms of Josiah, the destruction by Nebuchadnezzar. *Baruch* then continues the history to the Messianic kingdom and the final triumph of right, of which *Philo* speaks only in general terms, though it may have developed clearer views as it proceeded. For the present, my conjecture is that *Philo* ended with the Babylonian captivity, and not without an anticipation of the Return.

12. Conclusion. Character Of The Present Edition

12. I fear that we cannot regard the writer of *Philo* as a man of very lofty mind or of great literary talent. He has some imagination, and is sensible of the majesty of the Old Testament literature, but he has not the insight, the power, or the earnestness of the author of 4 *Esdras*, nor again the ethical perception of him who wrote the *Testaments of the Twelve Patriarchs*. From this point of view the obscurity which has hung over his book is not undeserved. Nevertheless it is a source by no means to be neglected by the student of Christian origins and of Jewish thought, and for that reason I have suggested that it should find a place in this series of translations.

I hope that the pretensions of this edition will not be misconceived. It is not a critical edition in the sense that it presents all the variants of all the authorities and lays the whole body of evidence before the reader. Such a presentation would only be possible if the text as well as the translation were included in this volume. (I do not myself, let me say in passing, believe that the result of a complete statement of various readings would differ very importantly from what the reader now has before him, seeing that the text depends upon a single thread of tradition.) Nor, again, will every available illustrative passage be found in such notes as I have written on the subject matter in Rabbinic literature especially it should be possible to find many more parallels. Notes of a linguistic kind, too, are out of place where a translation only is in question. Neither has every Biblical allusion been marked: as a rule, the reader who knows his Bible will easily recognize the phrases which the author weaves together often deftly enough. Besides these omissions, larger problems remain unsolved. There are not a few unhealed places in the text, and there are some whole episodes of which the bearing is very obscure.

On the other hand, I may claim that account has here been taken for the first time of a fairly representative selection of the authorities for the text, and that the relation of the book to some, at least, of its fellows has been elucidated; and I hope that the translation, in which I have followed as closely as possible the language of the Authorised Version (though I have kept the Latin forms of the proper names), may be found readable.

I have, further, provided a means of referring to passages in the text by a division into chapters and verses, or sections, which I think must prove useful. Something of the kind was much needed, for it has hitherto only been possible to cite by the pages of one or other of the sixteenth-century editions. My division is of course applicable to any future edition.

The present volume is, then, a step in the direction of a critical edition, but only a step. Like the first editor, Sichardus, I recognize its defects (or some of them) and should welcome the opportunity, if it ever came, of producing an improved form of the original text. As it is the kindness of the Society under whose auspices the book appears allows me to include in it a selection of the most important readings and some particulars of the Latinity of the original. For this indulgence my readers, as well as myself, will assuredly be grateful.

13. Synopsis Of The Contents

CHAPTER

I. Genealogy from Adam to Noah, with the names of the sons and daughters of the early patriarchs.

II. Genealogy from Cain to Lamech; the names of Cain's cities, short accounts of Jubal and Tubal, and the song of Lamech.

III. The Flood and the covenant with Noah, mainly in the words of Genesis, but with the addition of two important speeches of God.

IV. The descendants of Shem, Ham and Japhet, and the territories occupied by them. The genealogy continued to Abraham. In this occur accounts of the first appearing of the rainbow, the prophecy of Milcah, and the beginning of divination.

V. The review and census of the descendants of Noah.

VI. The Tower of Babel begun. Abraham's rescue from the fire.

VII. Destruction of the Tower, and dispersion of the builders.

VIII. The genealogy from Abraham to the going down into Egypt. The names of Job's children.

IX. The oppression in Egypt. Amram refuses to separate from his wife. Miriam's vision. The birth of Moses.

X. The plagues, the crossing of the Red Sea. Israel in the desert.

XI. The giving of the Law. The Decalogue.

XII. The Golden Calf.

XIII. The Tabernacle, and the institution of certain Feasts.

XIV. The numbering of the people.

XV. The spies.

XVI. Korah.

XVII. Aaron's Rod.

XVIII. Balaam.

XIX. The farewell and death of Moses.

XX. Joshua succeeds him. The spies sent to Jericho. Withdrawal of the manna, pillar of cloud, and fountain.

XXI. Joshua warned of his end: his prayer: he writes the Law upon stones and builds an altar.

XXII. The altar built by the tribes beyond Jordan. The sanctuary at Shiloh.

XXIII. Joshua's last speech, with the story of Abraham's vision and of the giving of the Law.

XXIV. His farewell and death.

XXV. Kenaz (Cenez) elected ruler by lot. Detection by the lot of sinners among the tribes. Their confessions: account of the Amorite idols.

XXVI. God directs the disposal of the accursed objects: the sinners are burned. The commands of God are carried out: account of the twelve precious stones.

XXVII. Kenaz's victory, single-handed, over the Amorites.

XXVIII. His last days: the speech of Phinehas: vision and death of Kenaz.

XXIX. Zebul succeeds: an inheritance given to the daughters of Kenaz: a sacred treasury founded: death of Zebul.

XXX. Israel oppressed by Sisera. Deborah's speech.

XXXI. The stars fight against Sisera: his death.

XXXII. Deborah's hymn, with the description of the sacrifice of Isaac and the giving of the Law.

XXXIII. Last words and death of Deborah.

XXXIV. Aod, the wizard of Midian, seduces Israel by his sorceries.

XXXV. The call of Gideon.

XXXVI. He defeats Midian: his sin and death.

XXXVII. Abimelech succeeds. [*Gap in the text.*] Parable of the trees. Death of Abimelech. [*Gap in the text.*]

XXXVIII. Jair apostatizes and is destroyed by fire.

XXXIX. Israel oppressed by Ammon. Jephthah is persuaded to help. His negotiations with Getal, King of Ammon: his vow: God's anger.

XL. Seila, Jephthah's daughter: her readiness to die: her lamentation and death. Death of Jephthah.

XLI. The Judges Abdon (Addo) and Elon.

XLII. Manoah and his wife Eluma. Samson promised.

XLIII. Birth, exploits and death of Samson.

XLIV. Micah and his mother Dedila. The idols described. God's anger.

XLV. The Levite Bethac at Nob. The Benjamite outrage.

XLVI. Israel attacks Benjamin and is thrice defeated. Prayer of Phinehas.

XLVII. Parable of the Lion, spoken by God in answer to Phinehas. Benjamin is defeated: names of the surviving chiefs. Death of Micah.

XLVIII. Departure of Phinehas from among men. Wives are found for the Benjamites. Conclusion of the period of the Judges.

XLIX. Israel is at a loss for a ruler. Lots are cast in vain. Advice of Nethez. The lot falls on Elkanah, who refuses to be ruler. God promises Samuel.

L. Peninnah's reproaches to Hannah: Hannah's prayer.

LI. Birth of Samuel: hymn of Hannah.

LII. Sin of Hophni and Phinehas. Eli rebukes them, their refusal to repent.

LIII. Call of Samuel: Eli's submission to God's will.

LIV. The ark captured by the Philistines: Saul brings the news. Death of Eli and of his daughter-in-law.

LV. Grief of Samuel. The ark and Dagon: the Philistines plagued: they take counsel as to the return of the ark: it is sent back.

LVI. The people ask for a king, prematurely. Saul comes to Samuel.

LVII. Samuel presents him to the people and he is made king.

LVIII. He is sent against Amalek, and spares Agag. Agag is slain, after begetting a son who is to be Saul's slayer.

LIX. Samuel anoints David: David's psalm: the lion and the bear.

LX. Saul oppressed by an evil spirit: David's song.

LXI. David's first victory, over Midian. Goliath defies Israel: David slays him (story of Orpah and Ruth).

LXII. Saul's envy of David. David's parting with Jonathan: their farewell speeches and covenant.

LXIII. The priests of Nob slain: God's sentence against Doeg. Death of Samuel.

LXIV. Saul expels the sorcerers to make a name for himself: God's anger. The Philistines invade: Saul goes to Sedecla, the witch of Endor. Appearance and speech of Samuel.

LXV. Defeat of Saul: he summons the Amalekite (Edab, son of Agag) to kill him. The text ends abruptly in the midst of a message from Saul to David.

There is more than one plausible way of dividing the book into episodes. The simplest is this--

1. Adam to the descent into Egypt, cc. I.-VIII.
2. Moses, IX.-XIX.
3. Joshua, XX.-XXIV.

4. The judges, XXV.-XLVIII.
. Samuel, Saul and David, XLIV-LXV.
A more elaborate subdivision would be-
Adam to Lamech, I.-II.
Noah and his descendants, III.-V.
Abraham to the death of Joseph, VI.-VIII.
The life of Moses, IX.-XIX.
Joshua, XX.-XXIV.
The Judges, the chief figures being--
Kenaz, XXV.-XXVIII.
Zebul, XXIX.
Deborah, XXX.-XXXIII.
Aod, XXXIV.
Gideon, XXXV.-XXXVI.
Jair, XXXVIII.
Jephthah, XXXIX.-XL.
Abdon, Elon, XLI.
Samson, XLII.-XLIII.
The events of the last chapters of the Book of Judges, XLIV.-XLVIII.
Life of Samuel, to the return of the ark, XLIX.-LV.
Saul's career, LVI.-LXV., David entering upon the scene in LIX.

A third and more artificial method of division (which is followed to some extent by the MS. R) is into portions corresponding to the Biblical books, viz.--
Genesis, I.-VIII.
Exodus, IX.-XIII.
Leviticus, part of XIII.
Numbers, XIV.-XVIII.
Deuteronomy, XIX.
Joshua, XX.-XXIV.
Judges, XXV.-XLVIII.
1 Samuel, XLIX.-LXV.

The space allotted to the period of the Judges emerges as the striking feature. It is rather greater than that given to the Pentateuch and Joshua, and more than double the share of 1 Samuel. And of it almost a third part is devoted to the doings of a person practically unknown to the Bible, namely, Kenaz.

Additional Note

A passage in Origen *On Romans* (IV. 12, p. 646) deserves to be quoted as being very much in the manner of Philo. "We have found," he says, "in a certain apocryphal book (in quodam secretiore libello) mention of an angel of grace who takes his name from grace, being called Ananchel, *i.e.* the grace of God: and the writing in question says that this angel was sent by God to Esther to give her favour in the sight of the king." just so in Philo appropriate angels are sent to Kenaz and to David and intervene to save the victims of Jair. I think it worth suggesting that the story of Esther found a place in *Philo*, and that this was the *secretior libellus* to which Origen refers.

NOTE

Phrases and sentences in *italics* mark quotations from the Old Testament: single words in *italics*, and short, are supplements of the translator.

The following signs are also employed:

[ ] Words wrongly inserted into the text.
( ) Alternative readings of importance.
< > (As p. 151) Words that have fallen out, restored by
<< >> As p. 100)} conjecture.
† † (As p. 89) Corrupt passages.

THE BIBLICAL ANTIQUITIES OF PHILO OR THE HISTORY OF PHILO FROM THE BEGINNING OF THE WORLD TO KING DAVID

Chapter 1

1. The beginning of the world. Adam begat three sons and one daughter, Cain, Noaba, Abel and Seth.

2. And Adam *lived after he begat Seth 700 years, and begat 12 sons and 8 daughters.*

3. And these are the names of the males: Eliseel, Suris, Elamiel, Brabal, Naat, Zarama, Zasam, Maathal, and Anath.

4. And these are his daughters: Phua, Iectas, Arebica, Sifa, Tecia, Saba, Asin.

5. *And Seth lived 105 years and begat Enos. And Seth lived after he begat Enos 707 years, and begat 3 sons and 2 daughters.*

6. And these are the names of his sons: Elidia, Phonna, and Matha: and of his daughters, Malida and Thila.

7. *And Enos lived 180 years and begat Cainan. And Enos lived after he begat Cainan 715 years, and begat 2 sons and a daughter.*

8. And these are the names of his sons: Phoë and Thaal; and of the daughter, Catennath.

9. *And Cainan lived 520 years and begat Malalech. And Cainan lived after he begat Malalech 730 years, and begat 3 sons and 2 daughters.*

10. And these are the names of the males: Athach, Socer, Lopha: and the names of the daughters, Ana and Leua.

11. *And Malalech lived 165 years and begat Jareth. And Malalech lived after he begat Jareth 730 years, and begat 7 sons and 5 daughters.*

12. And these are the names of the males: Leta, Matha, Cethar, Melie, Suriel, Lodo, Othim. And these are the names of the daughters: Ada and Noa, Iebal, Mada, Sella.

13. *And Jareth lived 172 years and begat Enoch. And Jareth lived after he begat Enoch 800 years and begat 4 sons and 2 daughters.*

14. And these are the names of the males: Lead, Anac, Soboac and Iectar: and of the daughters, Tetzeco, Lesse.

15. *And Enoch lived 165 years and begat Matusalam. And Enoch lived after he begat Matusalam 200 years, and begat 5 sons and 3 daughters.*

16. *But Enoch pleased God* at that time *and was not found, for God translated him.*

17. Now the names of his sons are: Anaz, Zeum, Achaun, Pheledi, Elith; and of the daughters, Theiz, Lefith, Leath.

18. *And Mathusalam lived 187 years and begot Lamech. And Mathusalam lived after he begat Lamech 782 years, and begot 2 sons and 2 daughters.*

19. And these are the names of the males: Inab and Rapho; and of the daughters, Aluma and Amuga.

20. *And Lamech lived 182 years and begot a son, and called him* according to his nativity *Noe, saying: This child will give rest to us* and to the earth from those who are therein, upon whom (*or* in the day when) a visitation shall be made because of the iniquity of their evil deeds.

21. *And Lamech lived after he begot Noe 585 years.*
22. *And Noe lived 300 years and begot 3 sons,*

Chapter 2

II. But Cain dwelt in the earth trembling, according as God appointed unto him after he slew Abel his brother; and the name of his wife was Themech.

2. *And Cain knew* Themech *his wife and she conceived and bare Enoch.*

3. Now Cain was 15 years old when he did these things; and from that time he began to build cities, until he had founded seven cities. And these are the names of the cities: The name of the first city according to the name of his son Enoch. The name of the second city Mauli, and of the third Leeth, and the name of the fourth Teze, and the name of the fifth Iesca; the name of the sixth Celeth, and the name of the seventh Iebbath.

4. And Cain lived after he begat Enoch 715 years and begat 3 sons and 2 daughters. And these are the names of his sons: Olad, Lizaph, Fosal; and of his daughters, Citha and Maac. And all the days of Cain were 730 years, and he died.

5. Then took Enoch a wife of the daughters of Seth, which bare him Ciram and Cuuth and Madab. But Ciram begat Matusael, and Matusael begat Lamech.

6. *But Lamech took unto himself two wives: the name of the one was Ada and the name of the other Sella.*

7. *And Ada bare him* Iobab: *he was the father of all that dwell in tents and herd flocks.* And again she bare him *Iobal, which was the first to teach all playing of instruments* (*lit.* every psalm of organs).

8. And at that time, when they that dwelt on the earth had begun to do evil, every one with his neighbour's wife, defiling them, God was angry. And he began to play upon the *lute* (*kinnor*) *and the harp* and on every instrument of sweet psalmody (*lit.* psaltery), and to corrupt the earth.

9. *But Sella bare Tubal* and Misa and Theffa, and this is that Tubal which showed unto men arts in lead and tin and iron and copper and silver and gold: and then began the inhabiters of the earth to make graven images and to worship them.

10. *Now Lamech said unto his two wives Ada and Sella: Hear my voice, ye wives of Lamech, give heed to my precept*: for I have corrupted men for myself, and *have taken away* sucklings from the breasts, that I might show my sons how to work evil, *and the inhabiters of the earth.* And now *shall vengeance be taken seven times of Cain, but of Lamech seventy times seven.*

CHAPTER 3

III. *And it came to pass when men had begun to multiply on the earth,* that beautiful *daughters were born unto them. And the sons of God saw the daughters of men that they were exceeding fair, and took them wives of all that they had chosen.*

2. *And God said: My spirit shall not judge among these men for ever, because they are of flesh; but their years shall be* 120. Upon whom he laid (*or* wherein I have set) the ends of the world, and in their hands wickednesses were not put out (or the law shall not be quenched).

3. *And God saw that in all the dwellers upon earth works of evil were fulfilled: and inasmuch as their thought was upon iniquity all their days, God* said: *I will blot out man* and all things that have budded upon the earth, *for it repenteth me that I have made him.*

4. *But Noe found grace* and mercy *before the Lord, and these are his generations. Noe, which was a righteous man and* undefiled *in his generation, pleased the Lord.* Unto whom God *said: The time of all men that dwell upon the earth is come, for their deeds are very evil. And now make thee an ark of* cedar wood, *and thus shalt thou make it.* 300 *cubits shall be the length thereof, and* 50 *cubits the breadth, and* 30 *cubits the height. And thou shall enter into the ark, thou and thy wife and thy sons and thy sons' wives with thee. And I will make my covenant with thee,* to destroy all the dwellers upon earth. *Now of clean beasts and of the fowls of the heaven that are clean thou shalt take by sevens male and female, that their seed may be saved alive upon the earth. But of unclean beasts and fowls thou shalt take to thee by twos male and female, and shalt take provision for thee and for them also.*

5. *And Noe did that which God commanded him and entered into the ark, he and all his sons with him. And it came to pass after* 7 *days that the water of the flood began to be upon the earth. And in that day all the depths were opened* and the great spring *of water and the windows of heaven, and there was rain upon the earth* 40 *days and* 40 *nights.*

6. And it was then the 1652 (1656) year from the time when God had made the heaven and the earth in the day when the earth was corrupted with the inhabiters thereof by reason of the iniquity of their works.

7. And when the flood continued 140 days upon the earth, Noe only and they that were with him in the ark remained alive: and when God remembered Noe, he made the water to diminish.

8. And it came to pass on the 90 day that God dried the earth, and said *unto Noe: Go out of the ark, thou* and all that are with thee, *and grow and multiply upon the earth. And Noe went out of the ark, he an d his sons and his sons' wives, and all the beasts and creeping things and fowls and cattle* brought he forth with him as God commanded him. *Then built Noe an altar unto the Lord, and took of all the cattle and of the clean fowls and offered burnt offerings on the altar*: and it was accepted of the Lord for a savour of rest.

9. *And God said: I will not again curse the earth for man's sake, for the guise of man's heart* hath left off *from his youth. And therefore I will not again destroy together all living as I have done.* But it shall be, when the dwellers upon earth have sinned, I will judge them by famine or by the sword or by fire or by pestilence (*lit.* death), and there shall be earthquakes, and they shall be scattered into places not inhabited (*or*, the places of *their* habitation shall be scattered). But I will not again spoil the earth with the water of a flood, and *in all the days of the earth seed time and harvest, cold and heat, summer and*

autumn, day and night shall not cease, until I remember them that dwell on the earth, *even* until the times are fulfilled.

10. But when the years of the world shall be fulfilled, then shall the light cease and the darkness be quenched: and I will quicken the dead and raise up from the earth them that sleep: and Hell shall pay his debt and destruction give back that which was committed unto him, that I may render unto every man according to his works and according to the fruit of their imaginations, *even* until I judge between the soul and the flesh. And the world shall rest, and death shall be quenched, and Hell shall shut his mouth. And the earth shall not be without birth, neither barren for them that dwell therein: and none shall be polluted that hath been justified in me. And there shall be another earth and another heaven, even an everlasting habitation.

11. *And the Lord spake* further *unto Noe and to his sons saying: Behold I will make my covenant with you and with your seed after you, and will not again spoil the earth with the water of a flood. And all that liveth and moveth therein shall be to you for meal. Nevertheless the flesh with the blood of the soul shall ye not eat. For he that sheddeth man's blood, his blood shall be shed; for in the image of God was man made. And ye, grow ye and multiply and fill the earth* as the multitude of fishes that multiply in the waters. And God said: This is the covenant that I have made betwixt me and you; *and it shall be when I cover the heaven with clouds, that my bow shall appear in the cloud, and it shall be for a memorial of the covenant betwixt me and you, and all the dwellers upon earth.*

CHAPTER 4

IV. *And the sons of Noe which went forth of the ark were Sem, Cham, and Japheth.*
2. *The sons of Japheth: Gomer, Magog, and Madai*, Nidiazech, *Tubal*, Mocteras, Cenez, *Riphath, and Thogorma, Elisa*, Dessin, Cethin, Tudant.

And the sons of Gomer: Thelez, Lud, Deberlet.
And the sons of Magog: Cesse, Thipha, Pharuta, Ammiel, Phimei, Goloza, Samanach.
And the sons of Duden: Sallus, Phelucta Phallita.
And the sons of Tubal: Phanatonova, Eteva.
And the sons of Tyras: Maac, Tabel, Ballana, Samplameac, Elaz.
And the sons of Mellech: Amboradat, Urach, Bosara.
And the sons of <<As>>cenez: Jubal, Zaraddana, Anac.
And the sons of Heri: Phuddet, Doad, Dephadzeat, Enoc.
And the sons of Togorma: Abiud, Saphath, Asapli, Zepthir.
And the sons of Elisa: Etzaac, Zenez, Mastisa, Rira.
And the sons of Zepti: Macziel, Temna, Aela, Phinon.
And the sons of Tessis: Meccul, Loon, Zelataban.
And the sons of Duodennin: Itheb, Beath, Phenech.

3. And these are they that were scattered abroad, and dwelt in the earth with the Persians and Medes, and in the islands that are in the sea. And Phenech, the son of Dudeni, went up and commanded that ships of the sea should be made: and then was the third part of the earth divided.

4. Domereth and his sons took Ladech; and Magog and his sons took Degal; Madam and his sons took Besto; Iuban (*sc.* Javan) and his sons took Ceel; Tubal and his sons took Pheed; Misech and his sons took Nepthi; <<T>>iras and his sons took <<Rôô>>; Duodennut and his sons took Goda; Riphath and his sons took Bosarra; Torgoma and his sons took Fud; Elisa and his sons took Thabola; Thesis (*sc.* Tarshish) and his sons took Marecham; Cethim and his sons took Thaan; Dudennin and his sons took Caruba.

5. And then began they to till the earth and to sow upon it: and when the earth was athirst, the dwellers therein cried unto the Lord and he heard them and gave rain abundantly, and it was so, when the rain descended upon the earth, that the bow appeared in the cloud, and the dwellers upon earth saw the memorial of the covenant and fell upon their faces and sacrificed, offering burnt offerings unto the Lord.

6. *Now the sons of Cham were Chus, Mestra, and Phuni, and Chanaan. And the sons of Chus: Saba*, and . . . Tudan.

And the sons of Phuni: [Effuntenus], Zeleutelup, Geluc, Lephuc.
And the sons of Chanaan were Sydona, Endain, Racin, Simmin, Uruin, Nenugin, Amathin, Nephiti, Telaz, Elat, Cusin.

7. *And Chus begat Nembroth. He began to be* proud *before the Lord.*

But Mestram begat Ludin and Megimin and Labin and Latuin and Petrosonoin and Ceslun: *thence came forth the Philistines* and the Cappadocians.

8. And then did they also begin to build cities: and these are the cities which they built: Sydon, and the parts that lie about it, that is Resun, Beosa, Maza, Gerara, Ascalon, Dabir, Camo, Tellun, Lacis, Sodom and Gomorra, Adama and Seboim.

9. *And the sons of Sem: Elam, Assur, Arphaxa, Luzi, Aram.* And the sons of Aram: Gedrum, Ese. *And Arphaxa begat Sale, Sale begat Heber, and unto Heber were born two sons: the name of the one was Phalech, for in his days the earth was divided, and the name of his brother was Jectan.*

10. *And Jectan begat Helmadam and Salastra and Mazaam, Rea, Dura, Uzia, Deglabal, Mimoel, Sabthphin, Evilac, Iubab.*

And the sons of Phalech: Ragau, Rephuth, Zepheram, Aculon, Sachar, Siphaz, Nabi, Suri, Seciur, Phalacus, Rapho, Phalthia, Zaldephal, Zaphis, and Arteman, Heliphas. These are the sons of Phalech, and these are their names, and they took them wives of the daughters of Jectan and begat sons and daughters and filled the earth.

11. But Ragau took him to wife Melcha the daughter of Ruth, and she begat him Seruch. And when the day of her delivery came she said: Of this child shall be born in the fourth generation one who shall set his dwelling on high, and shall be called perfect, and undefiled, and he shall be the father of nations, and his covenant shall not be broken, and his seed shall be multiplied for ever.

12. *And Ragau lived after he begat Seruch* 119 *years and begat* 7 *sons and* 5 *daughters.* And these are the names of his sons: Abiel, Obed, Salma, Dedasal, Zeneza, Accur, Nephes. And these are the names of his daughters: Cedema, Derisa, Seipha, Pherita, Theila.

13. *And Seruch lived* 29 *years and begat Nachor. And Seruch lived after he begat Nachor* 67 *years and begat* 4 *sons and* 3 *daughters.* And these are the names of the males: Zela, Zoba, Dica and Phodde. And these are his daughters: Tephila, Oda, Selipha.

14. *And Nachor lived* 34 *years and begat Thara. And Nachor lived after he begat Thara* 200 *years and begat* 8 *sons and* 5 *daughters.* And these are the names of the males: Recap, Dediap, Berechap, Iosac, Sithal, Nisab, Nadab, Camoel. And these are his daughters: Esca, Thipha, Bruna, Ceneta.

15. *And Thara lived* 70 *years and begat Abram, Nachor, and Aram. And Aram begat Loth.*

16. Then began they that dwelt on the earth to look upon the stars, and began to prognosticate by them and to make divination, and to make their sons and daughters pass through the fire. But Seruch and his sons walked not according to them.

17. And these are the generations of Noe upon the earth according to their languages and their tribes, out of whom the nations were divided upon the earth after the flood.

CHAPTER 5

V. Then came the sons of Cham, and made Nembroth a prince over themselves: but the sons of Japheth made Phenech their chief: *and* the sons of Sem gathered together and set over them Jectan to be their prince.

2. And when these three had met together they took counsel that they would look upon and take account of the people of their followers. And this was done while Noe was yet alive, *even* that all men should be gathered together: and they lived at one with each other, and the earth was at peace.

3. Now in the 340th year of the going forth of Noe out of the ark, after that God dried up the flood, did the princes take account of their people.

4. And *first* Phenech the son of Japheth looked upon them.

The sons of Gomer all of them passing by according to the sceptres of their captaincies were in number 5,800.

But of the sons of Magog all of them passing by according to the sceptres of their leading the number was 6,200.

And of the sons of Madai all of them passing by according to the sceptres of their captaincies were in number 5,700.

And the sons of Tubal. all of them passing by according to the sceptres of their captaincies were in number 9,400.

And the sons of Mesca all of them passing by according to the sceptres of their captaincies were in number 5,600.

The sons of Thiras all of them passing by according to the sceptres of their captaincies were in number 12,300.

And the sons of Ripha<<th>> passing by according to the sceptres of their captaincies were in number 14,500.

And the sons of Thogorma passing by according to the sceptres of their captaincy were in number 14,400.

But the sons of Elisa passing by according to the sceptres of their captaincy were in number 14,900.

And the sons of Thersis all of them passing by according to the sceptres of their captaincy were in number 12,100.

The sons of Cethin all of them passing by according to the sceptres of their captaincy were in number 17,300.

And the sons of Doin passing by according to the sceptres of their captaincies were in number 17,700.

And the number of the camp of the sons of Japheth, all of them men of might and all girt with their armour, which were set in the sight of their captains was 140,202 besides women and children.

The account of Japheth in full was in number 142,000.

5. And Nembroth passed by, he and the son(s) of Cham all of them passing by according to the sceptres of their captaincies were found in number 24,800.

The sons of Phua all of them passing by according to the sceptres of their captaincies were in number 27,700.

And the sons of Canaan all of them passing by according to the sceptres of their captaincies were found in number 32,800.

The sons of Soba all of them passing by according to the sceptres of their captaincies were found in number 4,300.

The sons of Lebilla all of them passing by according to the sceptres of their captaincies were found in number 22,300.

And the sons of Sata all of them passing by according to the sceptres of their captaincies were found in number 25,300.

And the sons of Remma all of them passing by according to the sceptres of their captaincies were found in number 30,600.

And the sons of Sabaca all of them passing by according to the sceptres of their captaincies were found in number 46,400.

And the number of the camp of the sons of Cham, all of them mighty men, and furnished with armour, which were set in the sight of their captaincies was in number 244,900 besides women and children.

6. And Jectan the son of Sem looked upon the sons of Elam, and they were all of them passing by according to the number of the sceptres of their captaincies in number 47,000.

And the sons of Assur all of them passing by according to the sceptres of their captaincies were found in number 73,000.

And the sons of Aram all of them passing by according to the sceptres of their captaincies were found in number 87,300.

The sons of Lud all of them passing by according to the sceptres of their captaincies were found in number 30,600.

[The number of the sons of Cham was 73,000.]

But the sons of Arfaxat all of them passing by according to the sceptres of their captaincies were in number 114,600.

And the whole number of them was 347,600. 7. The number of the camp of the sons of Sem, all of them setting forth in valour and in the commandment of war in the sight of their captaincies was † ix † besides women and children.

8. And these are the generations of Noe set forth separately, whereof the whole number together was 914,000. And all these were counted while Noe was yet alive, and in the presence of Noe 350 years after the flood. And all the days of Noe were 950 years, and he died.

CHAPTER 6

VI. Then all they that had been divided and dwelt upon the earth gathered together there after, and dwelt together; *and they set forth from the East and found a plain in the land of Babylon: and there they dwelt, and they said every man to his neighbour*: Behold, it will come to pass that we shall be scattered every man. from his brother, and in the latter days we shall be fighting one against another. Now, therefore, come and let us build for ourselves a tower, the head whereof shall reach unto heaven, and we shall make us a name and a renown upon the earth.

2. And they said everyone to his neighbour: Let us take bricks (*lit.* stones), and let us, each one, write our names upon the bricks and burn them with fire: and that which is thoroughly burned shall be for mortar and brick. (*Perhaps,* that which is not thoroughly burned shall be for mortar, and that which is, for brick.)

3. And they took every man their bricks, saving 12 men, which would not take them, and these are their names: Abraham, Nachor, Loth, Ruge, Tenute, Zaba, Armodath, Iobab, Esar, Abimahel, Saba, Auphin.

4. And the people of the land laid hands on them and brought them before their princes and said: These are the men that have transgressed our counsels and will not walk in our ways. And the princes said unto them: Wherefore would ye not set every man your bricks with the people of the land? And they answered and said: We will not set bricks with you, neither will we be joined with your desire. One Lord know we, and him do we worship. And if ye should cast us into the fire with your bricks, we will not consent to you.

5. And the princes were wroth and said: As they have said, so do unto them, and if they consent not to set bricks with you, ye shall burn them with fire together with your bricks.

6. Then answered Jectan which was the first prince of the captains: Not so, but there shall be given them a space of 7 days. And it shall be, if they repent of their evil counsels, and will set bricks along with us, they shall live; but if not, let them be burned according to your word. But he sought how he might save them out of the hands of the people; for he was of their tribe, and he served God.

7. And when he had thus said he took them and shut them up in the king's house: and when it was evening the prince commanded 50 mighty men of valour to be called unto him, and said unto them: Go forth and take to-night these men that are shut up in mine house, and put provision for them from my house upon 10 beasts, and the men bring ye to me, and their provision together with the beasts take ye to the mountains and wait for them there: and know this, that if any man shall know what I have said unto you, I will burn you with fire.

8. And the men set forth and did all that their prince commanded them, and took the men from his house by night; and took provision and put it upon beasts and took them to the hill country as he commanded them.

9. And the prince called unto him those 12 men and said to them: Be of good courage and fear not, for ye shall not die. For God in whom ye trust is mighty, and therefore be ye stablished in him, for he will deliver you and save you. And now lo, I have commanded So men to take [you with] provision from my house, and go before you into the hill country and wait for you in the valley: and I will give you other 50 men which shall guide you thither: go ye therefore and hide yourselves there in the valley, having water to drink that floweth down from the rocks: hold yourselves *there* for 30 days, until the anger of the people of the land be appeased and until God send his wrath upon them and break them. For I know that the counsel of iniquity which they have agreed to perform shall not stand, for their thought is vain. And it shall be when 7 days are expired and they shall seek for you, I will say unto them: They have gone forth and have broken the door of the prison wherein they were shut up and have fled by night, and I have sent 100 men to seek them. So will I turn them from their madness that is upon them.

10. And there answered him 11 of the men saying: Thy servants have found favour in thy sight, in that we are set free out of the hands of these proud men.

11. But Abram only kept silence, and the prince said unto him: Wherefore answerest thou not me, Abram, servant of God? Abram answered and said: Lo, I flee away to-day into the hill country, and if I escape the fire, wild beasts will come out of the mountains and devour us. Or our victuals will fail and we shall die of hunger; and we shall be found fleeing from the people of the land and shall fall in our sins. And now, as he liveth in whom I trust, I will not remove from my place wherein they have put me: and if there be any sin of mine so that I be indeed burned, the will of God be done. And the prince said unto him: Thy blood be upon thy head, if thou refuse to go forth with these. But if thou consent, thou shalt be delivered. Yet if thou wilt abide, abide as thou art. And Abram said: I will not go forth, but I will abide here.

12. And the prince took those 11 men and sent other 50 with them, and commanded them saying: Wait, ye also, in the hill country for 15 days with those 50 which were sent before you; and after that ye shall return and say We have not found them, as I said to the former ones. And know that if any man transgress one of all these words that I have spoken unto you, he shall be burned with fire. So the men went forth, and he took Abram by himself and shut him up where he had been shut up aforetime.

13. And after 7 days were passed, the people were gathered together and spake unto their prince saying: Restore us the men which would not consent unto us, that we may burn them with fire. And they sent captains to bring them, and they found them not, save Abram only. And they gathered all of them to their prince saying: The men whom ye shut up are fled and have escaped that which we counselled.

14. And Phenech and Nemroth said unto Jectan: Where are the men whom thou didst shut up? But he said: They have broken prison and fled by night: but I have sent 100 men to seek them, and commanded them if they find them that they should not only burn them with fire but give their bodies to the fowls of the heaven and so destroy them.

15. Then said they: This *fellow* which is found alone, let us burn him. And they took Abram and brought him before their princes and said to him: Where are they that were with thee? And he said: Verily at night I slept, and when I awaked I found them not.

16. And they took him and built a furnace and kindled it with fire, and put bricks burned with fire into the furnace. Then Jectan the prince being amazed (*lit.* melted) in his mind took Abram and put him with the bricks into the furnace of fire.

17. But God stirred up a great earthquake, and the fire gushed forth of the furnace and brake out into flames and sparks of fire and consumed all them that stood round about in sight of the furnace; and all they that were burned in that day were 83,500. But upon Abram was there not any the least hurt by the burning of the fire.

18. And Abram arose out of the furnace, and the fiery furnace fell down, and Abram was saved. And he went unto the 11 men that were hid in the hill country and told them all that had befallen him, and they came down with him out of the hill country rejoicing in the name of the Lord, and no man met them to affright them that day. And they called that place by the name of Abram, and in the tongue of the Chaldeans Deli, which is being interpreted, God.

Chapter 7

VII. And it came to pass after these things, that the people of the land turned not from their evil thoughts: and they came together again unto their princes and said: The people shall not be overcome for ever: and now let us come together and build us a city and a tower which shall never be removed.

2. And when they had begun to build, God saw the city and the tower which the children of men were building, *and he said: Behold, this is one people and their speech is one*, and this which they have begun to build the earth will not sustain, neither will the heaven suffer it, beholding it: and it shall be, if they be not now hindered, that they shall dare all things that they shall take in mind to do.

3. *Therefore, lo, I will divide their speech*, and scatter them over all countries, that they may not know every man his brother, neither every man understand the speech of his neighbour. And I will deliver them to the rocks, and they shall build themselves tabernacles of stubble and straw, and shall dig themselves caves and shall live therein like beasts of the field, and thus shall they continue before my face for ever, that they may never devise such things. And I will esteem them as a drop of water, and liken them unto spittle: and unto some of them their end shall come by water, and other of them shall be dried up with thirst.

4. And before all of them will I choose my servant Abram, and I will bring him out from their land, and lead him into the land which mine eye hath looked upon from the beginning when all the dwellers upon earth sinned before my face, and I brought *on them* the water of the flood: and *then* I destroyed not *that land*, but preserved it. Therefore the fountains of my wrath did not break forth therein, neither did the water of my destruction come down upon it. For there will I make my servant Abram to dwell, and I will make my covenant with him, and bless his seed, and will be called his God for ever.

5. Howbeit when the people that dwelt in the land had begun to build the tower, God divided their speech, and changed their likeness. And they knew not every man his brother, neither did each understand the speech of his neighbour. So it came to pass that when the builders commanded their helpers to bring bricks they brought water, and if they asked for water, the others brought them straw. And so their counsel was broken and the), ceased building the city: and *God scattered them thence over the face of all the earth. Therefore was the name of that place called Confusion, because there God confounded their speech, and scattered them thence over the face of all the earth.*

CHAPTER 8

VIII. *But Abram went forth thence and dwell in the land of Chanaan, and took with him Loth his brothers son, and Sarai his wife.* And because Sarai was barren and had no offspring, then Abram took Agar her maid, and she bare him Ismahel. And Ismahel begat 12 sons.

2. Then Loth departed from Abram and dwelt in Sodom [but Abram dwelt in the land of Cam]. And the men of Sodom were very evil and sinners exceedingly.

3. And God appeared unto Abraham saying: Unto thy seed will I give this land; and thy name shall be called Abraham, and Sarai thy wife shall be called Sara. Ana I will give thee of her an eternal seed and make my covenant with thee. And Abraham knew Sara his wife, and she conceived and bare Isaac.

4. And Isaac took him a wife of Mesopotamia, the daughter of Bathuel, which conceived and bare him Esau and Jacob.

5. And Esau took to him for wives Judin the daughter of Bereu, and Basemath the daughter of Elon, and Elibema the daughter of Anan, and Manem the daughter of Samahel. And <<Basemath>> *bare him Adelifan, and the sons of Adelifan were Temar, Omar, Seffor, Getan, Tenaz, Amalec.* And Judin bare Tenacis, Ieruebemas, *Bassemen, Rugil*: and the *sons of Rugil were Naizar, Samaza; and Elibema bare Auz, Iollam, Coro*. Manem bare Tenetde, Thenatela.

6. And Jacob took to him for wives the daughters Gen. of Laban the Syrian, Lia and Rachel, and two concubines, Bala and Zelpha. And Lia bare him Ruben, Simeon, Levi, Juda, Isachar, Zabulon, and Dina their sister. But Rachel bare Joseph and Benjamin. Bala bare Dan and Neptalim, and Zelpha bare Gad and Aser. These are the 12 sons of Jacob and one daughter.

7. And Jacob dwelt in the land of Chanaan, and Sichem the son of Emor the Correan forced his daughter Dina and humbled her. And Simeon and Levi the sons of Jacob went in and slew all their city with the edge of the sword, and took Dina their sister, and went out thence.

8. And thereafter Job took her to wife and begat of her 14 sons and 6 daughters, even 7 sons and 3 daughters before he was smitten with affliction, and thereafter when he was made whole 7 sons and 3 daughters. And these are their names: Eliphac, Erinoe, Diasat, Philias, Diffar, Zellud, Thelon: and his daughters Meru, Litaz, Zeli. And such as had been the names of the former, so were they also of the latter.

9. Now Jacob and his 12 sons dwelt in the land of Chanaan: and *his sons* hated their brother Joseph, whom also they delivered into Egypt, to Petephres the chief of the cooks of Pharao, and he abode with him 14 years.

10. And it came to pass after that the king of Egypt had seen a dream, that they told him of Joseph, and he declared him the dreams. And it was so after he declared his dreams, that Pharao made him prince over all the land of Egypt. At that time there was a famine in all the land, as Joseph had foreseen. And his brethren came down into Egypt to buy food, because in Egypt only was there food. And Joseph knew his brethren, and was made known to them, and dealt not evilly with them. And he sent and called his father out of the land of Chanaan, and he came down unto him.

11. *And these are the names of the sons of Israel which came down into Egypt with Jacob*, each one with his house. *The sons of Reuben, Enoch and Phallud, Esrom and Carmin; the sons of Simeon, Namuhel and Iamin and Dot and Iachin, and Saul the son of a Canaanitish woman.The sons of Levi, Gerson, Caat and Merari: but the sons of Juda, Auna, Selon, Phares, Zerami.The sons of Isachar, Tola and Phua, Job and Sombram. The sons of*

Zabulon, Sarelon and Iaillil. And Dina their sister bare 14 sons and 6 daughters. And these are the generations *of Lia whom she bare to Jacob. All the souls of sons and daughters were* 72.

12. *Now the sons of Dan were Usinam. The sons of Neptalim*, Betaal, Neemmu, Surem, Optisariel. *And these are the generations of Balla which she bare to Jacob. All the souls were* 8.

13. *But the sons of Gad:* . . . Sariel, Sua, Visui, Mophat *and Sar: their sister* the daughter of Seriebel, Melchiel. *These are the* generations *of Zelpha* the wife of Jacob *which she bare to him. And all the souls of sons and daughters were* in number 10.

14. *And the sons of Joseph, Ephraim and Manassen: and Benjamin* begat Gela, *Esbel, Abocmephec*, Utundeus. *And these were the souls which Rachel bare to Jacob*, 14. And they went down into Egypt and abode there 210 years.

CHAPTER 9

IX. And it came to pass after the departure of Joseph, *the children of Israel were multiplied and increased greatly. And there arose another king in Egypt which knew not Joseph: and he said to his people: Lo, this people is multiplied more than we. Come let us take counsel against them that they multiply not. And the king of Egypt commanded all his people saying: Every son that shall be born to the Hebrews, cast into the river, but keep the females alive.* And the Egyptians answered their king saying: Let us slay their males and keep their females, to give them to our bondmen for wives: and he that is born of them shall be a bondman and serve us. And this is that that did appear most evil before the Lord.

2. Then the elders of the people assembled the people with mourning and mourned and lamented saying: An untimely birth have the wombs of our wives suffered. Our fruit is delivered over to our enemies and now we are cut off. Yet let us appoint us an ordinance, that no man come near his wife, lest the fruit of their womb be defiled, and our bowels serve idols: for it is better to die childless, until we know what God will do.

3. And Amram answered and said: It will sooner come to pass that the age shall be utterly abolished and the immeasurable world fall, or the heart of the depths touch the stars, than that the race of the children of Israel should be diminished. And it shall be, when the covenant is fulfilled whereof God when he made it spake to Abraham saying: Surely thy sons shall dwell in a land that is not theirs, and shall be brought into bondage and afflicted 400 years.--And lo, since the word was passed which God spake to Abraham, there are 350 years. (And) since we have been in bondage in Egypt it is 130 years.

4. Now therefore I will not abide by that which ye ordain, but will go in and take my wife and beget sons, that we may be made many on the earth. For God will not continue in his anger, neither will he alway forget his people, nor cast forth the race of Israel to nought upon the earth, neither did he in vain make his covenant with our fathers: yea, when as yet we were not, God spake of these things.

5. Now therefore I will go and take my wife, neither will I consent to the commandment of this king. And if it be right in your eyes, so let us do all of us, for it shall be, when our wives conceive, they shall not be known to be great with child until 3 months are fulfilled, like as also our mother Thamar did, for her intent was not to fornication, but because she would not separate herself from the sons of Israel she took thought and said: It is better for me to die for sinning with my father-in-law than to be joined to Gentiles. And she hid the fruit of her womb till the 3rd month, for then was it perceived. And as she went to be put to death she affirmed it saying: The man whose is this staff and this ring and goatskin, of him have I conceived. And her device delivered her out of all peril.

6. Now therefore let us also do thus. And it shall be when the time of bringing forth is come, if it be possible, we will not cast forth the fruit of our womb. And who knoweth if thereby God will be provoked, to deliver us from our humiliation?

7. And the word which Amram had in his heart was pleasing before God: and God said: Because the thought of Amram is pleasing before me, and he hath not set at nought the covenant made between me and his fathers, therefore, lo now, that which is begotten of him shall serve me for ever, and by him will I do wonders in the house of Jacob, and will do by him signs and wonders for my people which I have done for none other, and will perform in them my glory and declare unto them my ways.

8. I the Lord will kindle for him my lamp to dwell in him, and will show him my covenant which no man hath seen, and manifest to him my great excellency, and my justice and judgments and will shine for him a perpetual light. For in ancient days I thought of him, saying: My spirit shall not be a mediator among these men for ever, for they are flesh, and their days shall be 120 years.

9. And Amram of the tribe of Levi went forth and took a wife of his tribe, and it was so when he took her, that the residue did after him and took their wives. Now he had one son and one daughter, and their names were Aaron and Maria,

10. And the spirit of God came upon Maria by night, and she saw a dream, and told her parents in the morning saying: I saw this night, and behold a man in a linen garment stood and said to me: Go and tell thy parents: behold, that which shall be born of you shall be cast into the water, for by him water shall be dried up, and by him will I do signs, and I will save my people, and he shall have the captaincy thereof alway. And when Maria had told her dream her parents believed her not.

11. But the word of the king of Egypt prevailed against the children of Israel and they were humiliated and oppressed in the work of bricks.

12. But Jochabeth conceived of Amram and hid *the child* in her womb 3 months, for she could not hide it longer: because the king of Egypt had appointed overseers of the region, that when the Hebrew women brought forth they should cast the males into the river straightway. And she took her child and made him an ark of the bark of a pine-tree and set the ark on the edge of the river.

13. Now the boy was born in the covenant of God and in the covenant of his flesh.

14. And it came to pass, when they cast him out, all the elders gathered together and chode with Amram saying: Are not these the words which we spake saying: "It is better for us to die childless than that our fruit should be cast into the water?" And when they said so, Amram hearkened not to them.

15. But the daughter of Pharao came down to wash in the river according as she had seen in a dream, and her maids saw the ark, and she sent one of them and took it and opened it. And when she saw the child and looked upon the covenant, that is, the testament in his flesh, she said: He is of the children of the Hebrews.

16. And she took him and nourished him and he became her son, and she called his name Moyses. But his mother called him Melchiel. And the child was nourished and became glorious above all men, and by him God delivered the children of Israel, as he had said.

CHAPTER 10

X. Now when the king of Egypt was dead another king arose, and afflicted all the people of Israel. But they cried unto the Lord and he heard them, and sent Moses and delivered them out of the land of Egypt: and God sent also upon them 10 plagues and smote them. Now these were the plagues, namely, blood, and frogs, and all manner of flies, hail, and death of cattle, locusts and gnats, and darkness that might be felt, and the death of the firstborn.

2. And when they had gone forth thence and were journeying, the heart of the Egyptians was yet again hardened, and they continued to pursue them, and found them by the Red Sea. And the children of Israel cried unto their God and spake to Moyses saying: Lo, now is come the time of our destruction, for the sea is before us and the multitude of enemies behind us, and we in the midst. Was it for this that God brought us out, or are these the covenants which he made with our fathers saying: To your seed will I give the land wherein ye dwell? and now let him do with us that which seemeth good in his sight.

3. Then did the children of Israel sever their counsels into three divisions of counsels, because of the fear of the time. For the tribe of Ruben and of Isachar and. of Zabulon and of Symeon said: Come, let us cast ourselves into the sea, for it is better for us to die in the water than to be slain of our enemies. And the tribe of Gad and of Aser and of Dan and Neptalim said: Nay, but let us return with them, and if they will give us our lives, we will serve them. But the tribe of Levi and of Juda and Joseph and the tribe of Benjamin said: Not so, but let us take our weapons and fight them, and God will be with us.

4. Moses also cried unto the Lord and said: O Lord God of our fathers, didst thou not say unto me: Go and tell the sons of Lia, God hath sent me unto You? And now, behold, thou hast brought thy people to the brink of the sea, and the enemy follow after them: but thou, Lord, remember thy name.

5. And God said: Whereas thou hast cried unto me, take thy rod and smite the sea, and it shall be dried up. And when Moses did all this, God rebuked the sea, and the sea was dried up: the seas of waters stood still and the depths of the earth appeared, and the foundations of the dwelling-place were laid bare at the noise of the fear of God and at the breath of the anger of my Lord.

6. And Israel passed over on dry land in the midst of the sea. And the Egyptians saw and went on to pursue after them, and God hardened their mind, and they knew not that they were entering into the sea. And so it was that while the Egyptians were in the sea God commanded the sea yet again, and said to Moses: Smite the sea yet once again. And he did so. And the Lord commanded the sea and it returned unto his waves, and covered the Egyptians and their chariots and their horsemen unto this day.

7. But as for his own people, he led them forth into the wilderness: forty years did he rain bread from heaven for them, and he brought them quails from the sea, and a well of water following them brought he forth for them. And in a pillar of cloud he led them by day and in a pillar of fire by night did he give light unto them.

CHAPTER 11

XI. *And in the 3rd month of the journeying of the children of Israel out of the land of Egypt, they came into the wilderness of Sinai.* And God remembered his word and said: I will give light unto the world, and lighten the habitable places, and make my covenant with the children of men, and glorify my people above all nations, for unto them will I put forth an eternal exaltation which shall be unto them a light, but unto the ungodly a chastisement.

2. And he said unto Moses: Behold, I will call thee to-morrow: be thou ready and tell my people: "For three days let not a man come near his wife," and on the 3rd day I will speak unto thee and unto them, and after that thou shalt come up unto me. And I will put my words in thy mouth and thou shalt enlighten my people. For I have given into thy hands an everlasting law whereby I will judge all the world. For this shall be for a testimony. For if men say: "We have not known thee, and therefore we have not served thee," therefore will I take vengeance upon them, because they have not known my law.

3. And Moses did as God commanded him, and sanctified the people and said unto them: *Be ye ready on the 3rd day*, for after 3 days will God make his covenant with you. And the people were sanctified.

4. *And it came to pass on the 3rd day that, lo, there were voices of thunderings (lit. them that sounded) and brightness of lightnings and the voice of instruments sounding aloud. And there was fear upon all the people that were in the camp. And Moses put forth the people to meet God.*

5. And behold the mountains burned with fire and the earth shook and the hills were removed and the mountains overthrown: the depths boiled, and all the habitable places were shaken: and the heavens were folded up and the clouds drew up water. And flames of fire shone forth and thunderings and lightnings were multiplied and winds and tempests made a roaring: the stars were gathered together and the angels ran before, until God established the law of an everlasting covenant with the children of Israel, and gave unto them an eternal commandment which should not pass away.

6. *And at that time the Lord spake unto his people all these words, saying: I am the Lord thy God which brought thee out of the land of Egypt, out of the house of bondage. Thou shalt not make to thyself graven gods, neither* shalt thou make any abominable image of the sun or the moon or any of the ornaments of the heaven, nor the *likeness of all things that are upon the earth* nor of such as creep in the waters or upon the earth. *I am the Lord thy God, a jealous God, requiting the sins* of them that sleep upon the living children of the ungodly, if they walk in the ways of their fathers; *unto the third and fourth generation, doing* (or *shewing*) *mercy unto* 1000 *generations to them that love me and keep my commandments.*

7. *Thou shall not take the name of the Lord thy God in vain*, that my ways be not made vain. *For God* abominateth *him that taketh his name in vain.*

8. *Keep the sabbath day to sanctify it. Six days do thy work, but the seventh day is the sabbath of the Lord. In it thou shall do no work, thou and all* thy labourers, saving that therein *ye praise the Lord in the congregation of the elders and glorify* the Mighty One *in the seat of the aged. For in six days the Lord made heaven and earth, the sea and all that are in them*, and all the world, the wilderness that is not inhabited, and all things that do labour, and all the order of the heaven, *and God rested the seventh day. Therefore God sanctified the seventh day*, because he rested therein.

9. *Thou shalt love thy father and my mother* and fear them: and then shall thy light rise, and I will command the heaven and it shall pay thee the rain thereof, and the earth shall hasten her fruit and thy days shall be many, and thou shalt dwell in thy land, and shalt not be childless, for thy seed shall not fail, even that of them that dwell therein.

10. *Thou shalt not commit adultery*, for thine enemies did not commit adultery with thee, but thou camest out with a high hand.

11. *Thou shall not kill*: because thine enemies got not the mastery over thee to slay thee, but thou beheldest their death.

12. *Thou shalt not bear false witness against thy neighbour*, speaking falsely, lest thy watchmen speak falsely against thee.

13. *Thou shall not covet thy neighbor's house, nor that which he hath*, lest others also covet thy land.

14. And when the Lord ceased speaking, the people feared with a great fear: and they saw the mountain burning with torches of fire, and they said to Moses: *Speak thou unto us, and let not God speak unto us, lest peradventure we die*. For, lo, to-day we know that God speaketh with man face to face, and man shall live. And now have we perceived of a truth how that the earth bare the voice of God with trembling. And Moses said unto them: Fear not, for this cause came this voice unto you, that ye should not sin (or, for this cause, that he might prove. you, God came unto you, that ye might receive the fear of him unto you, that ye sin not).

15. *And all the people stood afar off, but Moses drew near unto the cloud*, knowing that God was there. And then God spake unto him his justice and judgements, and kept him by him 40 days and 40 nights. And there did he command him many things, and showed him the tree of life, whereof he cut and took and put it into Mara, and the water of Mara was made sweet and followed them in the desert 40 years, and went up into the hills with them and came down into the plain. Also he commanded him concerning the tabernacle and the ark of the Lord, and the sacrifice of burnt offerings and of incense, and the ordinance of the table and of the candlestick and concerning the laver and the base thereof, and the shoulder-piece and the breastplate, and the very precious stones, that the children of Israel should make them so: and he shewed him the likeness of them to make them according to the pattern which he saw. And said unto him: Make for me a sanctuary and the tabernacle of my glory shall be among you.

CHAPTER 12

XII. And Moses came down: and whereas he was covered with invisible light--for he had gone down into the place where is the light of the sun and moon,--the light of his face overcame the brightness of the sun and moon, and he knew it not. And it was so, when he came down to the children of Israel, they saw him and knew him not. But when he spake, then they knew him. And this was like that which was done in Egypt when *Joseph knew his brethren but they knew not him*. And it came to pass after that, when Moses knew that his face was become glorious, he made him a veil to cover his face.

2. But while he was in the mount, the heart of the people was corrupted, and *they came together to Aaron saying: Make us gods* that we may serve them, as the other nations also have. For this Moses by whom the wonders were done before us, is taken from us. And Aaron said unto them: Have patience, for Moses will come and bring judgement near to us, and light up a law for us, and set forth from his mouth the great excellency of God, and appoint judgements unto our people.

3. And when he said this, they hearkened not unto him, that the word might be fulfilled which was spoken in the day when the people sinned in building the tower, when God said: And now if I forbid them not, *they will adventure all that they take in mind to do*, and worse. But Aaron feared, because the people was greatly strengthened, and said to them: Bring us the earrings of your wives. And the men sought every one his wife, and they gave them straightway, and they put them in the fire and they were made into a figure, and there came out a molten calf.

4. And the Lord said to Moses: Make haste hence, for the people is corrupted and hath dealt deceitfully with my ways which I commanded them. What and if the promises are at an end which I made to their fathers when I said: To your seed will I give this land wherein ye dwell? For behold the people is not yet entered into the land, even though they bear *my* judgements, *yet* have they forsaken me. And therefore I know that if they enter the land they will do yet greater iniquities. Now therefore I also will forsake them: and I will turn again and make peace with them, that a house may be built for me among them; and that house also shall be done away, because they will sin against me, and the race of men shall be unto me as a drop of a pitcher, and shall be counted as spittle.

5. And Moses hasted and came down and saw the calf, and he looked upon the tables and saw that they were not written: and he hasted and brake them; and his hands were opened and he became like a woman travailing of her firstborn, which when she is taken in her pangs her hands are upon her bosom, and she shall have no strength to help her to bring forth.

6. And it came to pass after an hour he said within *himself*: Bitterness prevaileth not for ever, neither hath evil the dominion alway. Now therefore will I arise, and strengthen my loins: for albeit they have sinned, *yet* shall not these things be in vain that were declared unto me above.

7. And he arose and brake the calf and cast it into the water, and made the people drink. And it was so, if any man's will in his mind were that the calf should be made, his tongue was cut off, but if any had been constrained thereto by fear, his face shone.

8. And then Moses went up into the mount and prayed the Lord, saying: Behold now, thou art God which hast planted this vineyard and set the roots thereof in the deep, and stretched out the shoots of it unto thy most high seat. Look upon it at this time, for the vineyard hath put forth her fruit and hath not known him that tilled her. And now if thou be wroth with thy vineyard and root it up out of the deep, and wither up the shoots from thy most high eternal seat, the deep will come no more to nourish it, neither thy throne to refresh that thy vineyard which thou hast burned.

9. For thou art he that art all light, and hast adorned thy house with precious stones and gold and perfumes and spices (*or* and jasper), and wood of balsam and cinnamon, and

with roots of myrrh and costum hast thou strewed thine house, and with divers meats and sweetness of many drinks hast thou satisfied it. If therefore thou have not pity upon thy vineyard, all these things are done in vain, Lord, and thou wilt have none to glorify thee. For even if thou plant another vineyard, neither will that one trust in thee, because thou didst destroy the former. For if verily thou forsake the world, who will do for thee that that thou hast spoken as God? And now let thy wrath be restrained from thy vineyard the more <<because of>> that thou hast said and that which remaineth to be spoken, and let not thy labour be in vain, neither let thine heritage be torn asunder in humiliation.

10. And God said to him: Behold I am become merciful according to thy words. Hew thee out therefore two tables of stone from the place whence thou hewedst the former, and write upon them again my judgements which were on the first.

CHAPTER 13

XIII. And Moses hasted and did all that God Ex. 34 commanded him, and came down and made the tables <<and the tabernacle>>, and the vessels thereof, and the ark and the lamps and the table and the altar of burnt offerings and the altar of incense and the shoulderpiece and the breastplate and the precious stones and the laver and the bases and all things that were shewn him. And he ordered all the vestures of the priests, the girdles and the *rest*, the mitre, the golden plate and the holy crown: he made also the anointing oil for the priests, and the priests themselves he sanctified. And when all things were finished the cloud covered all of them.

2. Then Moses cried unto the Lord, and God spake to him from the tabernacle saying: This is the law of the altar, whereby ye shall sacrifice unto me and pray for your souls. But as concerning that which ye shall offer me, offer ye of cattle the calf, the sheep and the she goat: but of fowls the turtle and the dove.

3, And if there be leprosy in your land, and it so be that the leper is cleansed, let them take for the Lord two live young birds, and wood of cedar and hyssop and scarlet; and he shall come to the priest, and he shall kill one, and keep the other. And he shall order the leper according to all that I have commanded in my law.

4. And it shall be when the times come round to you, ye shall sanctify me with a feast-day and rejoice before me at the feast
of the unleavened bread, and set bread before me, keeping a feast of remembrance because on that day ye came forth of the land of Egypt.

5. And in the feast of weeks ye shall set bread before me and make me an offering for your fruits.

6. But the feast of trumpets shall be for an offering for your watchers, because therein I oversaw my creation, that ye may be mindful of the whole world. In the beginning of the year, when ye show them me, I will acknowledge the number of the dead and of them that are born, and the fast of mercy. For ye shall fast unto me for your souls, that the promises of your fathers may be fulfilled.

7. Also the feast of tabernacles bring ye to me: ye shall take for me the pleasant fruit of the tree, and boughs of palm-tree and willows and cedars, and branches of myrrh: and I will remember the whole earth in rain, and the measure of the seasons shall be established, and I will order the stars and command the clouds, and the winds shall sound and the lightnings run abroad, and there shall be a storm of thunder, and this shall be for a perpetual sign. Also the nights shall yield dew, as I spake after the flood of the earth

8. when I (*or* Then he) gave him precept as concerning the year of the life of Noe, and said to him: These are the years which I ordained after the weeks wherein I visited the city of men, at what time I shewed them (*or* him) the place of birth and the colour (*or* and the serpent), and I (*or* he) said: This is. the place of which I taught the first man saying: If thou transgress not that I bade thee, all things shall be subject unto thee. But he transgressed my ways and was persuaded of his wife, and she was deceived by the serpent. And then was death ordained unto the generations of men.

9. And furthermore the Lord shewed (*or*, And the Lord said further: I shewed) him the ways of paradise and said unto him: These are the ways which men have lost by not walking in them, because they have sinned against me.

10. And the Lord commanded him concerning the salvation of the souls of the people and said: If they shall walk in my ways I will not forsake them, but will alway be merciful unto them, and will bless their seed, and the earth shall haste to yield her fruit, and there shall be rain for them to increase their gains, and the earth shall not be barren. Yet verily I know that they will corrupt their ways, and I shall forsake them, and they will forget the covenants which I made with their fathers. Yet will I not forget them for ever: for in the last

days they shall know that because of their sins their seed was forsaken; for I am faithful in my ways.

CHAPTER 14

XIV. *At that time God said unto him: Begin to number my people from 20 years and upwards* unto 40 years, that I may show your tribes all that I declared unto their fathers in a strange land. For by the 50th part *of them* did I raise them up out of the land of Egypt, but 40 and 9 parts of them died in the land of Egypt.

2. When thou hast ordered them and numbered them (*or*, While ye abode there. And when thou hast numbered them, etc.), write the tale of them, till I fulfil all that I spake unto their fathers, and set them firmly in their own land: for I will not diminish any word of those I have spoken unto their fathers, even of those which I said to them: Your seed shall be as the stars of heaven for multitude. By number shall they enter into the land, and in a short time shall they become without number.

3. Then Moses went down and numbered them, and the number of the people was 604,550. *But the tribe of Levi numbered he not among them, for so was it commanded him*; only he numbered them that were upwards of 50 years, of whom the number was 47,300. Also he numbered them that were below 20 years, and the number of them was 850,850. And he looked over the tribe of Levi and the whole number of them was CXX. CCXD. DCXX. CC. DCCC.

4. And Moses declared the number of them to God; and God said to him: These are the words which I spake to their fathers in the land of Egypt, and appointed a number, even 210 years, unto all that saw my wonders. Now the number of them all was 9000 times 10,000, 200 times 95,000 men, besides women, and I put to death the whole multitude of them because they believed me not, and the 50th part of them I was left and I sanctified them unto me. Therefore do I command the generation of my people to give me tithes of their fruits, to be before me for a memorial of how great oppression I have removed from them.

5. And when Moses came down and declared these things to the people, they mourned and lamented and abode in the desert two years.

Chapter 15

XV. And Moses sent spies to spy out the land, even 12 men, for so was it commanded him. And when they had gone up and seen the land, they returned to him bringing of the fruits of the land, and troubled the heart of the people, saying: Ye will not be able to inherit the land, for it is shut up with iron bars by their mighty men.

2. But two men out of the 12 spake not so, but said: Like as hard iron can overcome the stars, or as weapons can conquer the lightnings, or the fowls of the air put out the thunder, so can these men resist the Lord. For they saw how that as they went up the lightnings of the stars shone and the thunders followed, sounding with them.

3. And these are the names of the men: Chaleb the son of Jephone, the son of Beri, the son of Batuel, the son of Galipha, the son of Zenen, the son of Selimun, the son of Selon, the son of Juda. The other, Jesus the son of Naue, the son of Eliphat, the son of Gal, the son of Nephelien, the son of Emon, the son of Saul, the son of Dabra, the son of Effrem, the son of Joseph.

4. But the people would not hear the voice of the twain, but were greatly troubled, and spake saying: Be these the words which God spake to us saying: I will bring you into a land flowing with milk and honey? And how now doth he bring us up that we may fall on the sword, and our women shall go into captivity?

5. And when they said thus, the glory of God appeared suddenly, and he said to Moses: Doth this people thus persevere to hearken unto me not at all? Lo now the counsel which hath gone forth from me shall not be in vain. I will send the angel of mine anger upon them to break up their bodies with fire in the wilderness. And I will give commandment to mine angels which watch over them that they pray not for them, for I will shut up their souls in the treasuries of darkness, and I will say to my servants their fathers: Behold, this is the seed unto which I spake saying: *Your seed shall come into a land that is not theirs, and the nation whom they shall serve I will judge.* And I fulfilled my words and made their enemies to melt away, and subjected angels under their feet, and put a cloud for a covering of their heads, and commanded the sea, and the depths were broken before their face and walls of water stood up.

6. And there hath not been the like of this word since the day when I said: Let the waters under the heaven be gathered into one place, unto this day. And I brought them out, and slew their enemies and led them before me unto the Mount Sina. And I bowed the heavens and came down to kindle a lamp for my people, and to set bounds to all creatures. And I taught them to make me a sanctuary that I might dwell among them. But they have forsaken me and become faithless in my words, and their mind hath fainted, and now behold the days shall come when I will do unto them as they have desired and I will cast forth their bodies in the wilderness.

7. And Moses said: Before thou didst take seed wherewith to make man upon the earth, did I order his ways? therefore now let thy mercy suffer us unto the end, and thy pity for the length of days.

Chapter 16

XVI. At that time did he give him commandment concerning the fringes: and then did Choreb rebel and 200 men with him and spake saying: What if a law which we cannot bear is ordained for us?

2. And God was wroth and said: I commanded the earth and it gave me man, and unto him were born at the first two sons. And the elder arose and slew the younger, and the earth hasted and swallowed his blood. But I drove forth Cain, and cursed the earth and spake unto Sion saying: Thou shalt not any more swallow up blood. And now are the thoughts of men greatly polluted.

3. Lo, I will command the earth, and it shall swallow up body and soul together, and their dwelling shall be in darkness and in destruction, and they shall not die but shall pine away until I remember the world and renew the earth. And then shall they die and not live, and their life shall be taken away out of the number of all men: neither shall Hell vomit them forth again, and destruction shall not remember them, and their departure shall be as that of the tribe of the nations of whom I said, "I will not remember them," that is, the camp of the Egyptians, and the people whom I destroyed with the water of the flood. And the earth shall swallow them, and I will not do any more *unto them*.

4. And when Moses spake all these words unto the people, Choreb, and his men were yet unbelieving. And Choreb sent to call his seven sons which were not of counsel with him.

5. But they sent to him in answer saying: As the painter showeth not forth an image made by his art unless he be first instructed, so we also when we received the law of the Most Mighty which teacheth us his ways, did not enter . therein save that we might walk therein. Our father begat us [not], but the Most Mighty formed us, and now if we walk in his ways we shall be his children. But if thou believe not, go thine own way. And they came not up unto him.

6. And it came to pass after this that the earth opened before them, and his sons sent unto him saying: If thy madness be still upon thee, who shall help thee in the day of thy destruction? and he hearkened not unto them. And the earth opened her mouth and swallowed them up, and their houses, and four times was the foundation of the earth moved to swallow up the men, as it was commanded her. And thereafter Choreb and his company groaned, until the firmament of the earth should be delivered back.

7. But the assemblies of the people said unto Moses: We cannot abide round about this place where Choreb and his men have been swallowed up. And he said to them. Take up your tents from round about them, neither be ye joined to their sins. And they did so.

Chapter 17

XVII. Then was the lineage of the priests of God declared by the choosing of a tribe, and it was said unto Moses: *Take throughout every tribe one rod and put them in the tabernacle, and then shall the rod of him* to whomsoever my glory shall speak, *flourish, and I will take away the murmuring from my people.*

2. And Moses did so and set 12 rods, and the rod of Aaron came out, and put forth *blossom and yielded seed of almonds.*

3. And this likeness which was born there was like unto the work which Israel wrought while he was in Mesopotamia with Laban the Syrian, when he took rods of almond, and put them at the gathering of waters, and the cattle came to drink and were divided among the peeled rods, and brought forth [kids] white and speckled and parti-coloured.

4. Therefore was the synagogue of the people made like unto a flock of sheep, and as the cattle brought forth according to the almond rods, so was the priesthood established by means of the almond rods.

CHAPTER 18

XVIII. At that time Moses slew Seon and Og, the kings of the Amorites, and divided all their land unto his people, and they dwelt therein.

2. But Balac was the king of Moab, that lived over against them, and he was greatly afraid, and sent to Balaam the son of Beor the interpreter of dreams, which dwelt in Mesopotamia, and charged him saying: Behold I know how that in the reign of my father Sefor, when the Amorites fought against him, thou didst curse them and they were delivered up before him. And *now come and curse this people, for they are many, more than we, and will do thee great honour.*

3. And Balaam said: Lo, this is good in the sight of Balac, but he knoweth not that the counsel of God is not as man's counsel. And he knoweth not that the spirit which is given unto us is given for a time, and our ways are not guided except God will. *Now therefore abide ye here, and I will see what the Lord will say to me this night.*

4. And in the night *God said unto him: Who are the men that are come unto thee?* And Balaam said: Wherefore, Lord, dost thou tempt the race of man? They therefore cannot sustain it, for thou knewest more than they, all that was in the world, before thou foundedst it. And now enlighten thy servant if it be right that I go with them.

5. And God said to him: Was it not concerning this people that I spake unto Abraham in a vision saying: *Thy seed shall be as the stars of heaven*, when I raised him up above the firmament and showed him all the orderings of the stars, and required of him his son for a burnt offering? and he brought him to be laid upon the altar, but I restored him to his father. And because he resisted not, his offering was acceptable in my sight, and for the blood of him did I choose this people. And then I said unto the angels that work subtilly: Said I not of him: *To Abraham will I reveal all that I do?*

6. Jacob also, when he wrestled in the dust with the angel that was over the praises, did not let him go until he blessed him. And now, behold, thou thinkest to go with these, and curse them whom I have chosen. But if thou curse them, who is he that shall bless thee?

7. *And Balaam arose in the morning and said: Go your way, for God will not have me to come with you. And they went and told Balac* all that was said of Balaam. And *Balac sent yet again other men to Balaam* saying: Behold, I know that when thou offerest burnt offerings to God, God will be reconciled with man, and now ask yet again of thy Lord, and entreat by burnt offerings, as many as he will. For if peradventure he will be propitiated in my necessity, thou shalt have thy reward, if so be God accept thy offerings.

8. And Balaam said to them: Lo, the son of Sephor is foolish, and knoweth not that he dwelleth hard by (*lit.* round about) the dead: *And now tarry here this night and I will see what God will say unto me.* And God said to him: Go with them, and thy journey shall be an offence, and Balac himself shall go unto destruction. And he arose and went with them.

9. And his she-ass came by the way of the desert and saw the angel, and he opened the eyes of Balaam and he saw the angel and worshipped him on the earth. And the angel said to him: Haste and go on, for what thou sayest shall come to pass with him.

10. And he came unto the land of Moab and built an altar and offered sacrifices: and when he had seen a part of the people, the spirit of God abode not in him, and he took up his parable and said: Lo, Balac hath brought me hither unto the mount, saying: Come, run into the fire of these men. <<Lo>> I cannot abide that <<fire>> which waters quench, but that fire which consumeth water who shall endure? And he said to him: It is easier to take away the foundations and all the topmost part of them, and to quench the light of the sun and darken the shining of the moon, than for him who will to root up the planting of the Most Mighty or spoil his vineyard. And *Balac* himself hath not known it, because his mind is puffed up, to the intent his destruction may come swiftly.

11. For behold, I see the heritage which the Most Mighty showed me in the night, and lo the days come when Moab shall be amazed at that which befalleth her, for Balac desired to persuade the Most Mighty with gifts and to purchase decision with money. Oughtest thou not to have asked what he sent upon Pharao and upon his land because he would bring them into bondage? Behold an overshadowing vine, desirable exceedingly, and who shall be jealous against it, for it withereth not? But if any say in his counsel that the Most Mighty hath laboured in vain or chosen them to no purpose, lo now I see the salvation of deliverance which is to come unto them. I am restrained in the speech of my voice and I cannot express that which I see with mine eyes, for but a little is left to me of the holy spirit which abideth in me, since I know that in that I was persuaded of Balac I have lost the days of my life:

12. Lo, again I see the heritage of the abode of this people, and the light of it shineth above the brightness of lightning, and the running of it is swifter than arrows. And the time shall come when Moab shall groan, and they that serve Cham (Chemosh?) shall be weak, even such as took this counsel against them. But I shall gnash my teeth because I was deceived and did transgress that which was said to me in the night. Yet my prophecy shall remain manifest, and my words shall live, and the wise and prudent shall remember my words, for when I cursed I perished, and though I blessed I was not blessed. And when he had so said he held his peace. And Balac said: Thy God hath defrauded thee of many gifts from me.

13. Then Balaam said unto him: Come and let us advise what thou shalt do to them. Choose out the most comely women that are among you and that are in Midian and set them before them naked, and adorned with gold and jewels, and it shall be when they shall see them and lie with them, they will sin against their Lord and fall into your hands, for otherwise thou canst not subdue them.

14. And so saying Balaam turned away and returned to his place. And thereafter the people were led astray after the daughters of Moab, for Balac did all that Balaam had showed him.

Chapter 19

XIX. At that time Moses slew the nations, and gave half of the spoils to the people, and he began to declare to them the words of the law which God spake to them in Oreb.

2. And he spake to them, saying: Lo, I sleep with my fathers, and shall go unto my people. But I know that ye will arise and forsake the words that were ordained unto you by me, and God will be wroth with you and forsake you and depart out of your land, and bring against you them that hate you, and they shall have dominion over you, but not unto the end, for he will remember the covenant which he made with your fathers.

3. But then both ye and your sons and all your generations after you will arise and seek the day of my death and will say in their heart: Who will give us a shepherd like unto Moses, or such another judge to the children of Israel, to pray for our sins at all times, and to be heard for our iniquities?

4. Howbeit, *this day I call heaven and earth to witness against you*, for the heaven shall hear this and the earth shall take it in with her ears, that God hath revealed the end of the world, that he might covenant with you upon his high places, and hath kindled an everlasting lamp among you. Remember, ye wicked, how that when I spake unto you, ye answered saying: All that God hath said unto us we will hear and do. But if we transgress or corrupt our ways, he shall call a witness against us and cut us off.

5. But know ye that ye did eat the bread of angels 40 years. And now behold I do bless your tribes, before my end come. But ye, know ye my labour wherein I have laboured with you since the day ye came up out of the land of Egypt.

6. And when he had so said, God spake unto him the third time, saying: Behold, thou goest to sleep with thy fathers, and this people will arise and seek me, and will forget my law wherewith I have enlightened them, and I shall forsake their seed for a season.

7. But unto thee will I show the land before thou die, but thou shall not enter therein in this age, lest thou see the graven images whereby this people will be deceived and led out of the way. I will show thee the place wherein they shall serve me 740 (*l.* 850) years. And thereafter it shall be delivered into the hand of their enemies, and they shall destroy it, and strangers shall compass it about, and it shall be in that day as it was in the day when I brake the tables of the covenant which I made with thee in Oreb: and when they sinned, that which was written therein vanished away. Now that day was the 17th day of the 4th month.

8. And Moses went up into Mount Oreb, as God had bidden him, and prayed, saying: Behold, I have fulfilled the time of my life, even 120 years. And now I pray thee let thy mercy be with thy people and let thy compassion be continued upon thine heritage, Lord, and thy long-suffering in thy place upon the race of thy choosing, for thou hast loved them more than all.

9. And thou knowest that I was a shepherd of sheep, and when I fed the flock in the desert, I brought them unto thy Mount Oreb, and then first saw I thine angel in fire out of the bush; but thou calledst me out of the bush, and I feared and turned away my face, and thou sentest me unto them, and didst deliver them out of Egypt, and their enemies thou didst sink in the water. And thou gavest them a law and judgements whereby they should live. *For what man is he that hath not sinned against thee*? How shall thine heritage be established except thou have mercy on them? Or who shall yet be born without sin? Yet wilt thou correct them for a season, but not in anger.

10. Then the Lord shewed him the land and all that is therein and said: This is the land which I will give to my people. And he shewed him the place from whence the clouds draw up water to water all the earth, and the place whence the river receiveth his water, and the land of Egypt, and the place of the firmament, from whence the holy land only drinketh. He shewed him also the place from whence it rained manna for the people, and even unto the paths of paradise. And he shewed him the measures of the sanctuary, and the number

of the offerings, and the sign whereby men shall interpret (*lit.* begin to look; upon) the heaven, and said: These are the things which were forbidden to the sons of men because they sinned.

11. And now, thy rod wherewith the signs were wrought shall be for a witness between me and my people. And when they sin I shall be wroth with them and remember my rod, and spare them according to my mercy, and thy rod shall be in my sight for a remembrance all the days, and shall be like unto the bow wherein I made a covenant with Noe when he came out of the ark, saying: I will set my bow in the cloud, and it shall be a sign between me and men that the water of a flood be no more upon the earth.

12. But thee will I take hence and give thee sleep with thy fathers and give thee rest in thy slumber, and bury thee in peace, and all the angels shall lament for thee, and the hosts *of heaven* shall be sorrowful. But there shall not any, of angels or men, know thy sepulchre wherein thou art to be buried, but thou shalt rest therein until I visit the world, and raise thee up and thy fathers out of the earth [of Egypt] wherein ye shall sleep, and ye shall come together and dwell in an immortal habitation that is not subject unto time.

13. But this heaven shall be in my sight as a fleeting cloud, and like yesterday when it is past, and it shall be when I draw near to visit the world, I will command the years and charge the times, and they shall be shortened, and the stars shall be hastened, and the light of the sun make speed to set, neither shall the light of the moon endure, because I will hasten to raise up you that sleep, that in the place of sanctification which I shewed thee, all they that can live may dwell therein.

14. And Moses said: If I may ask yet one thing of thee, O Lord, according to the multitude of thy mercy, be not wroth with me. And shew me what measure of time hath passed by and what remaineth.

15. And the Lord said to him: An instant, the topmost part of a hand, the fulness of a moment, and the drop of a cup. And time hath fulfilled all. For 4½ have passed by, and 2½ remain.

16. And Moses when he heard was filled with under standing, and his likeness was changed gloriously: *and he died* in glory according *to the mouth of the Lord, and he buried him* as he had promised him, and the angels lamented at his death, and lightnings and torches and arrows went before him with one accord. And on that day the hymn of the hosts was not said because of the departure of Moses. Neither was there any day like unto it since the Lord made man upon earth, neither shall there be any such for ever, that he should make the hymn of the angels to cease because of a man; for he loved him greatly; and he buried him with his own hands on an high place of the earth, and in the light of the whole world.

CHAPTER 20

XX. And at that time God made his covenant with Jesus the son of Naue which remained of the men that spied out the land: for the lot had fallen upon them that they should not see the land because they spake evil of it, and for this cause that generation died.

2. Then said God unto Jesus the son of Naue: Wherefore mournest thou, and wherefore hopest thou in vain, thinking that Moses shall yet live? Now therefore thou waitest to no purpose, for Moses is dead. Take the garments of his wisdom and put them on thee, and gird thy loins with the girdle of his knowledge, and thou shalt be changed and become another man. Did I not speak for thee unto Moses my servant, saying: "He shall lead my people after thee, and into his hand will I deliver the kings of the Amorites"?

3. And Jesus took the garments of wisdom and put them on, and girded his loins with the girdle of understanding. And it came to pass when he put it on, that his mind was kindled and his spirit stirred up, and he said to the people: Lo, the former generation died in the wilderness because they spake against their God. And, behold now, know, all ye captains, this day that if ye go forth in the ways of your God, your paths shall be made straight.

4. But if ye obey not his voice, and are like your fathers, your works shall be spoiled, and ye yourselves broken, and your name shall perish out of the land, and then where shall be the words which God spake unto your fathers? For even if the heathen say: It may be God hath failed, because he hath not delivered his people, yet whereas they perceive that he hath chosen to himself other peoples, working for them great wonders, they shall understand that the Most Mighty accepteth not persons. But because ye sinned through vanity, therefore he took his power from you and subdued you. And now arise and set Your heart to walk in the ways of your Lord and he shall direct you.

5. And the people said unto him: Lo, this day see we that which Eldad and Modat prophesied in the days of Moses, saying: After that Moses resteth, the captainship of Moses shall be given unto Jesus the son of Naue. And Moses was not envious, but rejoiced when he heard them; and thenceforth all the people believed that thou shouldest lead them, and divide the land unto them in peace: and now also if there be conflict, be strong and do valiantly, for thou only shalt be leader in Israel.

6. And when he heard that, Jesus thought to send spies into Jericho. And he called Cenez and Seenamias his brother, the two sons of Caleph, and spake to them, saying: I and your father were sent of Moses in the wilderness and went up with other ten men: and they returned and spake evil of the lands and melted the heart of the people, and they were scattered and the heart of the people with them. But I and your father only fulfilled the word of the Lord, and lo, we are alive this day. And now will I send you to spy out the land of Jericho. Do like unto your father and ye also shall live.

7. And they went up and spied out the city. And when they brought back word, the people went up and besieged the city and burned it with fire.

8. And after that Moses was dead, the manna ceased to come down for the children of Israel, and then began they to eat the fruits of the land. And these are the three things which God gave his people for the sake of three persons, that is, the well of the water of Mara for Maria's sake, and the pillar of cloud for Aaron's sake, and the manna for the sake of Moses. And when these three came to an end, those three gifts were taken away from them.

9. Now the people and Jesus fought against the Amorites, and when the battle waxed strong against their enemies throughout all the days of Jesus, 30 and 9 kings which dwelt in the land were cut off. And Jesus gave the land by lot to the people, to every tribe according to the lots, according as he had received commandment.

10. Then came Caleph unto him and said: Thou knowest how that we two were sent by lot by Moses to go with the spies, and because we fulfilled the word of the Lord, behold we are alive at this day: and now if it be well-pleasing in thy sight, let there be given unto my son

Cenez for a portion the territory of the three (*or* the tribe of the) towers. And Jesus blessed him, and did so.

CHAPTER 21

XXI. And when Jesus was become old and well-stricken in years, God said to him: Behold, thou waxest old and well-stricken in days, and the land is become very great, and there is none to divide it (*or* take it by lot), and it shall be after thy departure this people will mingle with the inhabitants of the land and go astray after other gods, and I shall forsake them as I testified in my word unto Moses; but do thou testify unto them before thou diest.

2. And Jesus said: Thou knowest more than all, O Lord, what moveth the heart of the sea before it rageth, and thou hast tracked out the constellations and numbered the stars, and ordered the rain. Thou knowest the mind of all generations before they be born. And now, Lord, give unto thy people an heart of wisdom and a mind of prudence, and it shall be when thou givest these ordinances unto thine heritage, they shall not sin before thee and thou shall not be wroth with them.

3. Are not these the words which I spake before thee, Lord, when Achar stole of the curse, and the people were delivered up before thee, and I prayed in thy sight and said: Were it not better for us, O Lord, if we had died in the Red Sea, wherein thou drownedst our enemies? or if we had died in the wilderness, like our fathers, than to be delivered into the hand of the Amorites that we should be blotted out for ever?

4. Yet if thy word be about us, no evil shall befall us: for even though our end be removed unto death, thou livest which art before the world and after the world; and whereas a man cannot devise how to put one generation before another, he saith "God hath destroyed his people whom he chose": and behold, we shall be in Hell: yet thou wilt make thy word alive. And now let the fulness of thy mercies have patience with thy people, and choose for thine heritage a man which shall rule over thy people, he and his generation.

5. Was it not for this that our father Jacob spake, saying: *A prince shall not depart from Juda, nor a leader from his loins.* And now confirm the words spoken aforetime, that the nations of the earth and tribes of the world may learn that thou art everlasting.

6. And he said furthermore: O Lord, behold the days shall come and the house of Israel shall be like unto a brooding dove which setteth her young *in the nest* and will not forsake them nor forget her place. So, also, these shall turn from their deeds and fight against the salvation that shall be born unto them.

7. And Jesus went down from Galgala and built an altar of very great stones, and brought no iron upon them, as Moses had commanded, and set up great stones on mount Gebal, and whitened them and wrote on them the words of the law very plainly: and gathered all the people together and read in their ears all the words of the law.

8. And he came down with them and offered upon the altar peace-offerings, and they sang many praises, and lifted up the ark of the covenant of the Lord out of the tabernacle with timbrels and dances and lutes and harps and psalteries and all instruments of sweet sound.

9. And the priests and Levites were going up before the ark and rejoicing with psalms, and they set the ark before the altar, and lifted up on it yet again peace-offerings very many, and the whole house of Israel sang together with a loud voice saying: Behold, our Lord hath fulfilled that which he spake with our fathers saying: To your, seed will I give a land wherein to dwell, a land flowing with milk and honey. And lo, he hath brought us. into the land of our enemies and hath delivered them broken in heart before us, and he is the God which sent to our fathers in the secret places of souls, saying: Behold, the Lord hath done all that he spake unto us. And now know we of a truth that God hath confirmed all the words of the law which he spake to us in Oreb; and if our heart keep his ways it will be well with us, and with our sons after us.

10. And Jesus blessed them and said: The Lord grant your heart to continue therein (*or* in him) all the days, and if ye depart not from his name, the covenant of the Lord shall endure with you. And *he grant* that it be not corrupted, but that the dwelling-place of God be

builded among you, as he spake when he sent you into his inheritance with mirth and gladness.

CHAPTER 22

XXII. And it came to pass after these things, when Jesus and all Israel had heard that the children of Ruben and the children of Gad and the half tribe of Manasse which dwelt about Jordan had built them an altar and did offer sacrifices thereon and had made priests for the sanctuary, all the people were troubled above measure and came unto them to Silon.

2. And Jesus and all the elders spake to them saying: What be these works which are done among you, while as yet we are not settled in our land? Are not these the words which Moses spake to you in the wilderness saying: See that when ye enter into the land ye spoil not your doings, and corrupt all the people? And now wherefore is it that our enemies have so much abounded, save because ye do corrupt your ways and have made all this trouble, and therefore will they assemble against us and overcome us.

3. And the children of Ruben and the children of Gad and the half tribe of Manasse said unto Jesus and all the people of Israel: Lo now hath God enlarged the fruit of the womb of men, and hath set up a light that that which is in darkness may see, for he knoweth what is in the secret places of the deep, and with him light abideth. Now the Lord God of our fathers knoweth if any of us or if we ourselves have done this thing in the way of iniquity, but only for our posterity's sake, that their heart be not separated from the Lord our God lest they say to us: Behold now, our brethren which be beyond Jordan have an altar, to make offerings upon it, but we in this place that have no altar, let us depart from the Lord our God, because our God hath set us afar off from his ways, that we should not serve him.

4. And then verily spake we among ourselves: Let us make us an altar, that they may have a zeal to seek the Lord. And verily there be some of us that stand by and know that we are your brothers and stand guiltless before your face. Do ye therefore that which is pleasing in the sight of the Lord.

5. And Jesus said: Is not the Lord our king mightier than woo sacrifices? And wherefore taught ye not your sons the words of the Lord which ye heard of us? For if your sons had been *occupied* in the meditation of the law of the Lord, their mind would not have been led aside after a sanctuary made with hands. Or know ye not that when the people were forsaken for a moment in the wilderness when Moses went up to receive the tables, their mind was led astray, and they made themselves idols? And except the mercy of the God of your fathers had kept *us*, all the synagogues should have become a byword, and all the sins of the people should have been blazed abroad because of your foolishness.

6. Therefore now go and dig down the sanctuaries that ye have builded you, and teach your sons the law, and they shall be meditating therein day and night, that the Lord may be with them for a witness and a judge unto them all the days of their life. And God shall be witness and judge between me and you, and between my heart and your heart, that if ye have done this thing in subtlety it shall be avenged upon you, because you would destroy your brothers: but if ye have done it ignorantly as ye say, God will be merciful unto you for your sons' sake. And all the people answered: Amen, Amen.

7. And Jesus and all the people of Israel offered for them 1,000 rams for a sin-offering (*lit.* the word of excusing), and prayed for them and sent them away in peace: and they went and destroyed the sanctuary, and fasted and wept, both they and their sons, and prayed and said: O God of our fathers, that knowest before the heart of all men, thou knowest that our ways were not wrought in iniquity in thy sight, neither have we swerved from thy ways, but have served thee all of us, for we are the work of thy hands:
now *therefore* remember thy covenant with the sons of thy servants.

8. And after that Jesus went up unto Galgala, and reared up the tabernacle of the Lord, and the ark of the covenant and all the vessels thereof, and set it up in Silo, and put there the Demonstration and the Truth (*i.e.* the Urim and *Thummim*). And at that time Eleazar the priest which served the altar did teach by the Demonstration all them of the people that came

to inquire of the Lord, for thereby it was shown unto them, but in the new sanctuary that was in Galgala, Jesus appointed even unto this day the burnt offerings that were offered by the children of Israel every year.

    9. For until the house of the Lord was builded in Jerusalem, and so long as the offerings were made in the new sanctuary, the people were not forbidden to offer therein, because the Truth and the Demonstration revealed all things in Silo. And until the ark was set by Solomon in the sanctuary of the Lord they went on sacrificing there unto that day. But Eleazar the son of Aaron the priest of the Lord ministered in Silo.

Chapter 23

XXIII. And Jesus the son of Naue ordered the people and divided unto them the land, being a mighty man of valour. And while yet the adversaries of Israel were in the land, the days of Jesus drew near that he should die, and he sent and called all Israel throughout all their land with their wives and their children, and said unto them: Gather yourselves together before the ark of the covenant of the Lord in Silo and I will make a covenant with you before I die.

2. And when all the people were gathered together on the 16th day of the 3rd month before the face of the Lord in Silo with their wives and their children, Jesus said unto them: Hear, O Israel, behold I make with you the covenant of this law which the Lord ordained with our fathers in Oreb, and therefore tarry ye here this night and see what God will say unto me concerning You.

3. And as the people waited there that night, the Lord appeared unto Jesus in a vision and spake saying: According to all these words will I speak unto this people.

4. And Jesus came in the morning and assembled all the people and said unto them: Thus saith the Lord: One rock was there from whence I digged out your father, and the cutting of that rock brought forth two men, whose names were Abraham and Nachor, and out of the chiselling of that place were born two women whose names were Sara and Melcha. And they dwelled together beyond the river. And Abraham took Sara *to wife* and Nachor took Melcha.

5. And when the people of the land were led astray, every man after his own devices, Abraham believed in me and was not led aside after them. And I saved him out of the fire and took him and brought him over into all the land of Chanaan. And I spake unto him in a vision saying: Unto thy seed will I give this land. And he said unto me: Behold now thou hast given me a wife and she is barren. And how shall I have *seed* of that womb that is shut up?

6. And I said unto him: *Take for me a calf of three years old and a she-goat of three years and a ram of three years, a turtledove and a pigeon.* And he took them as I commanded him. And *I sent a sleep upon him* and compassed him about with fear, and *I set* before him the place of fire wherein the works of them that commit iniquity against me shall be avenged, and I showed him the torches of fire whereby the righteous which have believed in me shall be enlightened.

7. And I said unto him: These shall be for a witness between me and thee that I will give thee seed of the womb that is shut up. And I will liken thee unto the dove, because thou hast received for me the city which thy sons shall (begin to) build in my sight. But the turtle-dove I will liken unto the prophets which shall be born of thee. And the ram will I liken unto the wise men which shall be born of thee and enlighten thy sons. But the calf I will liken unto the multitude of the peoples which shall be multiplied through thee. And the she-goat I will liken unto the women whose wombs I will open and they shall bring forth. These things shall be for a witness betwixt us that I will not transgress my words.

8. And I gave him Isaac and formed him in the womb of her that bare him, and commanded it that it should restore him quickly and render him unto me in the 7th month. And for this cause every woman that bringeth forth in the 7th month, her child shall live: because upon him did I call my glory, and showed forth the new age.

9. And I gave unto Isaac Jacob and Esau, and unto Esau I gave the land of Seir for an heritage. And Jacob and his sons went down into Egypt. And the Egyptians brought your fathers low, as ye know, and I remembered your fathers, and sent Moses my friend and delivered them from thence and smote their enemies.

10. And I brought them out with a high hand and led them through the Red Sea, and laid the cloud under their feet, and brought them out through the depth, and brought them beneath the mount Sina, and I *bowed the heavens and came down*, and I congealed the flame of the fire, and stopped up the springs of the deep, and impeded the course of the stars, and

tamed the sound of the thunder, and quenched the fulness; of the wind, and rebuked the multitude of the clouds, and stayed their motions, and interrupted the storm of the hosts, that I should not break my covenant, for all things were moved at my coming down, and all things were quickened at my advent, and I suffered not my people to be scattered, but gave unto them my law, and enlightened them, that if they did these things they may live and have length of days and not die.

11. And I have brought you into this land and given you vineyards. Ye dwell in cities which ye built not. And I have fulfilled the covenant which I spake unto your fathers.

12. And now if ye obey your fathers, I will set my heart upon you for ever, and will overshadow you, and your enemies shall no more fight against you, and your land shall be renowned throughout all the world and your seed be elect in the midst of the peoples, which shall say: Behold the faithful people; because they believed the Lord, therefore hath the Lord delivered them and planted them. And therefore will I plant you as a desirable vineyard and will rule you as a beloved flock, and I will charge the rain and the dew, and they shall satisfy you all the days of your life.

13. And it shall be at the end that the lot of every one of you shall be in eternal life, both for you and your seed, and I will receive your souls and lay them up in peace, until the time of the age is fulfilled, and I restore you unto your fathers and your fathers unto you, and they shall know at your hand that it is not in vain that I have chosen you. These are the words that the Lord hath spoken unto me this night.

14. And all the people answered and said: The Lord is our God, and him only will we serve. And all the people made a great feast that day and a renewal thereof for 28 days.

Chapter 24

XXIV. And after these days Jesus the son of Naue assembled all the people yet again, and said unto them: Behold now the Lord hath testified unto you this day: I have called heaven and earth to witness to you that if ye will continue to serve the Lord ye shall be unto him a peculiar people. But if ye will not serve him and will obey the gods of the Amorites in whose land ye dwell, say so this day before the Lord and go forth. *But I and my house will serve the Lord.*

2. And all the people lifted up their voice and wept saying: Peradventure the Lord will account us worthy, and it is better for us to die in the fear of him, than to be destroyed out of the land.

3. And Jesus the son of Naue blessed the people and kissed them and said unto them: Let your words be for mercy before our Lord, and let him send his angel, and preserve you: Remember me after my death, and *remember ye* Moses the friend of the Lord. And let not the words of the covenant which he hath made with you depart from you all the days of your life. And he, sent them away and they departed every man to his inheritance.

4. But Jesus laid himself upon his bed, and sent and called Phineës the son of Eleazar the priest and said unto him: Behold now I see with mine eyes the transgression of this people wherein they will begin to deceive: but thou, strengthen thy hands in the time that thou art with them, And he kissed him and his father and his sons and blessed him and said: The Lord God of your fathers direct your ways and *the ways* of this people.

5. And when he ceased speaking unto them, *he drew up his feet into the bed* and slept with his fathers. And his sons *laid their hands upon his eyes.*

6. And then all Israel gathered together to bury him, and they lamented him with a great lamentation, and thus said they in their lamentation: Weep ye for the wing of this swift eagle, for he hath flown away from us. And weep ye for the strength of this lion's whelp, for he is hidden from us. Who now will go and report unto Moses the righteous, that we have had forty years a leader like unto him? And they fulfilled their mourning and *buried him* with their own hands *in the mount Effraim* and returned every man unto his tent. And after the death of Jesus the land of Israel was at rest.

CHAPTER 25

XXV. And the Philistines sought to fight with the men of Israel: and they inquired of the Lord and said: Shall we go up and fight against the Philistines? and God said to them: If ye go up with a pure heart, fight; but if your heart is defiled, go not up. And they inquired yet again saying: How shall we know if all the heart of the people be alike? and God said to them: Cast lots among your tribes, and it shall be unto every tribe that cometh under the lot, that it shall be set apart into one lot, and then shall ye know whose heart is clean and whose is defiled.

2. And the people said: Let us first appoint over us a prince, and so cast lots. And the angel of the Lord said to them: Appoint. And the people said: Whom shall we appoint that is worthy, Lord? And the angel of the Lord said to them: Cast the lot upon the tribe of Caleb, and he that is shown by the lot, even he shall be your prince. And they cast the lot for the tribe of Caleb and it came out upon Cenez, and they made him ruler over Israel.

3. And Cenez said to the people: Bring your tribes unto me and hear ye the word of the Lord. And the people gathered together and Cenez said to them: Ye know that which Moses the friend of the Lord charged you, that ye should not transgress the law to the right hand or to the left. And Jesus also who was after him gave you the same charge. And now, lo, we have heard of the mouth of the Lord that your heart is defiled. And the Lord hath charged us to cast lots among your tribes to know whose heart hath departed from the Lord our God. Shall not the fury of anger come upon the people? But I promise you this day that even if a man of mine own house come out in the lot of sin, he shall not be saved alive, but shall be burned with fire. And the people said: Thou hast spoken a good counsel, to perform it.

4. And the tribes were brought before him, and there were found of the tribe of Juda 345 men, and of the tribe of Ruben 560, and of the tribe of Simeon 775, and of the tribe of Levi 150, and of the tribe of Zabulon 655 (*or* 645), and of the tribe of Isachar 665, and of the tribe of Gad 380. Of the tribe of Aser 665, and of the tribe of Manasse 480, and of the tribe of Effraim 468, and of the tribe of Benjamin 267. And all the number of them that were found by the lot of sin was 6110. And Cenez took them all and shut them up in prison, till it should be known what should be done with them.

5. And Cenez said: Was it not of this that Moses the friend of the Lord spake saying: *There is a strong root among you bringing forth gall and bitterness*? Now blessed be the Lord who hath revealed all the devices of these men, neither hath he suffered them to corrupt his people by their evil works. Bring hither therefore the Demonstration and the Truth and call forth Eleazar the priest, and let us inquire of the Lord by him.

6. Then Cenez and Eleazar and all the elders and the whole synagogue prayed with one accord saying: Lord God of our fathers, reveal unto thy servants the truth, for we are found not believing in the wonders which thou didst for our fathers since thou broughtest them out of the land of Egypt unto this day. And the Lord answered and said: First ask them that were found, and let them confess their deeds which they did subtilly, and afterwards they shall be burned with fire.

7. And Cenez brought them forth and said to them: Behold now ye know how that Achiar confessed when the lot fell on him, and declared all that he had done. And now declare unto me all your wickedness and your inventions: who knoweth, if ye tell us the truth, even though ye die now, yet God will have mercy upon you when he shall quicken the dead?

8. And one of them named Elas said unto him: Shall not death come now upon us, that we shall die by fire? Nevertheless I tell thee, my Lord, there are none inventions like unto these which we have made wickedly. But if thou wilt search out the truth plainly, ask severally the men of every tribe, and so shall some one of them that stand by perceive the difference of their sins.

9. And Cenez asked them of his own tribe and they told him: We desired to imitate and make the calf that they made in the wilderness. And after that he asked the men of the tribe of Ruben, which said: We desired to sacrifice unto the gods of them that dwell in the land. And he asked the men of the tribe of Levi, which said: We would prove the tabernacle, whether it were holy. And he asked the remnant of the tribe of Isachar, which said: We would inquire by the evil spirits of the idols, to see whether they revealed plainly: and he asked the men of the tribe of Zabulon, which said: We desired to eat the flesh of our children and to learn whether God hath care for them. And he asked the remnant of the tribe of Dan, which said: The Amorites taught us that which they did, that we might teach our children. And lo, they are hid under the tent of Elas, who told thee to inquire of us. Send therefore and thou shall find them. And Cenez sent and found them.

10. And thereafter asked he them that were left over of the tribe of Gad, and they said: We committed adultery with each other's wives. And he asked next the men of the tribe of Aser, which said: We found seven golden images which the Amorites called the holy Nymphs, and we took them with the precious stones that were set upon them, and hid them: and lo, now they are laid up under the top of the mount Sychem. Send therefore and thou shalt find them. And Cenez sent men and removed them thence.

11. Now these are the Nymphs which when they were called upon did show unto the Amorites their works in every hour. For these are they which were devised by seven evil men after the flood, whose names are these: <? Cham> Chanaan, Phuth, Selath, Nembroth, Elath, Desuath. Neither shall there be again any like similitude in the world graven by the hand of the artificer and adorned with variety of painting, but they were set up and fixed for the consecration *(i.e.* the holy place?) of idols. *Now* the stones were precious, brought from the land of Euilath, among which was a crystal and a prase (*or* one crystalline and one green), and they shewed their fashion, being carved after the manner of a stone pierced with open-work, and another of them was graven on the top, and another as it were marked with spots (*or* like a spotted chrysoprase) so shone with its graving as if it shewed the water of the deep lying beneath.

12. And these are the precious stones which the Amorites had in their holy places, and the price of them was above reckoning. For when any entered in by night, he needed not the light of a lantern, so much did the natural light of the stones shine forth. Wherein that one gave the greatest light which was cut after the form of a stone pierced with open-work, and was cleansed with bristles; for if any of the Amorites were blind, he went and put his eyes thereupon and recovered his sight. Now when Cenez found them, he set them apart and laid them up till he should know what should become of them.

13. And after that he asked them that were left of the tribe of Manasse, and they said: We did only defile the Lord's sabbaths. And he asked the forsaken of the tribe of Effraim, which said: We desired to pass our sons and our daughters through the fire, that we might know if that which was said were manifest. And he asked the forsaken of the tribe of Benjamin, which said: We desired at this time to examine the book of the law, whether God had plainly written that which was therein, or whether Moses had taught it of himself.

Chapter 26

XXVI. And when Cenez had taken all these words and written them in a book and read them before the Lord, God said to him: Take the men and that which was found with them and all their goods and put them in the bed of the river Phison, and burn them with fire that mine anger may cease from them.

2. And Cenez said: Shall we burn these precious stones also with fire, or sanctify them unto thee, for among us there are none like unto them? And God said to him: If God should receive in his own name any of the accursed thing, what should man do? Therefore now take these precious stones and all that was found, both books and men: and when thou dealest so with the men, set apart these stones with the books, for fire will not avail to burn them, and afterwards I will shew thee how thou must destroy them. But the men and all that was found thou shalt burn with fire. And thou shalt assemble all the people, and say to them: Thus shall it be done unto every man whose heart turneth away from his God.

3. And when the fire hath consumed those men, then the books and the precious stones which cannot be burned with fire, neither cut with iron, nor blotted out with water, lay them upon the top of the mount beside the new altar; and I will command a cloud, and it shall go and take up dew and shed it upon the books, and shall blot out that which is written therein, for they cannot be blotted out with any other water than such as hath never served men. And thereafter I will send my lightning, and it shall burn up the books themselves.

4. But as concerning the precious stones, I will command mine angel and he shall take them and go and cast them into the depths of the sea, and I will charge the deep and it shall swallow them up, for they may not continue in the world because they have been polluted by the idols of the Amorites, And I will command another angel, and he shall take for me twelve stones out of the place whence these seven were taken; and thou, when thou findest them in the top of the mount where he shall lay them, take and put them on the shoulder-piece over against the twelve stones which Moses set therein in the wilderness, and sanctify them in the breastplate (*lit.* oracle) according to the twelve tribes: and say not, How shall I know which stone I shall set for which tribe? Lo, I will tell thee the name of the tribe answering unto the name of the stone, and thou shall find both one and other graven.

5. And Cenez went and took all that had been found and the men with it, and assembled all the people again, and said to them: Behold, ye have seen all the wonders which God hath shewed us unto this day, and lo, when we sought out all that had subtilly devised evil against the Lord and against Israel, God hath revealed them according to their works, and now cursed be every man that deviseth to do the like among you, brethren. And all the people answered Amen, Amen. And when he had so said, he burned all the men with fire, and all that was found with them, saving the precious stones.

6. And after that Cenez desired to prove whether the stones could be burned with fire, and cast them into the fire. And it was so, that when they fell therein, forthwith the fire was quenched. And Cenez took iron to break them, and when the sword touched them the iron thereof was melted; and thereafter he would at the least blot out the books with water; but it came to pass that the water when it fell upon them was congealed. And when he saw that, he said: Blessed be God who hath done so great wonders for the children of men, and made Adam the first-created and shewed him all things; that when Adam had sinned thereby, then he should deny him all these things, lest if he shewed them unto the race of men they should have the mastery over them.

7. And when he had so said, he took the books and the stones and laid them on the top of the mount by the new altar as the Lord had commanded him, and took a peace-offering and burnt-offerings, and offered upon the new altar 2000, offering them all for a burnt sacrifice. And on that day they kept a great feast, he and all the people together.

8. And God did that night as he spake unto Cenez, for he commanded a cloud, and it went and took dew from the ice of paradise and shed it upon the books and blotted them out. And after that an angel came and burned them up, and another angel took the precious stones and cast them into the heart of the sea, and he charged the depth of the sea, and it swallowed them up. And another angel went and brought twelve stones and laid them hard by the place whence he had taken those seven. And he graved thereon the names of the twelve tribes.

9. And Cenez arose on the morrow and found those twelve stones on the top of the mount where himself had laid those seven. And the graving of them was so as if the form of eyes was portrayed upon them.

10. And the first stone, whereon was written the name of the tribe of Ruben, was like a sardine stone. The second stone was graven with a tooth (*or* ivory), and therein was graven the name of the tribe of Simeon, and the likeness of a topaz was seen in it; and on the third stone was graven the name of the tribe of Levi, and it was like unto an emerald. But the fourth stone was called a crystal, wherein was graven the name of the tribe of Juda, and it was likened to a carbuncle. The fifth stone was green, and upon it was graven the name of the tribe of Isachar, and the colour of a sapphire stone was therein. And of the sixth stone the graving was as if it had been inscribed, (*or* as a chrysoprase) speckled with diverse markings, and thereon was written the tribe of Zabulon, And the jasper stone was likened unto it.

11. Of the seventh stone the graving shone and shewed within itself, as it were, *enclosed* the water of the deep, and therein was written the name of the tribe of Dan, which stone was like a ligure. But the eighth stone was cut out with adamant, and therein was written the name of the tribe of Neptalim, and it was like an amethyst. And of the ninth stone the graving was pierced, and it *was* from Mount Ophir, and therein was written the tribe of Gad, and an agate stone was likened unto it. And of the tenth stone the graving was hollowed, and gave the likeness of a stone of Theman, and there was written the tribe of Aser, and a chrysolite was likened unto it. And the eleventh stone was an elect stone from Libanus, and thereon was written the name of the tribe of Joseph, and a beryl was. likened to it. And the twelfth stone was cut out of the height of Sion (*or* the quarry), and upon it was written the tribe of Benjamin; and the onyx stone was likened unto it.

12. And God said to Cenez: Take these stones and put them in the ark of the covenant of the Lord with the tables of the covenant which I gave unto Moses in Oreb, and they shall be there with them until Jahel arise to build an house in my name, and then he shall set them before me upon the two cherubim, and they shall be in my sight for a memorial of the house of Israel.

13. And it shall be when the sins of my people are filled up, and their enemies have the mastery over their house, that I will take these stones and the former together with the tables, and lay them up in the place whence they were brought forth in the beginning, and they shall be there until I remember the world, and visit the dwellers upon earth. And then will I take them and many other better than they, from that *place* which *eye hath not seen nor ear heard neither hath it come up into the heart of man*, until the like cometh to pass unto the world, and the just shall have no need for the light of the sun nor of the shining of the moon, for the light of the precious stones shall be their light.

14. And Cenez arose and said: Behold what good things God hath done for men, and because of their sins have they been deprived of them all. And now know I this day that the race of men is weak, and their life shall be accounted as nothing.

15. And so saying, he took the stones from the place where they were laid, and as he took them there was as it were the light of the sun poured out upon them, and the earth shone with their light. And Cenez put them in the ark of the covenant of the Lord with the tables as it was commanded him, and there they are unto this day.

Chapter 27

XXVII. And after this he armed of the people 300,000 men and went up to fight against the Amorites, and slew on the first day 800,000 men, and on the second day he slew about 500,000.

2. And when the third day came, certain men of the people spake evil against Cenez, saying: Lo now, Cenez alone lieth in his house with his wife and his concubines, and sendeth us to battle, that we may be destroyed before our enemies.

3. And when the servants of Cenez heard, they brought him word. And he commanded a captain of fifty, and he brought of them thirty-seven men who spake against him and shut them up in ward.

4. And their names are these: Le and Uz, Betul, Ephal, Dealma, Anaph, Desac, Besac, Gethel, Anael, Anazim, Noac, Cehec, Boac, Obal, Iabal, Enath, Beath, Zelut, Ephor, Ezeth, Desaph, Abidan, Esar, Moab, Duzal, Azath, Phelac, Igat, Zophal, Eliesor, Ecar, Zebath, Sebath, Nesach and Zere. And when the captain of fifty had shut them up as Cenez commanded, Cenez said: When the Lord hath wrought salvation for his people by my hand, then will I punish these men.

5. And so saying, Cenez commanded the captain of fifty, saying: Go and choose of my servants 300 men, and as many horses, and let no man of the people know of the hour when I shall go forth to battle; but only in what hour I shall tell thee, prepare the men that they be ready this night.

6. And Cenez sent messengers, spies, to see where was the multitude of the camp of the Amorites. And the messengers went and spied, and saw that the multitude of the camp of the Amorites was moving among the rocks devising to come and fight against Israel. And the messengers returned and told him according to this word. And Cenez arose by night, he and 300 horsemen with him, and took a trumpet in his hand and began to go down with the 300 men. And it came to pass, when he was near to the camp of the Amorites, that he said to his servants: Abide here and I will go down alone and view the camp of the Amorites. And it shall be, if I blow with the trumpet ye shall come down, but if not, wait for me here.

7. And Cenez went down alone, and before he went down he prayed, and said: O Lord God of our fathers, thou hast shewn unto thy servant the marvellous things which thou hast prepared to do by thy covenant in the last days: and now, send unto thy servant one of thy wonders, and I will overcome thine adversaries, that they and all the nations and thy people may know that the Lord delivereth not by the multitude of an host, neither by the strength of horsemen, when they shall perceive the sign of deliverance which thou shalt work for me this day (*or* horsemen, and that thou, Lord, wilt perform a sign of salvation with me this day). Behold, I will draw my sword out of the scabbard and it shall glitter in the camp of the Amorites: and it shall be, if the Amorites perceive that it is I, Cenez, *then* I *shall* know that thou hast delivered them into mine hand. But if they perceive not that it is I, and think that it is another, then I *shall* know that thou hast not hearkened unto me, but hast delivered me unto mine enemies. But and if I be indeed delivered unto death, I shall know that because of mine iniquities the Lord hath not heard me, and hath delivered me unto mine enemies; but he will not destroy, his inheritance by my death.

8. And he set forth after he had prayed, and heard the multitude of the Amorites saying: Let us arise and fight against Israel: for we know that our holy Nymphs are there among them and will deliver them into our hands.

9. And Cenez arose, for the spirit of the Lord clothed him as *a garment*, and he drew his sword, and when the light of it shone upon the Amorites like sharp lightning, they saw it, and said: Is not this the sword of Cenez which hath made our wounded many? Now is the word justified which we spake, saying that our holy Nymphs have delivered them into our

hands. Lo, now, this day shall there be feasting for the Amorites, when our enemy is delivered unto us. Now, therefore, arise and let everyone gird on his sword and begin the battle.

10. And it came to pass when Cenez heard their words, he was clothed with the spirit of might and changed into another man, and went down into the camp of the Amorites and began to smite them. And the Lord sent before his face the angel Ingethel (*or* Gethel), who is set over the hidden things, and worketh unseen, (and another) angel of might helping with him: and Ingethel smote the Amorites with blindness, so that every man that saw his neighbour counted them his adversaries, and they slew one another. And the angel Zeruel, who is set over strength, bare up the arms of Cenez lest they should perceive him; and Cenez smote of the Amorites forty and five thousand men, and they themselves smote one another, and fell forty and five thousand men.

11. And when Cenez had smitten a great multitude, he would have loosened his hand from his sword, for the handle of the sword clave, that it could not be loosed, and his right hand had taken into it the strength of the sword. Then they that were left of the Amorites fled into the mountains; but Cenez sought how he might loose his hand: and he looked with his eyes and saw a man of the Amorites fleeing, and he caught him and said to him: I know that the Amorites are cunning: now therefore shew me how I may loose my hand from this sword, and I will let thee go. And the Amorite said: Go and take a man of the Hebrews and kill him, and while his blood is yet warm hold thine hand beneath and receive his blood, so shall thine hand be loosed. And (Zenez said: As the Lord liveth, if thou hadst said, Take a man of the Amorites, I would have taken one of them and saved thee alive: but forasmuch as thou saidest "of the Hebrews" that thou mightest show thine hatred, thy mouth shall be against thyself, and according as thou hast said, so will I do unto thee. And when he had thus said Cenez slew him, and while his blood was yet warm, he held his hand beneath and received it therein, and it was loosed.

12. And Cenez departed and put off his garments, and cast himself into the river and washed, and came up again and changed his garments, and returned to his young men. Now the Lord cast upon them a heavy sleep in the night, and they slept and knew not any thing of all that Cenez had done. And Cenez came and awaked them out of sleep; and they looked [upon him] with their eyes and saw, and behold, the field was full of dead bodies: and they were astonished in their mind, and looked every man on his neighbour. And Cenez said unto them: Why marvel ye? Are the ways of the Lord as the way of men? For with men a multitude prevaileth, but with God that which he appointeth. And therefore if God hath willed to work deliverance for this people by my hands, wherefore marvel ye? Arise and gird on every man your swords, and we will go home to our brethren.

13. And when all Israel heard the deliverance that was wrought by the hands of Cenez, all the people came out with one accord to meet him, and said: Blessed be the Lord which hath made thee ruler over his people, and hath shown that those things are sure which he spake unto thee: that which we heard by speech we see now with our eyes, for the work of the word of God is manifest.

14. And Cenez said unto them: Ask now your brethren, and let them tell you how greatly they laboured with me in the battle. And the men that were with him said: As the Lord liveth, we fought not, neither knew we *anything*, save only when we awaked, we saw the field full of dead bodies. And the people answered: Now know we that when the Lord appointeth to work deliverance for his people, he hath no need of a multitude, but only of sanctification.

15. And Cenez said to the captain of fifty which had shut up those men in prison: Bring forth those men that we may hear their words. And when he had brought them forth, Cenez said to them: Tell me, what saw ye in me that ye murmured among the people? And they said: Why askest thou us? Why askest thou us? Now therefore command that we be burned with fire, for we die not for this sin that we have now spoken, but for that former one wherein those men were taken which were burned in their sins; for then we did consent unto their sin, saying: Peradventure the people will not perceive us; and then we did escape the

people. But now have we been (rightly) made a public example by our sins in that we fell into slandering of thee. And Cenez said: If ye yourselves therefore witness against yourselves, how shall I have compassion upon you? And Cenez commanded them to be burned with fire, and cast their ashes into the place where they had burned the multitude of the sinners, even into the brook Phison.

      16. And Cenez ruled over his people fifty and seven years, and there was fear upon all his enemies all his days.

Chapter 28

XXVIII. And when the days of Cenez drew nigh that he should die, he sent and called all men (*or* all the elders), and the two prophets Jabis and Phinees, and Phinees the son of Eleazar the priest, and said to them: Behold now, the Lord hath showed me all his marvellous works which he hath prepared to do for his people in the last days.

2. And now will I make my covenant with you this day, that ye forsake not the Lord your God after my departing. For ye have seen all the marvels *which came* upon them that sinned, and all that they declared, confessing their sins of their own accord, and how the Lord our God made an end of them for that they transgressed his covenant. Wherefore now spare ye them of your house and your sons, and abide in the ways of the Lord your God, that the Lord destroy not his inheritance.

3. And Phinees, the son of Eleazar the priest, said: If Cenez the ruler bid me, and the prophets and the people and the elders, I will speak a word which I heard of my father when he was a-dying, and will not keep silence concerning the commandment which he commanded me when his soul was being received. And Cenez the ruler and the prophets said: Let Phinees say on. Shall any other speak before the priest which keepeth the commandments of the Lord our God, and that, seeing that truth proceedeth out of his mouth, and out of his heart a shining light?

4. Then said Phinees: My father, when he was a-dying, commanded me saying: Thus shalt thou say unto the children of Israel when they, are gathered together unto the assembly: The Lord appeared unto me the third day before this in a dream in the night, and said unto me: Behold, thou hast seen, and thy father before thee, how greatly I have laboured for my people; and it shall be after thy death that this people shall arise and corrupt their ways, departing from my commandments, and I shall be exceeding wroth with them. Yet will I remember the time which was before the ages, *even* in the time when there was not a man, and therein was no iniquity, when I said that the world should be, and they that should come should praise me therein, and I will plant a great vineyard, and out of it will I choose a plant, and order it and call it by my name, and it shall be mine for ever. But when I have done all that I have spoken, nevertheless my planting, which is called after me, will not know me, the planter thereof, but will corrupt his fruit, and will not yield me his fruit. These are the things which my father commanded me to speak unto this people.

5. And Cenez lifted up his voice, and the elders, and all the people with one accord, and wept with a great lamentation until the evening and said: Shall the shepherd destroy his flock to no purpose, except it continue in sin against him? And shall it not be he that shall spare according to the abundance of his mercy, seeing he hath spent great labour upon us?

6. Now while they were set, the holy spirit that dwelt in Cenez leapt upon him and took away from him his *bodily* sense, and he began to prophesy, saying: Behold now I see that which I looked not for, and perceive that I knew not. Hearken now, ye that dwell on the earth, even as they that sojourned therein prophesied before me, when they saw this hour, *even* before the earth was corrupted, that ye may know the prophecies appointed aforetime, all ye that dwell therein.

7. Behold now I see flames that burn not, and I hear springs of water awaked out of sleep, and they have no foundation, neither do I behold the tops of the mountains, nor the canopy of the firmament, but all things unappearing and invisible, which have no place whatsoever, and although mine eye knoweth not what it seeth, mine heart shall discover that which it may learn (or say).

8. Now out of the flame which I saw, and it burned not, I beheld, and lo a spark came up and as it were builded for itself a floor under heaven, and the likeness of the floor thereof was as a spider spinneth, in the fashion of a shield. And when the foundation was laid, I beheld, and from that spring there was stirred up as it were a boiling froth, and behold, it

changed itself as it were into another foundation; and between the two foundations, even the upper and the lower, there drew near out of the light of the invisible place as it were forms of men, and they walked to and fro: and behold, a voice saying: These shall be for a foundation unto men and they shall dwell therein 7000 years.

  9. And the lower foundation was a pavement and the upper was of froth, and they that came forth out of the light of the invisible place, they are those that shall dwell therein, and the name of that man is <Adam>. And it shall be, when he hath (*or* they have) sinned against me and the time is fulfilled, that the spark shall be quenched and the spring shall cease, and so they shall be changed.

  10. And it came to pass after Cenez had spoken these words that he awaked and his sense returned unto him: but he knew not that which he had spoken neither that which he had seen, but this only he said to the people: If the rest of the righteous be such after they are dead, it is better for them to die to the corruptible world, that they see not sin. And when Cenez had so said, he died and slept with his fathers, and the people mourned for him 30 days.

Chapter 29

XXIX And after these things the people appointed Zebul ruler over them, and at that time he gathered the people together and said unto them: Behold now, we know all the labour wherewith Cenez laboured with us in the days of his life. Now if he had had sons, they should have been princes over the people, but inasmuch as his daughters are yet alive, let them receive a greater inheritance among the people, because their father in his life refused to give it unto them, lest he should be called covetous and greedy of gain. And the people said: Do all that is right in thine eyes.

2. Now Cenez had three daughters whose names are these: Ethema the firstborn, the second Pheila, the third Zelpha. And Zebul gave to the firstborn all that was round about the land of the Phœnicians, and to the second he gave the olive yard of Accaron, and to the third all the tilled land that was about Azotus. And he gave them husbands, namely to the firstborn Elisephan, to the second Odiel, and to the third Doel.

3. Now in those days Zebul set up a treasury for the Lord and said unto the people: Behold, if any man will sanctify unto the Lord gold and silver, let him bring it to the Lord's treasury in Sylo: only let not any that hath stuff belonging to idols think to sanctify it to the Lord's treasures, for the Lord desireth not the abominations of the accursed things, lest ye disturb the synagogue of the Lord, for the wrath that is passed by sufficeth. And all the people brought that which their heart moved them to bring, both men and women, even gold and silver. And all that was brought was weighed, and it was 20 talents of gold, and 250 talents of silver.

4. And Zebul judged the people twenty and five years. And when he had accomplished his time, he sent and called all the people and said: Lo, now I depart to die. Look ye to the testimonies which they that went before us testified, and let not your heart be like unto the waves of the sea, but like as the wave of the sea under standeth not save only those things which are in the sea, so let your heart also think upon nothing save only those things which belong unto the law. And Zebul slept with his fathers, and was buried in the sepulchre of his father.

CHAPTER 30

XXX Then had the children of Israel no man whom they might appoint as judge over them: and their heart fell away, and they forgot the promise, and transgressed the ways which Moses and Jesus the servants of the Lord had commanded them, and were led away after the daughters of the Amorites, and served their gods.

2. And the Lord was wroth with them, and sent his angel and said: Behold, I chose me one people out of all the tribes of the earth, and I said that my glory should abide with them in this world, and I sent unto them Moses my servant, to declare unto them my great majesty and my judgements, and they have transgressed my ways. Now therefore behold I will stir up their enemies and they shall rule over them, and then shall all *the* people[s] say: Because we have transgressed the ways of God and of our fathers, therefore are these things come upon us. Yet there shall a woman rule over them which shall give them light 40 years.

3. And after these things the Lord stirred up against them Jabin king of Asor, and he began to fight against them, and he had as captain of his might Sisara, who had 8000 chariots of iron. And he came unto the mount Effrem and fought against the people, and Israel feared him greatly, and the people could not stand all the days of Sisara.

4. And when Israel was brought very low, all the children of Israel gathered together with one accord unto the mount of Juda and said: We did call ourselves blessed more than *all* people, and now, lo, we are brought so low, more than all nations, that we cannot dwell in our land, and our enemies bear rule over us. And now who hath done all this unto us? Is it not our iniquities, because we have forsaken the Lord God of our fathers, and have walked in those things which could not profit us? Now therefore come let us fast seven days, both men and women, and from the least (*sic*) even to the sucking child. Who knoweth whether God will be reconciled unto his inheritance, that he destroy not the planting of his vineyard?

5. And after the people had fasted 7 days, sitting in sackcloth, the Lord sent unto them on the 7th day Debbora, who said unto them: Can the sheep that is appointed to the slaughter answer before him that slayeth it, when both he that slayeth < . . . > and he that is slain keepeth silence, when he is sometimes provoked against it? Now ye were born to be a flock before our Lord. And he led you into the height of the clouds, and subdued angels beneath your feet, and appointed unto you a law, and gave you commandments by prophets, and chastised you by rulers, and shewed you wonders not a few, and for your sake commanded the luminaries and they stood still in the places where they were bidden, and when your enemies came upon you he rained hailstones upon them and destroyed them, and Moses and Jesus and Cenez and Zebul gave you commandments. And ye have not obeyed them.

6. For while they lived, ye shewed yourselves as it were obedient unto your God, but when they died, your heart died also. And ye became like unto iron that is thrust into the fire, which when it is melted by the flame becometh as water, but when it is come out of the fire returneth unto its hardness. So ye also, while they that admonish you burn you, do show the effect, and when they are dead ye forget all things.

7. And now, behold, the Lord will have compassion upon you this day, not for your sakes, but for his covenant's sake which he made with your fathers and for his oath's sake which he sware, that he would not forsake you for ever. But know ye that after my decease ye will begin to sin in your latter days. Wherefore the Lord will perform marvellous things among you, and will deliver your enemies into your hands. For your fathers are dead, but God, which made a covenant with them, is life.

CHAPTER 31

XXXI. And Debbora sent and called Barach and said to him: Arise and gird up thy loins as a man, and go down and fight against Sisara, For I see the constellations greatly moved in their ranks and preparing to fight for you. I see also the lightnings unmoveable in their courses, and setting forth to stay the wheels of the chariots of them that boast in the might of Sisara, who saith: I will surely go down in the arm of my might to fight against Israel, and will divide the spoil of them among my servants, and their fair women will I take unto me for concubines. Therefore hath the Lord spoken concerning him that the arm of a weak woman shall overcome him, and maidens shall take his spoil, and he also himself shall fall into the hands of a woman.

2. And when Debbora and the people and Barach went down to meet their enemies, immediately the Lord disturbed the goings of his stars, and spake unto them saying: Hasten and go ye, for our (*or* your) enemies fall upon you: confound their arms and break the strength of their hearts, for I am come that my people may prevail. For though it be that my people have sinned, yet will I have mercy on them. And when this was said, the stars went forth as it was commanded them and burned up their enemies. And the number of them that were gathered (*or* burned) and slain in one hour was 90 times 97,000 men. But Sisara they destroyed not, for so it was commanded them.

3. And when Sisara had fled on his horse to deliver his soul, Jahel the wife of Aber the Cinean decked herself with her ornaments and came out to meet him: now the woman was very fair: and when she saw him she said: Come in and take food, and sleep: and in. the evening I will send my servants with thee, for I know that thou wilt remember me and recompense me. And Sisara came in, and when he saw roses scattered upon the bed he said: If I be delivered, O Jahel, I will go unto my mother and thou shalt (*or* Jahel shall) be my wife.

4. And thereafter was Sisara athirst and he said to Jahel: Give me a little water, for I am faint and my soul burneth by reason of the flame which I beheld in the stars. And Jahel said unto him: Rest a little while and then thou shalt drink.

5. And when Sisara was fallen asleep, Jahel went to the flock and milked milk therefrom. And as she milked she said: Behold now, remember, O Lord, when thou didst divide every tribe and nation upon the earth, didst thou not choose out Israel only, and didst not liken him to any beast save only unto the ram that goeth before the flock and leadeth it? Behold therefore and see how Sisara hath thought *in his heart* saying: I will go and punish the flock of the Most Mighty. And lo, I will take of the milk of the beasts whereunto thou didst liken thy people, and will go and give him to drink, and when he hath drunk he shall become weak, and after that I will kill him. And this shall be the sign that thou shalt give me, O Lord, that, whereas Sisara sleepeth, when I go in, if he wake and ask me forthwith, saying: Give me water to drink, *then* I *shall* know that my prayer hath been heard.

6. So Jahel returned and entered in, and Sisara awaked and said to her: Give me to drink, for I burn mightily and my soul is inflamed. And Jahel took wine and mingled it with the milk and gave him to drink, and he drank and fell asleep.

7. But Jahel took a stake in her left hand and drew near unto him saying: If the Lord give me this sign I *shall* know that Sisara shall fall into my hands. Behold I will cast him upon the ground from off the bed whereon he sleepeth, and it shall be, if he perceive it not, that I shall know that he is delivered up. And Jahel took Sisara and pushed him from off the bed upon the earth, but he perceived it not, for he was exceeding faint. And Jahel said: Strengthen in me, O Lord, mine arm this day for thy sake and thy people's sake, and for them that put their trust in thee. And Jahel 'took the stake and set it upon his temple and smote with the hammer. And as he died Sisara' said to Jahel: Lo, pain hath come upon me, Jahel, and I die like a woman. And Jahel said unto him: Go boast thyself before thy father in hell, and tell him

that thou hast fallen into (*or* say, I have been delivered into) the hands of a woman. And she made an end and slew him and laid his body *there* until Barach should return.

8. Now the mother of Sisara was called Themech, and she sent unto her friends saying: Come, let us go forth together to meet my son, and ye shall see the daughters of the Hebrews whom my son will bring hither to be his concubines.

9. But Barach returned from following after Sisara and was greatly vexed because he found him not, and Jahel came forth to meet him, and said: Come, enter in, thou blessed of God, and I will deliver thee thine enemy whom thou followedst after and hast not found. And Barach went in and found Sisara dead, and said: Blessed be the Lord which sent his spirit and said: Into the hands of a woman shall Sisara be delivered. And when he had so said he cut off the head of Sisara and sent it unto his mother, and gave her a message saying: Receive thy son whom thou didst look for to come with spoil.

Chapter 32

XXXII. *Then Debbora and Barach the son of Abino* and all the people together *sang* an hymn unto the Lord *in that day*, saying: Behold, from on high hath the Lord shewn unto us his glory, even as he did aforetime when he sent forth his voice to confound the tongues of men. And he chose out our nation, and took Abraham our father out of the fire, and chose him before all his brethren, and kept him from the fire and delivered him from the bricks of the building of the tower, and gave him a son in the latter days of his old age, and brought him out of the barren womb, and all the angels were jealous against him, and the orderers of the hosts envied him.

2. And it came to pass, when they were jealous against him, God said unto him: Slay for me the fruit of thy belly and offer for my sake that which I gave thee. And Abraham did not gainsay him and set forth immediately. And as he went forth he said to his son: Lo, now, my son, I offer thee for a burnt offering and deliver thee into his hands who gave thee unto me.

3. And the son said to his father: Hear me, father. If a lamb of the flock is accepted for an offering to the Lord for an odour of sweetness, and if for the iniquities of men sheep are appointed to the slaughter, but man is set to inherit the world, how then sayest thou now unto me: Come and inherit a life secure, and a time that cannot be measured? What and if I had not been born in the world to be offered a sacrifice unto him that made me? And it shall be my blessedness beyond all men, for there shall be no other *such thing*; and in me shall the generations be instructed, and by me the peoples shall understand that the Lord hath accounted the soul of a man worthy to be a sacrifice unto him.

4. And when his father had offered him upon the altar and had bound his feet to slay him, the Most Mighty hasted and sent forth his voice from on high saying: Kill not thy son, neither destroy the fruit of thy body: for now have I showed forth *myself* that I might appear to them that know me not, and have shut the mouths of them that always speak evil against thee. And thy memorial shall be before me for ever, and thy name and the name of this *thy son* from one generation to another.

5. And to Isaac he gave two sons, which also were from a womb shut up, for at that time their mother was in the third year of her marriage. And it shall not be so with any other woman, neither shall any wife boast herself so, that cometh near to her husband in the third year. And there were born to him two sons, even Jacob and Esau. And God loved Jacob, but Esau he hated because of his deeds.

6. And it came to pass in the old age of their father, that Isaac blessed Jacob and sent him into Mesopotamia, and there he begat 12 sons, and they went down into Egypt and dwelled there.

7. And when their enemies dealt evilly with them, the people cried unto the Lord, and their prayer was heard, and he brought them out thence, and led them unto the mount Sina, and brought forth unto them the foundation of understanding which he had prepared from the birth of the world; and then the foundation was moved, the hosts sped forth the lightnings upon their courses, and the winds sounded out of their storehouses, and the earth was stirred from her foundation, and the mountains and the rocks trembled in their fastenings, and the clouds lifted up their waves against the flame of the fire that it should not consume the world.

8. Then did the depth awake from his springs, and all the waves of the sea came together. Then did Paradise give forth the breath of her fruits, and the cedars of Libanus were moved from their roots. And the beasts of the field were terrified in the dwellings of the forests, and all his works gathered together to behold the Lord when he ordained a covenant with the children of Israel. And all things that the Most Mighty said, these hath he observed, having for witness Moses his beloved.

9. And when he was dying *God* appointed unto him the firmament, and shewed him these witnesses whom now we have, saying: Let the heaven whereinto thou hast entered and the earth wherein thou hast walked until now be a witness between me and thee and my people. For the sun and the moon and the stars shall be ministers unto us (*or* you).

10. And when Jesus arose to rule over the people, it came to pass in the day wherein he fought against the enemies, that the evening drew near, while yet the battle was strong, and Jesus said to the sun and the moon: O ye ministers that were appointed between the Most Mighty and his sons, lo now, the battle goeth on still, and do ye forsake your office? Stand still therefore to-day and give light unto his sons, and put darkness upon our enemies. And they did so.

11. And now in these days Sisara arose to make us his bondmen, and we cried unto the Lord our God, and he commanded the stars and said: Depart out of your ranks, and burn mine enemies, that they may know my might. And the stars came down and overthrew their camp and kept us safe without any labour.

12. Therefore will we not cease to sing praises, neither shall our mouths keep silence from telling of his marvellous works: for he hath remembered his promises both new and old, and hath shown us his deliverance,: and therefore doth Jahel boast herself among women, because she alone hath brought this good way to success, in that with her own hands she slew Sisara.

13. O earth, go thou, go, ye heavens and lightnings, go, ye angels and hosts, [go ye] and tell the fathers in the treasure-houses of their souls, and say: The Most Mighty hath not forgotten the least of all the promises which he made with us, saying: Many wonders will I perform for your sons. And now from this day forth it shall be known that whatsoever God hath said unto men that he will perform, he will perform it, even though man die.

14. Sing praises, sing praises, O Debbora (*or*, if man delay to sing praises to God, yet sing thou, O Debbora), and let the grace of an holy spirit awake in thee, and begin to praise the works of the Lord: for there shall not again arise such a day, wherein the stars shall bear tidings and overcome the enemies of Israel, as it was commanded them. From this time forth if Israel fall into a strait, let him call upon these his witnesses together with their ministers, and they shall go upon an embassy to the most High, and he will remember this day, and will send a deliverance to his covenant.

15. And thou, Debbora, begin to speak of that thou sawest in the field: how that the people walked and went forth safely, and the stars fought on their part (*or*, how that, like peoples walking, so went forth the stars and fought). Rejoice, O land, over them that dwell in thee, for in thee is the knowledge of the Lord which buildeth his stronghold in thee. For it was of right that God took out of thee the rib of him that was first formed, knowing that out of his rib Israel should be born. And thy forming shall be for a testimony of what the Lord hath done for his people.

16. Tarry, O ye hours of the day, and hasten not onward, that we may declare that which our understanding can bring forth, for night will come upon us. And it shall be like the night when God smote the firstborn of the Egyptians for the sake of his firstborn.

17. And then shall I cease from my hymn because the time will be hastened (*or* prepared) for his righteous ones. For I will sing unto him as in the renewing of the creation, and the people shall remember this deliverance, and it shall be for a testimony unto them. Let the sea also bear witness, with the deeps thereof, for not only did God dry it up before the face of our fathers, but he did also overthrow the camp from its setting and overcame our enemies.

18. And when Debbora made an end of her words she went up with the people together unto Silo, and they offered sacrifices and burnt offerings and sounded upon the broad trumpets. And when they sounded and had offered the sacrifices, Debbora said: This shall be for a testimony of the trumpets between the stars and the Lord of them.

Chapter 33

XXXIII. And Debbora went down thence, and judged Israel 40 years. And it came to pass when the day of her death drew near, that she sent and gathered all the people and said unto them: Hearken now, my people. Behold, I admonish you as a woman of God, and give you light as one of the race of women; obey me now as your mother, and give ear to my words, as men that shall yourselves die.

2. Behold, I depart to die by the way of all flesh, whereby ye also shall go: only direct your heart unto the Lord your God in the time of your life, for after your death ye will not be able to repent of those things wherein ye live.

3. For death is now sealed up, and accomplished, and the measure and the time and the years have restored that which was committed to them. For even if ye seek to do evil in hell after your death, ye will not be able, because the desire of sin shall cease, and the evil creation shall lose its power, and hell, which receiveth that that is committed to it, will not restore it unless it be demanded by him that committed it. Now, therefore, my sons, obey ye my voice while ye have the time of life and the light of the law, *and* direct your ways.

4. And when Debbora spake these words, all the people lifted up their voice together and wept, saying: Behold now, mother, thou diest and forsakest thy sons; and to whom dost thou commit them? Pray thou, therefore, for us, and after thy departure thy soul shall be mindful of us for ever.

5. And Debbora answered and said to the people: While a man yet liveth he can pray for himself and for his sons; but after his end he will not be able to entreat nor to remember any man. Therefore, hope not in your fathers, for they will not profit you unless ye be found like unto them. But then your likeness shall be as the stars of the heaven, which have been manifested unto you at this time.

6. And Debbora died and slept with her fathers and was buried in the city of her fathers, and the people mourned for her 70 days. And as they bewailed her, thus they spake a lamentation, saying: Behold, a mother is perished out of Israel, and an holy one that bare rule in the house of Jacob, which made fast the fence about her generation, and her generation shall seek after her. And after her death the land had rest seven years.

XXXIV. And at that time there came up a certain Aod of the priests of Madian, and he was a wizard, and he spake unto Israel, saying: Wherefore give ye ear to your law? Come and I will shew you such a thing as your law is not. And the people said: What canst thou shew us that our law hath not? And he said to the people: Have ye ever seen the sun by night? And they said: Nay. And he said: Whensoever ye will, I will shew it unto you, that ye may know that our gods have power, and will not deceive them that serve them. And they said: Shew us.

2. And he departed and wrought with his magic, commanding the angels that were set over sorceries, because for a long time he did sacrifice unto them.

3. <<*For this was formerly in the power of the angels and was*>> performed by the angels before they were judged, and they would have destroyed the unmeasurable world; and because they transgressed, it came to pass that the angels had no longer the power. For when they were judged, then the power was not committed unto the rest: and by these *signs* (or *powers*) do they work who minister unto men in sorceries, until the unmeasurable age shall come.

4. And at that time Aod by art magic shewed unto the people the sun by night. And the people were astonished and said: Behold, what great things can the gods of the Madianites do, and we knew it not!

5. And God, willing to try Israel whether they were yet in iniquity, suffered *the angels*, and their work had good success, and the people of Israel were deceived and began to serve the gods of the Madianites. And God said: I will deliver them into the hands of the Madianites, inasmuch as by them are they deceived. And he delivered them into their hands, and the Madianites began to bring Israel into bondage.

CHAPTER 35

XXXV. Now Gedeon was the son of Joath, the most mighty man among all his brethren. And when it was the time of summer, he came to the mountain, having sheaves with him, to thresh them there, and escape from the Madianites that pressed upon him. And the angel of the Lord met him, and said unto him: Whence comest thou and where is thine entering in?

2. He said to him: Why askest thou me whence I come? for straitness encompasseth me, for Israel is fallen into affliction, and they are verily delivered into the hands of the Madianites. And where are the wonders which our fathers have told us, saying: The Lord chose Israel alone before all the peoples of the earth? Lo, now he hath delivered us up, and hath forgotten the promises which he made to our fathers. For we should have chosen rather to be delivered unto death once for all, than that his people should be punished thus time after time.

3. And the angel of the Lord said unto him: It is not for nothing that ye are delivered up, but your own inventions have brought these things upon you, for like as ye have forsaken the promises which ye received of the Lord, these evils are come upon you, and ye have not been mindful of the commandments of God, which they commanded you that were before you. Therefore are ye come into the displeasure of your God. But he will have mercy upon you, as no man hath mercy, *even* upon the race of Israel, and that not for your sakes, but because of them that are fallen asleep.

4. And now come, I will send thee, and thou shalt deliver Israel out of the hand of the Madianites. For thus saith the Lord: Though Israel be not righteous, yet because the Madianites are sinners, therefore, knowing the iniquity of my people, I will forgive them, and after that I will rebuke them for that they have done evil, but upon the Madianites I will be avenged presently.

5. And Gedeon said: Who am I and what is my father's house, that I should go against the Madianites to battle? And the angel said unto him: Peradventure thou thinkest that as is man's way so is the way of God. For men look upon the glory of the world and upon riches, but God looketh upon that which is upright and good, and upon meekness. Now therefore go, gird up thy loins, and the Lord shall be with thee, for thee hath he chosen to take vengeance of his enemies, like as, behold, he hath bidden thee.

6. And Gedeon said to him: *Let not my Lord be wroth if I speak* a word. Behold, Moses, the first of all the prophets, besought the Lord for a sign, and it was given him. But who am I, except the Lord that hath chosen me give me a sign that I may know that I go aright. And the angel of the Lord said unto him: Run and take for me water out of the pit yonder and pour it upon this rock, and I will give thee a sign. And he went and took it as he commanded him.

7. And the angel said unto him: Before thou pour the water upon the rock, ask what thou wouldst have it to become, either blood, or fire, or that it appear not at all. And Gedeon said: Let it become half of it blood and half fire. And Gedeon poured out the water upon the rock, and it came to pass when he had poured it out, that the half part became flame, and the half part blood, and they were mingled together, that is, the fire and the blood, yet the blood did not quench the fire, neither did the fire consume the blood. And when Gedeon saw that, he asked for yet. other signs, and they were given him. Are not these written in the book of the Judges?

Chapter 36

XXXVI. And Gedeon took 300 men and departed and came unto the uttermost part of the camp of Madian, and he heard every man speaking to his neighbour and saying: Ye shall see a confusion above reckoning, of the sword of Gedeon, coming upon us, for God hath delivered into his hands the camp of the Madianites, and he will begin to make an end of us, even the mother with the children, because our sins are filled up, even as also our gods have shewed us and we believed them not. And now arise, let us succour our souls and fly.

2. And when Gedeon heard these words, immediately he was clothed with the spirit of the Lord, and, being endued with power, he said unto the 300 men: Arise and let every one of you gird on his sword, for the Madianites are delivered into our hands. And the men went down with him, and he drew near and began to fight. And they blew the trumpet and cried out together and said: The sword of the Lord is upon us. And they slew of the Madianites about 120,000 men, and the residue of the Madianites fled.

3. And after these things Gedeon came and gathered the people of Israel together and said unto them: Behold, the Lord sent me to fight your battle, and I went according as he commanded me. And now I ask one petition of you: turn not away your face; and let every man of you give me the golden armlets which ye have on your hands. And Gedeon spread out a coat, and every man cast upon it their armlets, and they were all weighed, and the weight of them was found to be 12 talents (*or* 12,000 shekels). And Gedeon took them., and of them he made idols and worshipped them.

4. And God said: One way is *verily* appointed, that I should not rebuke Gedeon in his lifetime, even because when he destroyed the sanctuary of Baal, then all men said: Let Baal avenge himself. Now, therefore, if I chastise him for that he hath done evil against me, ye will say: It was not God that chastised him, but Baal, because he sinned aforetime against him. Therefore now shall Gedeon die in a good old age, that they may not have whereof to speak. But after that Gedeon is dead I will punish him once, because he hath transgressed against me. And Gedeon died in a good old age and was buried in his own city.

Chapter 37

XXXVII. And he had a son by a concubine whose name was Abimelech; the same slew all his brethren, desiring to be ruler over the people.

[*A leaf gone.*]

2. Then all the trees of the field came together unto the fig-tree and said: Come, reign over us. And the fig-tree said: Was I indeed born in the kingdom or in the rulership over the trees? or was I planted to that and that I should reign over you? And therefore even as I cannot reign over you, neither shall Abimelech obtain continuance in his rulership. After that the trees came together unto the vine and said: Come, reign over us. And the vine said: I was planted to give unto men the sweetness of wine, and I am preserved by rendering unto them my fruit. But like as I cannot reign over you, so shall the blood of Abimelech be required at your hand. And after that the trees came unto the apple and said: Come, reign over us. And he said: It was commanded me to yield unto men a fruit of sweet savour. Therefore I cannot reign over you, and Abimelech shall die by stones.

3. Then came the trees unto the bramble and said: Come, reign over us. And the bramble said: When the thorn was born, truth did shine forth in the semblance of a thorn. And when our first father was condemned to death, the earth was condemned to bring forth thorns and thistles. And when the truth enlightened Moses, it was by a thorn bush that it enlightened him. Now therefore it shall be that by me the truth shall be heard of you. Now if ye have spoken in sincerity unto the bramble that it should in truth reign over you, sit ye under the shadow of it: but if with dissembling, then let fire go forth and devour and consume the trees of the field. For the apple-tree was made for the chastisers, and the fig-tree was made for the people, and the vine[yard] was made for them that were before us.

4. And now shall *the bramble* be unto you even as Abimelech, which slew his brethren with wrong, and desireth to rule over you. If Abimelech be worthy of them (*or* Let Abimelech be a fire unto them) whom he desireth to rule, let him be as the bramble which was made to rebuke the foolish among the people. And there went forth fire out of the bramble and devoured the trees that are in the field.

5. After that Abimelech ruled over the people for one year and six months, and he died hard by a certain tower, whence a woman cast down upon him the half of a millstone.

[*A gap of uncertain length in the text.*]

Chapter 38

XXXVIII. (Then did Jair judge Israel 22 years.) The same built a sanctuary to Baal, and led the people astray saying: Every man that sacrificeth not unto Baal shall die. And when all the people sacrificed, seven men only would not sacrifice whose names are these: Dephal, Abiesdrel, Getalibal, Selumi, Assur, Jonadali, Memihel.

2. The same answered and said unto Jair: Behold, we remember the precepts which they that were before us commanded us, and Debbora our mother, saying: Take heed that ye turn not away your heart to the right hand or to the left, but attend unto the law of the Lord day and night. Now therefore why dost thou corrupt the people of the Lord and deceive them, saying: Baal is God, let us worship him? And now if he be God as thou sayest, let him speak as a God, and then we will sacrifice unto him.

3. And Jair said: Burn them with fire, for they have blasphemed Baal. And his servants took them to burn them with fire. And when they cast them upon the fire there went forth Nathaniel, the angel which is over fire, and quenched the fire and burned up the servants of Jair: but the seven men he made to escape, so that no man of the people saw them, for he had smitten the people with blindness.

4. And when Jair came to the place (*or* it came to the place of Jair) he also was burned. But before he burned him, the angel of the Lord said unto him: Hear the word of the Lord before thou diest. Thus saith the Lord: I raised thee up out of the land of Egypt, and appointed thee ruler over my peoples. But thou hast risen and corrupted my covenant, and hast led them astray, and hast sought to burn my servants in the flame, because they reproved thee, which though they be burned with corruptible fire, yet now are they quickened with living fire and are delivered. But thou shalt die, saith the Lord, and in the fire wherein thou shalt die, therein shalt thou have thy dwelling. And thereafter he burned him, and came even unto the pillar of Baal and overthrew it, and burned up Baal with the people that stood by, even 1000 men.

Chapter 39

XXXIX. And after these things came the children of Ammon and began to fight against Israel and took many of their cities. And when the people were greatly straitened, they gathered together in Masphath, saying every man to his neighbours: Behold now, we see the strait which encompasseth us, and the Lord is departed from us, and is no more with us, and our enemies have taken our cities, and there is no leader to go in and out before our face. Now therefore let us see whom we may set over us to fight our battle.

2. *Now Jepthan the Galaadite was a mighty man of valour*, and because he was jealous of his brothers, they had cast him out of his land, and he went and *dwelt in the land of Tobi. And vagrant men gathered themselves unto him* and abode with him.

3. And it came to pass when Israel was overcome in battle, that they came into the land of Tobi to Jepthan and said unto him: Come, rule over the people. For who knoweth whether thou wast therefore preserved to this day or wast therefore delivered out of the hands of thy brethren that thou mightest at this time bear rule over thy people?

4. And Jepthan said unto them: Doth love so return after hatred, or doth time overcome all things? For ye did cast me out of my land and out of my father's house; and now are ye come unto me when ye are in a strait? And they said unto him: If the God of our fathers remembered not our sins, but delivered us when we had sinned against him and he had given us over before the face of our enemies, and we were oppressed by them, why wilt thou that art a mortal man remember the iniquities which happened unto us, in the time of our affliction? Therefore be it not so before thee, lord.

5. And Jepthan said: God indeed is able to be unmindful of our sins, seeing he hath time and place to repose himself of his long-suffering, for he is God; but I am mortal, made of the earth: whereunto I shall return, and where shall I cast away mine anger, and the wrong wherewith ye have injured me? And the people said unto him: Let the dove instruct thee, whereunto Israel was likened, for though her young be taken away from her, yet departeth she not out of her place, but spurneth away her wrong and forgetteth it as it were in the bottom of the deep.

6. And Jepthan arose and went with them and gathered all the people, and said unto them: Ye know how that when our princes were alive, they admonished us to follow our law. And Ammon and his sons turned away the people from their way wherein they walked, to serve other gods which should destroy them. Now therefore set your hearts in the law of the Lord your God, and let us entreat him with one accord. And so will we fight against our adversaries, and trust and hope in the Lord that he will not deliver us up for ever. *For* although our sins do overabound, nevertheless his mercy filleth *all* the earth.

7. And the whole people prayed with one accord, both men and women, boys and sucklings. And when they prayed they said: Look, O Lord, upon the people whom thou hast chosen, and spoil not the vine which thy right hand hath planted; that this people may be before thee for an inheritance, whom thou hast possessed from the beginning, and whom thou hast preferred alway, and for whose sake thou hast made the habitable places, and brought them into the land which thou swarest unto them; deliver us not up before them that hate thee, O Lord.

8. And God repented him of his anger and strengthened the spirit of Jepthan. And he sent a message unto Getal the king of the children of Ammon and said: Wherefore vexest thou our land and hast taken my cities, or wherefore afflictest thou us? Thou hast not been commanded of the God of Israel to destroy them that dwell in the land. Now therefore restore unto me my cities, and mine anger shall cease from thee. But if not, know that I will come up unto thee and repay thee for the former things, and recompense thy wickedness upon thine head: rememberest thou not how thou didst deal deceitfully with the people of Israel in the

wilderness? And the messengers of Jepthan spake these words unto the king of the children of Ammon.

9. And Getal said: Did Israel take thought when he took the land of the Amorites? Say therefore: Know ye that now I will take from thee the remnant of thy cities and will repay thee thy wickedness and will take vengeance for the Amorites whom thou hast wronged. And Jepthan sent yet again to the king of the children of Ammon saying: Of a truth I perceive that God hath brought thee hither that I may destroy thee, unless thou rest from thine iniquity wherewith thou wilt vex Israel. And therefore I will come unto thee and show myself unto thee. For they are not, as ye say, gods which have given you the inheritance that ye possess. But because ye have been led astray after stones, fire shall follow after you unto vengeance.

10. And because the king of the children of Ammon would not hear the voice of Jepthan, Jepthan arose and armed all the people to go forth and fight in the borders saying: When the children of Ammon are delivered into my hands and I am returned, any that first meeteth with me shall be for a burnt offering unto the Lord.

11. And the Lord was very wroth and said: Behold, Jepthan hath vowed that he will offer unto me that which meeteth with him first. Now therefore if a dog meet with Jepthan first, shall a dog be offered unto me? And now let the vow of Jepthan be upon his firstborn, even upon the fruit of his body, and his prayer upon his only begotten daughter. But I will verily deliver my people at this time, not for his sake, but for the prayer which Israel hath prayed.

Chapter 40

XL. And Jepthan came and fought against the children of Ammon, and the Lord delivered them into his hand, and he smote threescore of their cities. And Jepthan returned in peace. And the women came out to meet him with dances. And he had an only begotten daughter; the same came out first in the dances to meet her father. And when Jepthan saw her he fainted and said: Rightly is thy name called Seila, that thou shouldest be offered for a sacrifice. And now who will put my heart in the balance and weigh my soul? and I will stand and see whether one will outweigh *the other*, the rejoicing that is come or the affliction which cometh upon me? for in that I have opened my mouth unto my Lord in the song of *my* vows, I cannot call it back again.

2. And Seila his daughter said unto him: And who is it that can be sorrowful in their death when they see the people delivered? Rememberest thou not that which was in the days of our fathers, when the father set his son for a burnt offering and he gainsaid him not, but consented unto him rejoicing? And he that was offered was ready, and he that offered was glad.

3. Now therefore annul not anything of that thou has vowed, but grant unto me one prayer. I ask of thee before I die a small request: I beseech thee that before I give up my soul, I may go into the mountains and wander (*or* abide) among the hills and walk about among the rocks, I and the virgins that are my fellows, and pour out my tears there and tell the affliction of my youth; and the trees of the field shall bewail me and the beasts of the field shall lament for me; for I am not sorrowful for that I die, neither doth it grieve me that I give up my soul: but whereas my father was overtaken in his vow, [and] if I offer not myself willingly for a sacrifice, I fear lest my death be not acceptable, and that I shall lose my life to no purpose. These things will I tell unto the mountains, and after that I will return. And her father said: Go.

4. And Seila the daughter of Jepthan went forth, she and the virgins that were her fellows, and came and told it to the wise men of the people. And no man could answer her words. And after that she went into the mount Stelac, and by night the Lord thought upon her, and said: Lo, now have I shut up the tongue of the wise among my people before this generation, that they could not answer the word of the daughter of Jepthan, that my word might be fulfilled, and my counsel not destroyed which I had devised: and I have seen that she is more wise than her father, and a maiden of understanding more than all the wise which are here. And now let her life be given her at her request, and her death shall be precious in my sight at all times.

5. And when the daughter of Jepthan came unto the mount Stelac, she began to lament. And this is her lamentation wherewith she mourned and bewailed herself before she departed, and she said: Hearken, O mountains, to my lamentation, and look, O hills, upon the tears of mine eyes, and be witness, O rocks, in the bewailing of my soul. Behold how I am accused, but my soul shall not be taken away in vain. Let my words go forth into the heavens, and let my tears be written before the face of the firmament, that the father overcome not (*or* fight not against) his daughter whom he hath vowed to offer up, that her ruler may hear that his only begotten daughter is promised for a sacrifice.

6. Yet I have not been satisfied with my bed of marriage, neither filled with the garlands of my wedding. For I have not been arrayed with brightness, sitting in my maidenhood; I have not used my precious ointment, neither hath my soul enjoyed the oil of anointing which was prepared for me. O my mother, to no purpose hast thou borne thine only begotten, and begotten her upon the earth, for hell is become my marriage chamber. Let all the mingling of oil which thou hast prepared for me be poured out, and the white robe which my mother wove for me, let the moth eat it, and the crown of flowers which my nurse plaited for me aforetime, let it wither, and the coverlet which she wove of violet and purple for my

virginity, let the worm spoil it; and when the virgins, my fellows, tell of me, let them bewail me with groaning for *many* days.

7. Bow down your branches, O ye trees, and lament my youth. Come, ye beasts of the forest, and trample upon my virginity. For my years are cut off, and the days of my life are waxen old in darkness.

8. And when she had so said, Seila returned unto her father, and he did all that he had vowed, and offered burnt offerings. Then all the maidens of Israel gathered together and buried the daughter of Jepthan and bewailed her. And the children of Israel made a great lamentation and appointed in that month, on the 14th day of the month, that they should come together every year and lament for the daughter of Jepthan four days. And they called the name of her sepulchre according to her own name Seila.

9. And Jepthan judged the children of Israel ten years, and died, and was buried with his fathers.

CHAPTER 41

XLI. And after him there arose a judge in Israel, Addo the son of Elech of Praton, and he also judged the children of Israel eight years. In his days the king of Moab sent messengers unto him saying: Behold now, thou knowest that Israel hath taken my cities: now therefore restore them in recompense. And Addo said: Are ye not yet instructed by that which hath befallen the children of Ammon, unless peradventure the sins of Moab be filled up? And Addo sent and took of the people 20,000 men and came against Moab, and fought against them and slew of them 45,000 men. And the remnant fled before him. And Addo returned in peace and offered burnt offerings and sacrifices unto his Lord, and died, and was buried in Ephrata his city.

2. And at that time the people chose Elon and made him judge over them, and he judged Israel twenty years. In those days they fought against the Philistines and took of them twelve cities. And Elon died and was buried in his city.

3. But the children of Israel forgat the Lord their God and served the gods of the dwellers in the land. Therefore were they delivered unto the Philistines and served them forty years.

CHAPTER 42

XLII. Now there was a man of the tribe of Dan, whose name was Manue, the son of Edoc, the son of Odo, the son of Eriden, the son of Phadesur, the son of Dema, the son of Susi, the son of Dan. And he had a wife whose name was Eluma, the daughter of Remac. And she was barren and bare him no child. And when Manue her husband said to her day by day: Lo, the Lord hath shut up thy womb, that thou shouldest not bear; set me free, therefore, that I may take an other wife lest I die without issue. And she said: The Lord hath not shut up me from bearing, but thee, that I should bear no fruit. And he said to her: Let the law make plain our trial.

2. And as they contended day by day and both of them were sore grieved because they lacked fruit, upon a certain night the woman went up into the upper chamber and prayed saying: Do thou, O Lord God of all flesh, reveal unto me whether unto my husband or unto me it is not given to beget children, or to whom it is forbidden or to whom allowed to bear fruit, that to whom it is forbidden, the same may mourn for his sins, because he continueth without fruit. Or if both of us be deprived, reveal this also unto us, that we may bear our sin and keep silence before thee.

3. And the Lord hearkened to her voice and sent her his angel in the morning, and said unto her: Thou art the barren one that bringeth not forth, and thou art the womb which is forbidden, to bear fruit. But now hath the Lord heard thy voice and looked upon thy tears and opened thy womb. And behold thou shalt conceive and bear a son and shall call his name Samson, for he shall be holy unto thy Lord. But take heed that he taste not of any fruit of the vine, neither eat any unclean thing, for as himself hath said, he shall deliver Israel from the hand of the Philistines. And when the angel of the Lord had spoken these words he departed from her.

4. And she came unto her husband into the house and said unto him: Lo, I lay mine hand upon my mouth and will keep silence before thee all my days, because it was in vain that I boasted myself, and believed not thy words. For the angel of the Lord came unto me to-day, and showed me, saying: Eluma, thou art barren, but thou shalt conceive and bear a son.

5. And Manue believed not his wife. And he was ashamed and grieved and went up, he also, into the upper chamber and prayed saying: Lo, I am not worthy to hear the signs and wonders which God hath wrought in us, or to see the face of his messenger.

6. And it came to pass while he thus spake, the angel of the Lord came yet again unto his wife. Now she was in the field and Manue was in his house. And the angel said unto her: Run and call unto thine husband, for God hath accounted him worthy to hear my voice.

7. And the woman ran and called to her husband, and he hasted and came unto the angel in the field in Ammo (?), which said unto him: Go in unto thy wife and do quickly all these things. But he said to him: Yet see thou to it, Lord, that thy word be accomplished upon thy servant. And he said: It shall be so.

8. And Manue said unto him: If I were able, I would persuade thee to enter into mine house and eat bread with me, and know that when thou goest away I would give thee gifts to take with thee that thou mightest offer a sacrifice unto the Lord thy God. And the angel said unto him: I will not go in with thee into thine house, neither eat thy bread, neither will I receive thy gifts. For if thou offerest a sacrifice of that which is not thine, I can not show favour unto thee.

9. And Manue built an altar upon the rock, and offered sacrifices and burnt offerings. And it came to pass when he had cut up the flesh and laid it upon the holy place, the angel put forth *his hand* and touched it with the end of his sceptre. And there came forth fire out of the rock and consumed the burnt offerings and sacrifices. And the angel went up from him with the flame of the fire.

10. But Manue and his wife when they saw that, fell upon their faces and said: We shall surely die, because we have seen the Lord face to face. And it sufficed *me* not that I saw him, but I did also ask, his name, knowing not that he was the minister of God. Now the angel that came was called Phadahel.

Chapter 43

XLIII. And it came to pass in the time of those days, that Eluma conceived and bare a son and called his name Samson. And the Lord was with him. And when he was begun to grow up, and sought to fight against the Philistines, he took him a wife of the Philistines. And the Philistines burned her with fire, for they were brought very low by Samson.

2. And after that Samson entered into (*or* was enraged against) Azotus. And they shut him in and compassed the city about and said: Behold, now is our adversary delivered into our hands. Now therefore let us gather ourselves together and succour the souls one of another. And when Samson was arisen in the night and saw the city closed in he said: Lo, now, these fleas have shut me up in their city. And now shall the Lord be with me, and I will go forth by their gates and fight against them.

3. And he went and set his left hand under the bar of the gate and shook it and threw down the gate of the wall. One of the gates he held in his right hand for a shield, and the other he laid upon his shoulders and bare it away, and because he had no sword he pursued after the Philistines with it, and killed therewith 25,000 men. And he lifted up all the purtenances of the gate and set them up on a mountain.

4. Now concerning the lion which he slew, and the jawbone of the ass wherewith he smote the Philistines, and the bands which he brake off from his arms as it were of themselves, and the foxes which he caught, are not these things written in the book of the Judges?

5. Then Samson went down unto Gerara, a city of the Philistines, and saw there an harlot whose name was Dalila, and was led away after her, and took her to him to wife. And God said: Behold, now Samson is led astray by his eyes and hath forgotten the mighty works which I have wrought with him, and is mingled with the daughters of the Philistines, and hath not considered my servant Joseph which was in a strange land and became a crown unto his brethren because he would not afflict his seed. Now therefore shall his concupiscence be a stumbling-block unto Samson, and his mingling shall be his destruction, and I will deliver him to his enemies and they shall blind him. Yet in the hour of his death will I remember him, and will avenge him yet once upon the Philistines.

6. And after these things his wife was importunate unto him, saying unto him: Show me thy strength, and wherein is thy might. So shall I know that thou lovest me. And when Samson had deceived her three times, and she continued importunate unto him every day, the fourth time he showed her his heart. But she made him drunk, and when he slumbered she called a barber, and he shaved the seven locks of his head, and his might departed from him, for so had himself revealed unto her. And she called the Philistines, and they smote Samson, and blinded him, and put him in prison.

7. And it came to pass in the day of their banqueting, that they called for Samson that they might mock him. And he being-bound between two pillars prayed saying: O Lord God of my fathers, hear me yet this once, and strengthen me that I may die with these Philistines: for this sight of the eyes which they have taken from me was freely given unto me by thee. And Samson added saying: Go forth, O my soul, and be not grieved. Die, O my body, and weep not for thyself.

8. And he took hold upon the two pillars of the house and shook them. And the house fell and all that was in it and slew all them that were round about it, and the number of them was 40,000 men and women. And the brethren of Samson came down and all his father's house, and took him and buried him in the sepulchre of his father. And he judged Israel twenty years.

Chapter 44

XLIV. And in those days there was no prince in Israel: but every man did that which was pleasing in his sight.

2. At that time Michas arose, the son of Dedila the mother of Heliu, and he had 1000 drachms of gold and four wedges of molten gold, and 40 didrachms of silver. And his mother Dedila said unto him: My son, hear my voice and thou shalt make thee a name before thy death: take thou that gold and melt it, and thou shalt make thee idols, and they shall be to thee gods, and thou shalt become a priest to them.

3. And it shall be that whoso will inquire by them, they shall come to thee and thou shalt answer them. And there shall be in thine house an altar and a pillar built, and of that gold thou hast, thou shalt buy thee incense for burning and sheep for sacrifices. And it shall be that whoso will offer sacrifice, he shall give for sheep 7 didrachms, and for incense, if he will burn it, he shall give one didrachm of silver of *full* weight. And thy name shall be Priest, and thou shalt be called a worshipper of the gods.

4. And Michas said unto her: Thou hast well counselled me, my mother, how I may live: and now shall thy name be greater than my name, and in the last days these things shall be required of thee.

5. And Michas went and did all that his mother had commanded him. And he carved out and made for himself three images of boys, and of calves, and a lion and an eagle and a dragon and a dove. And it was so that all that were led astray came to him, and if any would ask for wives, they inquired of him by the dove; and if for sons, by the image of the boys: but he that would ask for riches took counsel by the likeness of the eagle, and he that asked for strength by the image of the lion: again, if they asked for men and maidens they inquired by the images of calves, but if for length of days, they inquired by the image of the dragon. And his iniquity was of many shapes, and his impiety was full of guile.

6. Therefore then, when the children of Israel departed from the Lord, the Lord said: Behold I will root out the earth and destroy all the race of men, because when I appointed great things upon mount Sina, I showed myself unto the children of Israel in the tempest and I said that they should not make idols, and they consented that they should not carve the likeness of gods. And I appointed to them they should not take my name in vain, and they chose this, even not to take my name in vain. And I commanded them to keep the sabbath day, and they consented unto me to sanctify themselves. And I said to them that they should honour their father and mother: and they promised that they would so do. And I appointed unto them not to steal, and they consented. And I bade them do no murder, and they received it, that they should not. And I commanded them not to commit adultery, and they refused not. And I appointed unto them to bear no false witness, and not to covet every man his neighbour's wife or his house or anything that is his: and they accepted it.

7. And now, whereas I spake unto them that they should not make idols, they have made the works of *all* those gods that are born of corruption by the name of *a* graven *image*. And also of them through whom all things have been corrupted. For mortal men made them, and the fire served in the melting of them: the act of men brought them forth, and hands have wrought them, and understanding contrived them. And whereas they have received them, they have taken my name in vain, and have given my name to graven images, and upon the sabbath day which they accepted, to keep it, they have wrought abominations therefrom. Because I said unto them that they should love their father and mother, they have dishonoured me their maker. And for that I said to them they should not steal, they have dealt thievishly in their understanding with graven images. And whereas I said they should not kill, they do kill them when they deceive. And when I had commanded them not to commit adultery, they have played the adulterer with their jealousy. And where they did choose not to bear false witness,

they have received false witness from them whom they cast out, and have lusted after strange women.

8. Therefore, behold, I abhor the race of men, and to the end I may root out my creation, they that die shall be multiplied above the number of them that are born. For the house of Jacob is defiled with iniquities and the impieties of Israel are multiplied and I cannot [*some words lost*] wholly destroy the tribe of Benjamin, because that they first were led away after Michas. And the people of Israel also shall not be unpunished, but it shall be to them an offence for ever to the memory of all generations.

9. But Michas will I deliver unto the fire. And his mother shall pine away in his sight, living upon the earth, and worms shall issue forth out of her body. And when they shall speak one to the other, she shall say as it were a mother rebuking her son: Behold what a sin hast thou committed. And he shall answer as it were a son obedient to his mother and dealing craftily: And thou hast wrought yet greater iniquity. And the likeness of the dove which he made shall be to put out his eyes, and the likeness of the eagle shall be to shed fire from the wings of it, and the images of the boys he made shall be to scrape his sides, and for the image of the lion which he made, it shall be unto him as mighty ones tormenting him.

10. And thus will I do not only unto Michas but to all them also that sin against me. And now let the race. of men know that they shall not provoke me by their own inventions. Neither unto them only that make idols shall this chastisement come, but it shall be to every man, that with what sin he hath sinned therewith shall he be judged. Therefore if they shall speak lies before me, I will command the heaven and it shall defraud them of rain. And if any will covet the goods of his, neighbour, I will command death and it shall deny them the fruit of their body. And if they swear by my name falsely I will not bear their prayer. And when the soul parteth from the body, then they shall say: Let us not mourn for the things which we have suffered, but because whatsoever we have devised, that shall we also receive.

Chapter 45

XLV. And it came to pass at that time that a certain man of the tribe of Levi came to Gabaon, and when he desired to abide there, the sun set. And when he would enter in there, they that dwelt there suffered him not. And he said to his lad: Go on, lead the mule, and we will go to the city of Noba, peradventure they will suffer us to enter in there. And he came thither and sat in the street of the city. And no man said unto him: Come into my house.

2. But there was there a certain Levite whose name was Bethac. The same saw him and said unto him: Art thou Beel of my tribe? And he said: I am. And he said to him: Knowest thou not the wickedness of them that dwell in this city? Who counselled thee to enter in hither? Haste and go out hence, and come into my house wherein I dwell, and abide there to-day, and the, Lord shall shut up their heart before us, as he shut up the men of Sodom before the face of Lot. And he entered into the city and abode there that night.

3. And all the dwellers in the city came together and said unto Bethac: Bring forth them that came unto thee this day, and if not we will burn them and thee with fire. And he went out unto them and said to them: Are not they our brethren? Let us not deal evilly with them, lest our sins be multiplied against us. And they answered: It was never so, that strangers should give commands to the indwellers. And they entered in with violence and took out him and his concubine and cast them forth, and they, 'Let the man go, but they abused his concubine until she died; for she had transgressed against her husband at one time by sinning with the Amalekites, and therefore did the Lord God deliver her into the hands of sinners.

4. And when it was day Beel went out and found his concubine dead. And he laid her upon the mule and hasted and went out and came to Gades. And he took her body and divided it and sent it into *all* parts (*or* by portions) throughout the twelve tribes, saying: These things were done unto me in the city of Noba, for the dwellers therein rose up against me to slay me and took my concubine and shut me up and slew her. And if this is pleasing before your face) keep ye silence, and let the Lord be judge: but if ye will avenge it, the Lord shall help you.

5. And all the men, even the twelve tribes, were confounded. And they gathered together unto Silo and said every man to his neighbour: Hath such iniquity been done in Israel?

6. And the Lord said unto the Adversary: Seest thou how this foolish people is disturbed? In the hour when they should have died, even when Michas dealt craftily to deceive the people with these, *that is*, with the dove and the eagle and with the image of men and calves and of a lion and of a dragon, then were they not moved. And therefore because they were not provoked to anger, let their counsel *now* be vain and their heart moved, that they who allow evil may be consumed as well as the sinners.

Chapter 46

XLVI. And when it was day the people of Israel were greatly moved and said: Let us go up and search out the sin that is done, that the iniquity may be taken away from us. And they spake thus, and said: Let us inquire first of the Lord and learn whether he will deliver our brethren into our hands. And if not, let us forbear. And Phinees said unto them: Let us offer the Demonstration and the Truth. And the Lord answered them and said: Go up, for I will deliver them into your hands. But he deceived them, that he might accomplish his word.

2. And they went up to battle and came to the city of Benjamin and sent messengers saying: Send us the men that have done this wickedness and we will spare you, but requite to every man his evil doing. And the people of Benjamin hardened their heart and said unto the people of Israel: Wherefore should we deliver our brethren unto you? If ye spare *them* not, we will even fight against you. And the people of Benjamin came out against the children of Israel and pursued after them, and the children of Israel fell before them and they smote of them 45,000 men.

3. And the heart of the people was very sore vexed, and they came weeping and mourning unto Silo and said: Behold, the Lord hath delivered us up before the dwellers in Noba. Now let us inquire of the Lord which among us hath sinned. And they inquired of the Lord and he said unto them: If ye will, go up and fight, and they shall be delivered into your hands; and then it shall be told you wherefore ye fell before them. And they went up the second day to fight against them. And the children of Benjamin came out and pursued after Israel and smote of them 46,000 men.

4. And the heart of the people was altogether melted and they said: Hath God willed to deceive his people? or hath he so ordained because of the evil that is done that as well the innocent should fall as they that do evil? And when they spake thus they fell down before the ark of the covenant of the Lord and rent their clothes and put ashes upon their heads both they and Phinees the son of Eleazar the priest, which prayed and said: What is this deceit wherewith thou hast deceived us, O Lord? If it be righteous before thy face which the children of Benjamin have done, wherefore didst thou not tell us, that we might consider it? But if it was not pleasing in thy sight, wherefore didst thou suffer us to fall before them?

Chapter 47

XLVII. And Phinees added and said: O God of our fathers, hear my voice, and tell thy servant this day if it is well done in thy sight, or if peradventure the people have sinned and thou wouldest destroy their evil, that thou mightest correct among us also them that have sinned against thee. For I remember in my youth when Jambri sinned in the days of Moses thy servant, and I verily entered in, and was zealous in my soul, and lifted up both of them upon my sword, and the remnant would have risen against me to put me to death, and thou sentest thine angel and didst smite of them 24,000 men and deliver me out of their hands.

2. And now thou hast sent the eleven tribes and brought them hither saying: Go and smite them. And when they went they were delivered up. And now they say that the declarations of thy truth are lying before thee. And now, O Lord God of our fathers, hide it not from thy servant, but tell us wherefore thou hast done this iniquity against us.

3. And when the Lord saw that Phinees prayed earnestly before him, he said to him: By myself have I sworn, saith the Lord, that had I not sworn, I would not have remembered thee in that thou hast spoken, neither would I have answered you this day. And now say unto the people: Stand up and hear the word of the Lord,

4. Thus saith the Lord: There was a certain mighty lion in the midst of the forest, and unto him all the beasts committed the forest that he should guard it by his power, lest perchance other beasts should come and lay it waste. And while the lion guarded it there came beasts of the field from another forest and devoured all the young of the beasts and laid waste the fruit of their body, and the lion saw it and held his peace. Now the beasts were at peace, because they had entrusted the forest unto the lion, and perceived not that their young were destroyed.

5. And after a time there arose a very small beast of those that had committed the forest unto the lion, and devoured the least of the whelps of another very evil beast. And lo, the lion cried out and stirred up all the beasts of the forest, and they fought among themselves, and every one fought against his neighbour.

6. And when many beasts were destroyed, another whelp out of another forest like unto it, saw *it*, and said: Hast thou not destroyed as many beasts? What iniquity is this, that in the beginning when many beasts and their young were destroyed unjustly by other evil beasts, and when all the beasts should have been moved to avenge themselves, seeing the fruit of their body was despoiled to no purpose, then thou didst keep silence and spakest not, but now one whelp of an evil beast hath perished, and thou hast stirred up the whole forest that all the beasts should devour one another without cause, and the forest be diminished. Now therefore thou oughtest first to be destroyed, and so the remnant be established. And when the young of the beasts heard that, they slew the lion first, and put over them the whelp in his stead, and so the rest of the beasts were subject together.

7. Michas arose and made you rich by that which he committed, both he and his mother. And there were evil things and wicked, which none devised before them, but in his subtlety he made graven images, which had not been made unto that day, and no man was provoked, but ye were all led astray, and did see the fruit of your body spoiled, and held your peace even as that evil lion.

8. And now when ye saw how that this man's concubine which suffered evil, died, ye were moved all of you and came unto me saying: Wilt thou deliver the children of Benjamin into our hands? Therefore did I deceive you and said: I will deliver them unto you. And now I have destroyed them which then held their peace, and so will I take vengeance on all that have done wickedly against me. But you, go ye up now, for I will deliver them unto you.

9. And all the people arose with one accord and went. And the children of Benjamin came out against them and thought that they would over come them as heretofore. And they knew not that their wickedness was fulfilled upon them. And when they had come on as at

first, and were pursuing after them, the people fled from the face of them to give them place, and then they arose out of their ambushes, and the children of Benjamin were in the midst of them.

10. Then they which were fleeing turned back, and the men of the city of Noba were slain, both men and women, even 85,000 men, and the children of Israel burned the city and took the spoils and destroyed all things with the edge of the sword. And no man was left of the children of Benjamin save only 600 men which fled and were not found in the battle. And all the people returned unto Silo and Phinees the son of Eleazar the priest with them.

11. Now these are they that were left of the race of Benjamin, the princes of the tribe, of ten families whose names are these: of the 1st family: Ezbaile, Zieb, Balac, Reindebac, Belloch; and of the 2nd family: Nethac, Zenip, Phenoch, Demech, Geresaraz; and of the 3rd family: Jerimuth, Veloth, Amibel, Genuth, Nephuth, Phienna; and of the 4th city: Gemuph, Eliel, Gemoth, Soleph, Raphaph, and Doffo; and of the 5th family: Anuel, Code, Fretan, Remmon, Peccan, Nabath; and of the 6th family: Rephaz, Sephet, Araphaz, Metach, Adhoc, Balinoc; and of the 7th family: Benin, Mephiz, Araph, Ruimel, Belon, Iaal, Abac; and (of) the (8th, 9th and) 10th family: Enophlasa, Melec, Meturia, Meac; and the rest of the princes of the tribe which were left, in number threescore.

12. And at that time did the Lord requite unto Michas and unto his mother all the things that he had spoken. And Michas was melted with fire and his mother was pining away, even as the Lord had spoken concerning them.

Chapter 48

XLVIII. At that time also Phinees laid himself down to die, and the Lord said unto him: Behold thou hast overpassed the 120 years that were ordained unto all men. And now arise and go hence and dwell in the mount Danaben and abide there many years, and I will command mine eagle and he shall feed thee there, and thou shalt not comedown any more unto men until the time come and thou be proved in the time. And then shalt thou shut the heaven, and at thy word it shall be opened. And after that thou shalt be lifted up into the place whither they that were before thee were lifted up, and shalt be there until I remember the world. And then will I bring you and ye shall taste what is death.

2. And Phinees went up and did all that the Lord commanded him. Now in the days when he appointed him to be priest, he anointed him in Silo.

3. And at that time, when he went up, then it came to pass that the children of Israel when they kept the passover commanded the children of Benjamin saying: Go up and take wives for yourselves by force.. because we cannot give you our daughters, for we sware in the time of our anger: and it cannot be that a tribe perish out of Israel. And the children of Benjamin went up and seized for themselves wives and built Gabaon for them selves and began to dwell there.

4. And whereas in the meanwhile the children of Israel were at rest, they had no prince in those days, and every man did that which was right in his own eyes.

5. These are the commandments and the judgments and the testimonies and the manifestations that were in the days of the judges of Israel, before a king reigned over them.

CHAPTER 49

XLIX And at that time the children of Israel began to inquire of the Lord, and said: Let us; all cast lots, that we may see who there is that can rule over us like Cenez, for peradventure we shall find a man that can deliver us from our afflictions, for it is not expedient that the people should be without a prince.

2. And they cast the lot and found no man; and the people were greatly grieved and said: The people is not worthy to be heard by the Lord, for he hath not answered us. Now therefore let us cast lots even by tribes, if perchance God will be appeased by a multitude, for we know that he will be reconciled unto them that are worthy *of him*. And they cast lots by tribes, and upon no tribe did the lot come forth. And Israel said: Let us choose one of ourselves, for we are in a strait, for we perceive that God abhorreth his people, and that his soul is displeased at us.

3. And one answered and said unto the people, whose name was Nethez: It is not he that hateth us, but we ourselves have made ourselves to be hated, that God should forsake us. And therefore, even though we die, let us not forsake him, but let us flee unto him *for refuge*; for we have walked in our evil ways and have not known him that made us, and therefore will our device be vain. For I know that God will not cast us off for ever, neither will he hate his people unto all generations: therefore now be ye strong and let us pray yet again and cast lots by cities, for although our sins be enlarged, yet will his long-suffering not fail.

4. And they cast lots by cities, and the lot came upon Armathem. And the people said: Is Armathem accounted righteous beyond all the cities of Israel, that he hath chosen her thus before all the cities? And every man said to his neighbour: In that same city which hath come forth by lot let us cast the lot by men, and let us see whom the Lord hath chosen out of her.

5. And they cast the lot by men, and it took no man save Elchana, for upon him the lot leapt out, and the people took him And said: Come and be ruler over us. And Elchana said unto the people: I cannot be a prince over this people, neither can I judge who can be a prince over you. But if my sins have found me out, that the lot should leap upon me, I will slay myself, that ye defile me not; for it is just that I should die for my *own* sins only and not have to bear the weight of the people.

6. And when the people saw that it was not the will of Elchana to take the leadership over them, they prayed again unto the Lord saying: O Lord God of Israel, wherefore hast thou forsaken thy people in the victory of the enemy and neglected thine heritage in the time of trouble? Behold even he that was taken by the lot hath not accomplished thy commandment; but only this *hath come about*, that the lot leapt out upon him, and we believed that we had a prince. And lo, he also contendeth against the lot. Whom shall we yet require, or unto whom shall we flee, and where is the place of our rest? For if the ordinances are true which thou madest with our fathers, saying: I will enlarge your seed, and they shall know of this, then it were better that thou saidst to us, I will cut off your seed, than that thou shouldest have no regard to our root.

7. And God said unto them: If indeed I recompensed you according to your evil deeds, I ought not to give ear unto your people; but what shall I do, because my name cometh to be called upon you? And now know ye that Elchana upon whom the lot hath fallen cannot rule over you, but it is rather his son that shall be born of him; he shall be prince over you and shall prophesy; and from henceforth there shall not be wanting unto you a prince for many years.

8. And the people said: Behold, Lord, Elchana hath ten sons, and which of them shall be a prince or shall prophesy? And God said: Not any of the sons of Phenenna can be a prince over the people, but he that is born of the barren woman whom I have given him to wife, he shall be a prophet before me, and I will love him even as I loved Isaac, and his name

shall be before me for ever. And the people said: Behold now, it may be that God hath remembered us, to deliver us from the hand of them that hate us. And in that day they offered peace offerings and feasted in their orders.

Chapter 50

L. Now [whereas] Elchana had two wives, the name of the one was Anna and the name of the other Phenenna. And because Phenenna had sons, and Anna had none, Phenenna reproached her, saying: What profiteth it thee that Elchana thine husband loveth thee? but thou art a dry tree. I know moreover that he will love me, because he delighteth to see my sons standing about him like the planting of an oliveyard.

2. And so it was, when she reproached her every day, and Anna was very sore at heart, and she feared God from her youth, it came to pass when the good day of the passover drew on, and her husband went up to do sacrifice, that Phenenna reviled Anna saying: A woman is not *indeed* beloved even if her husband love her or her beauty. Let not Anna therefore boast herself of her beauty, but he that boasteth let him boast when he seeth his seed before his face; and when it is not so among women, even the fruit of their womb, then shall love become of no account. For what profit was it unto Rachel that Jacob loved her? except there had been given her the fruit of her womb, *surely* his love would have been to no purpose? And when Anna heard that, her soul was melted within her and *her eyes* ran down with tears.

3. And her husband saw her and said: *Wherefore art thou sad, and eatest not, and why is thy heart within thee cast down*? Is not thy behaviour better than the ten sons of Phenenna? And Anna hearkened to him and arose after she had eaten, and came unto Silo to the house of the Lord where Heli the priest abode, whom Phinees the son of Eleazar the priest had presented as it was commanded him.

4. And Anna prayed and said: Hast not thou, O Lord, examined the heart of all generations before thou formedst the world? But what is the womb that is born open, or what one that is shut up dieth, except thou will it? And now let my prayer go up before thee this day, lest I go down hence empty, for thou knowest my heart, how I have walked before thee from the days of my youth.

5. And Anna would not pray aloud as do all men, for she took thought at that time saying: Lest perchance I be not worthy to be heard, and it shall be that Phenenna will envy me yet more and reproach me as she daily saith: Where is thy God in whom thou trustest? And I know that it is not she that hath many sons that is enriched, neither she that lacketh them is poor, but whoso aboundeth in the will of God, she is enriched. For they that know for what I have prayed, if they perceive that I am not heard in my prayer, will blaspheme. And I shall not only have a witness in mine own soul, for my tears also are handmaidens of my prayers.

6. And as she prayed, Heli the priest, seeing that she was afflicted in her mind and carried herself like one drunken, said unto her: Go, put away thy wine from thee. And she said: Is my prayer so heard that I am called drunken? *Verily* I am drunken with sorrow and have drunk the cup of my weeping.

7. And Heli the priest said unto her: Tell me thy reproach. And she said unto him: I am the wife of Elchana, and because God hath surely shut up my womb, therefore I prayed before him that I might not depart out of this world unto him Without fruit, neither die without leaving mine own image. And Heli the priest said unto her: Go, for I know wherefore thou hast prayed, and. thy prayer is heard.

8. But Heli the priest would not tell her that a prophet was foreordained to be born of her: for he had heard when the Lord spake concerning him. And Anna came unto her house, and was consoled of her sorrow, *yet* she told no man of that for which she had prayed.

CHAPTER 51

LI. And in the time of those days she conceived and bare a son and called his name Samuel, which is interpreted Mighty, according as God called his name when he prophesied of him. And Anna sat and gave suck to the child until he was two years old, and when she had weaned him, she went up with him bearing gifts in her hands, and the child was very fair and the Lord was with him.

2. And Anna set the child before the face of Heli and said unto him: This is the desire which I desired, and this is the request which I sought. And Heli said unto her: Not thou only didst seek it, but the people *also* prayed for this. It is not thy request alone, but it was promised aforetime unto the tribes; and by this child is thy womb justified, that thou shouldest set up prophecy before the people, and appoint the milk of thy breasts for a fountain unto the twelve tribes.

3. And when Anna heard that, she prayed and said: Come ye at my voice, all ye peoples, and give ear unto my speech, all ye kingdoms, for my mouth is opened that I may speak, and my lips are commanded that I may sing praises unto the Lord. Drop, O my breasts, and give forth your testimonies, for it is appointed to you to give suck. For he shall be set up that is suckled by you, and by his words shall the people be enlightened, and he shall shew unto the nations their boundaries, and his horn shall be greatly exalted.

4. And therefore will I utter my words openly, for out of me shall arise the ordinance of the Lord, and all men shall find the truth. Haste ye not to talk proudly, neither to utter high words out of your mouth, but delight yourselves in boasting when the light shall come forth out of which wisdom shall be born, that they be not called rich which have most possessions, neither they that have borne abundantly be termed mothers: for the barren hath been satisfied, and she that was multiplied in sons is become empty;

5. For the Lord killeth with judgement, and quickeneth in mercy: for the ungodly are in this world: therefore quickeneth he the righteous when he will, but the ungodly he will shut up in darkness. But unto the righteous he preserveth their light, and when the ungodly are dead, then shall they perish, and when the righteous are fallen asleep, then shall they be delivered. And so shall all judgement endure until he be revealed which holdeth *it*.

6. Speak thou, speak thou, O Anna, and keep not silence: sing praises, O daughter of Bathuel, be cause of thy wonders which God hath wrought with thee. Who is Anna, that a prophet should come out of her? or who is the daughter of Bathuel, that she should bring forth a light foil the peoples? Arise thou also, Elchana, and gird up thy loins. Sing praises for the signs of the Lord: For of thy son did Asaph prophesy in the wilderness saying: *Moses and Aaron among his priests and Samuel among them*. Behold the word is accomplished and the prophecy come to pass. And these things endure thus, until they give an horn unto his anointed, and power cleaveth unto the throne of his king. Yet let my son stand here and minister, until there arise a light unto this people.

7. And they departed thence and set forth with mirth, rejoicing and exulting in heart for all the glory that God had wrought with them. But the people went down with one accord unto Silo with timbrels and dances, with lutes and harps, and came unto Heli the priest and offered Samuel unto him, whom they set before the face of the Lord and anointed him and said: Let the prophet live among the people, and let him be long a light unto this nation.

Chapter 52

LII. But Samuel was a very young child and knew nothing of all these things. And whilst he served before the Lord, the two sons of Heli, which walked not in the ways of their fathers, began to do wickedly unto the people and multiplied their iniquities. And they dwelt hard by the house of Bethac, and when the people came together to sacrifice, Ophni and Phinees came and provoked the people to anger, seizing the oblations before the holy things were offered unto the Lord.

2. And this thing pleased not the Lord, neither the people, nor their father. And their father spake thus unto them: What is this report that I hear of you? Know ye not that I have received the place that Phinees committed unto me? And if we waste that we have received, what shall we say if he that committed it require it again, and vex us for that which he committed *unto us*? Now therefore make straight your ways, and walk in good paths, and your deeds shall endure. But if ye gainsay *me* and refrain not from your evil devices, ye will destroy yourselves, and the priesthood will be in vain, and that which was sanctified will come to nought. And then will they say: To no purpose did the rod of Aaron spring up, and the flower that was born of it is come to nothing.

3. Therefore while ye are yet able, my sons, correct that ye have done ill, and the men against whom ye have sinned will pray for you. But if ye will not, but persist in your iniquities, I shall be guiltless, and I shall not only sorrow lest (*or* and now I shall not blot out these great evils in you, lest) I hear of the day of your death before I die, but also if this befall (*or* but even if this befall not) I shall be clear of blame: and though I be afflicted, ye shall nevertheless perish.

4. And his sons obeyed him not, for the Lord had given sentence concerning them that they should die, because they had sinned: for when *their father* said to them: Repent you of your evil way, they said: When we grow old, then will we repent. And for this cause it was not given unto them that they should repent when they were rebuked of their father, because they had always been rebellious, and had wrought very unjustly in despoiling Israel. But the Lord was angry with Heli.

CHAPTER 53

LIII. But Samuel was ministering before the Lord and knew not as yet what were the oracles of the Lord: for he had not yet heard the oracles of the Lord, for he was 8 years old.

2. But when God remembered Israel, he would reveal his words unto Samuel, and Samuel did sleep in the temple of the Lord. And it came to pass when God called unto him, that he considered first, and said: Be hold now, Samuel is young that he should be (or though he be) beloved in my sight; nevertheless because he hath not yet heard the voice of the Lord, neither is he confirmed unto the voice of the Most Highest, yet is he like unto Moses my servant: but unto Moses I spake when he was 80 years old, but Samuel is 8 years old. And Moses saw the fire first and his heart was afraid. And if Samuel shall see the fire now, how shall he abide it? There fore now shall there come unto him a voice as of a man, and not as of God. And when he under standeth, then I will speak unto him as God.

3. And at midnight a voice out of heaven called him: and Samuel awoke and perceived as it were the voice of Heli, and ran unto him and spake saying: Wherefore hast thou awaked me, father? For I was afraid, because thou didst never call me in the night. And Heli said: Woe is me, can it be that an unclean spirit hath deceived my son Samuel? And he said to him: Go and sleep, for I called thee not. Nevertheless, tell me if thou remember, how often he that called thee cried. And he said: Twice. And Heli said unto him: Say now, of whose voice wast thou aware, my son? And he said: Of thine, therefore ran I unto thee.

4. And Heli said: In thee do I behold the sign that men shall have from this day forward for ever, .that if one call unto another twice in the night or at noonday, they shall know that it is an evil spirit. But if he call a third time, they shall know that it is an angel. And Samuel went away and slept.

5. And he heard the second time a voice from heaven, and he arose and ran unto Heli and said unto him: Wherefore called he me, for I heard the voice of Elchana my father? Then did Heli under stand that God did begin to call him. And Heli said: In those two voices wherewith God hath called unto thee, he likened himself to thy father and to thy master, but now the third time *he will speak as* God.

6. And he said unto him: With thy right ear attend and with thy left refrain. For Phinees the priest commanded us, saying: The right ear heareth the Lord by night, and the left ear an angel. Therefore, if thou hear with thy right ear, say thus: Speak what thou wilt, for I hear thee, for thou hast formed me; but if thou hear with the left ear, come and tell me. And Samuel went away and slept as Heli had commanded him.

7. And the Lord added and spake yet a third time, and the right ear of Samuel was filled *with the voice*. And when he perceived that the speech of his father had come down unto him, Samuel turned upon his other side, and said: If I be able, speak, for thou hast formed me (*or* knowest well concerning me).

8. And God said unto him: Verily I enlightened the house of Israel in Egypt and chose unto me at that time Moses my servant for a prophet, and by him I wrought wonders for my people, and avenged them of mine enemies as I would, and I took my people into the wilderness, and enlightened them as they beheld.

9. And when one tribe rose up against another tribe, saying: Wherefore are the priests alone holy? I would not destroy them, but I said unto them: Give ye every one his rod, and it shall be that he whose rod flourisheth I have chosen him for the priesthood. And when they had all given their rods as I commanded, then did I command the earth of the tabernacle that the rod of Aaron should flourish, that his line might be manifested for many days. And now they which did flourish have abhorred my holy things.

10. Therefore, lo, the days shall come that I will cut off (*lit.* stop) the flower that came forth at that time, and I will go forth against them because they do transgress the word which I spake unto my servant Moses, saying: *If thou meet with a nest, thou shalt not take the*

mother with the young, therefore it shall befall them that the mothers shall die with the children, and the fathers perish with the sons.

11. And when Samuel heard these words his heart was melted, and he said: Hath it thus come against me in my youth that I should prophesy unto the destruction of him that fostered me? and how then was I granted at the request of my mother? and who is he that brought me up? how hath he charged me to bear evil tidings?

12. And Samuel arose in the morning and would not tell it unto Heli. And Heli said unto him: Hear now, my son. Behold, before thou wast born God promised Israel that he would send thee unto them to prophesy. And now, when thy mother came hither and prayed, for she knew not that which had been done, I said unto her: Go forth, for that which shall be born of thee shall be a son unto me. Thus spake I unto thy mother, and thus hath the Lord directed thy way. And even if thou chasten thy nursing-father, as the Lord liveth, hide thou not from me the things that thou hast heard.

13. Then Samuel was, afraid, and told him all the words that he had heard. And he said: *Can the thing formed answer him that formed it*? So also can I not answer when he will take away that which he hath given, even the faithful giver, the holy one which hath prophesied, for I am subject unto his power.

Chapter 54

LIV. And in those days the Philistines assembled their camp to fight against Israel, and the children of Israel went out to fight with them. And when the people of Israel had been put to flight in the first battle, they said: Let us bring up the ark of the covenant of the Lord, peradventure it Will fight with us, because in it are the testimonies of the Lord which he ordained unto our fathers in Oreb.

2. And as the ark went up with them, when it was come into the camp, the Lord thundered and said: This time shall be likened unto that which was in the wilderness, when they took the ark without my commandment, and destruction befel them. So also, at this time, shall the people fall, and the ark shall be taken, that I may punish the adversaries of my people because of the ark, and rebuke my people because they have sinned.

3. And when the ark was come into the battle, the Philistines went forth to meet the children of Israel, and smote them. And there was there a certain Golia, a Philistine, which came even unto the ark, and Ophni and Phinees the sons of Heli and Saul the son of Cis held the ark. And Golia took *it* with his left hand and slew Ophni and Phinees.

4. But Saul, because he was light on his feet, fled from before him; and he rent his clothes, Sam. and put ashes on his head, and came unto Heli the priest. And Heli said unto him: Tell me what hath befallen in the camp? And Saul said unto him: Why askest thou me these things? for the people is overcome, and God hath forsaken Israel. Yea, and the priests also are slain with the sword, and the ark is delivered unto the Philistines.

5. And when Heli heard of the taking of the ark, he said: Behold, Samuel prophesied of me and my sons that we should die together, but the ark he named not unto me. And now the testimonies are delivered up unto the enemy, and what can I more say? Behold, Israel is perished from the truth, for the judgements are taken away from him. And because Heli despaired wholly, he fell off from his seat. And they died in one day, even Heli and Ophni and Phinees his sons.

6. And Heli's son's wife sat and travailed; and when she heard these things, all her bowels were melted. And the midwife said unto her: Be of good cheer, neither let thy soul faint, for a son is born to thee. And she said to her: Lo now is one soul born and we four die, that is, my father and his two sons and his daughter-in-law. And she called his name, Where is the glory? saying: The glory of God is perished in Israel because the ark of the Lord is taken captive. And when she had thus said she gave up the ghost.

CHAPTER 55

LV. But Samuel knew nothing of all these things, because three days before the battle God sent him *away*, saying unto him: Go and look upon the place of Arimatha, there shall be thy dwelling. And when Samuel heard what had befallen Israel, he came and prayed unto the Lord) saying: Behold, now, in vain is understanding denied unto me that I might see the destruction of my people. And now I fear lest my days grow old in evil and my years be ended in sorrow, for whereas the ark of the Lord is not with me, why should I yet live?

2. And the Lord said unto him: Be not grieved, Samuel, that the ark is taken away. I will bring it again, and them that have taken it will I overthrow, and will avenge my people of their enemies. And Samuel said: Lo, even if thou avenge them in time, according to thy longsuffering, yet what shall we do which die now? And God said to him: Before thou diest thou shalt see the end which I will bring upon mine enemies, whereby the Philistines shall perish *and shall be slain* by scorpions and by all manner of noisome creeping things.

3. And when the Philistines had set the ark of the Lord that was taken in the temple of Dagon their god, and were come to enquire of Dagon concerning their going forth, they found him fallen on his face and his hands and feet laid before the ark. And they went forth on the first morning, having crucified his priests. And on the second day they came and found as on the day before, and the destruction was greatly multiplied among them.

4. Therefore the Philistines gathered together in Accaron, and said every man to his neighbour: Behold now, we see that the destruction is enlarged among us, and the fruit of our body perisheth, for the creeping things that are sent upon us destroy them that are with child and the sucklings and them also that give suck. And they said: Let us see wherefore the hand of the Lord is strong against us. Is it for the ark's sake? for every day is our god found fallen upon his face before the ark, and we have slain our priests to no purpose once and again.

5. And the wise men of the Philistines said: Lo, now by this may we know if the Lord have sent destruction upon us for his ark's sake or if a chance affliction is come upon us for a season?

6. And now, whereas all that are with child and give suck die, and they that give suck are made childless, and they, that are suckled perish, we also will take kine that give suck and yoke them to a new cart, and set the ark upon it, and shut up the young of the kine. And it shall be, if the kine indeed go forth, and turn not back to their young, we shall know that we have suffered these things for the ark's sake; but if they refuse to go, yearning after their young, we shall know that the time of our fall is come upon us.

7. And certain of the wise men and diviners answered: Assay ye not only this, but let us set the kine at the head of the three ways that are about Accaron. For the middle way leadeth to Accaron, and the way on the right hand to Judæa, and the way on the left hand to Samaria. And direct ye the kine that bear the ark in the middle way. And if they set forth by the right-hand way straight unto Judæa, we shall know that of a truth the God of the Jews hath laid us waste; but if they go by those other ways, we shall know that an evil (*lit.* mighty) time hath befallen us, for now have we denied our gods.

8. And the Philistines took milch kine and yoked them to a new cart and set the ark thereon, and set them at the head of the three ways, and their young they shut up at home. And the kine, albeit they lowed and yearned for their young, went forward nevertheless by the right-hand way that leadeth to Judæa. And then they knew that for the ark's sake they were laid waste.

9. And all the Philistines assembled and brought the ark again unto Silo with timbrels and pipes and dances. And because of the noisome creeping things that laid them waste, they made seats of gold and sanctified the ark.

10. And in that plaguing of the Philistines, the number was of them that died being with child 75,000, and of the sucking children 65,000, and of them that gave suck 55,000, and of men 25,000. And the land had rest seven years.

Chapter 56

LVI. And at that time the children of Israel required a king in their Just. And they gathered together unto Samuel, and said: Behold, now, thou art grown old, and thy sons walk not in the ways of the Lord; now, therefore, appoint a king over us to judge betwixt us, for the word is fulfilled which Moses spake unto our fathers in the wilderness, saying: Thou shalt surely appoint over thee a prince of your brethren.

2. And when Samuel heard mention of the kingdom, he was sore grieved in his heart, and said: Behold now I see that there is no more (*or* not yet) for us a time of a perpetual kingdom, neither of building the house of the Lord our God, inasmuch as these desire a king before the time. And now, if the Lord refuse it altogether (*or* But even if the Lord so will), it seemeth unto me that a king cannot be established.

3. And the Lord said unto him in the night: Be not grieved, for I will send them a king which shall lay them waste, and he himself shall be laid waste thereafter. Now he that shall come unto thee to-morrow at the sixth hour, he it is that shall reign over them.

4. And on the next day, Saul, the son of Cis, was coming from Mount Effrem, seeking the asses of his father; and when he was come to Armathem, he entered in to inquire of Samuel for the asses. Now he was walking hard by Baam, and Saul said unto him: Where is he that seeth? For at that time a prophet was called Seer. And Samuel said unto him: I am he that seeth. And he said: Canst thou tell me of the asses of my father? for they are lost.

5. And Samuel said unto him: Refresh thyself with me this day, and in the morning I will tell thee that whereof thou camest to inquire. And Samuel said unto the Lord: Direct, O Lord, thy people, and reveal unto me what thou hast determined concerning them. And Saul refreshed himself with Samuel that day and rose in the morning. And Samuel said unto him: Behold, know thou that the Lord hath chosen thee to be prince over his people at this time, and hath raised up thy ways, and thy time shall be directed.

6. And Saul said to Samuel: Who am 1, and what is my father's house, that my lord should speak thus unto me? For I understand not what thou sayest, because I am a youth. And Samuel said to Saul: Who will grant that thy word should come even unto accomplishment of itself, that thou mayest live many days? but consider this, that thy words shall be likened unto the words of a prophet, whose name shall be Hieremias.

7. And as Saul went away that day, the people came unto Samuel, saying: Give us a king as thou didst promise us. And he said to them: Behold, the king shall come unto you after three days. And lo, Saul came. And there befell him all the signs which Samuel had told him. Are not these things written in the book of the Kings?

Chapter 57

LVII. And Samuel sent and gathered all the people, and said unto them: Lo, ye and your king *are here*, and I am betwixt you, as the Lord commanded me.

2. And therefore I say unto you, before the face of your king, even as my lord Moses; the servant of God, said unto your fathers in the wilderness, when the synagogue of Core arose against him: Ye know that I have not taken aught of you, neither have I wronged any of you; and because certain lied at that time and said, Thou didst take, the earth swallowed them up.

3. Now, therefore, do ye whom the Lord hath not punished answer before the Lord and before his anointed, if it be for this cause that ye have required a king, because I have evil entreated you, and the Lord shall be your witness. But if, now the word of the Lord is fulfilled, I am free, and my father's house.

4. And the people answered: We are thy servants and our king with us; because we are unworthy to be judged by a prophet, therefore said we: Appoint a king over us to judge us. And all the people and the king wept with a great lamentation, and said: Let Samuel the prophet live. And when the king was appointed they offered sacrifices unto the Lord.

5. And after that Saul fought with the Philistines one year, and the battle prospered greatly.

CHAPTER 58

LVIII. And at that time the Lord said unto Samuel: Go and say unto Saul: Thou art sent to destroy Amalech, that the words may be fulfilled which Moses my servant spake saying: I will destroy the name of Amalech out of the land whereof I spake in mine anger. And forget not to destroy every soul of them as it is commanded thee.

2. And Saul departed and fought against Amalech, and , saved alive Agag the king of Amalech because he said to him: I will shew thee hidden treasures. Therefore he spared him and saved him alive and brought him unto Armathem.

3. And God said unto Samuel: Hast thou seen how the king is corrupted with money even in a moment, and hath saved alive Agag king of Amalech and his wife? Now therefore suffer Agag and his wife to come together this night, and to-morrow thou shalt slay him; but his wife they shall preserve till she bring forth a male child, and then she also shall die, and he that is born of her shall be an offence unto Saul. But thou, arise on the morrow and slay Agag: for the sin of Saul is written before my face alway.

4 And when Samuel was risen on the morrow, Saul came forth to meet him and said unto him: The Lord hath delivered our enemies into our hands as he said. And Samuel said to Saul: Whom hath Israel wronged? for before the time was come that a king should rule over him, he demanded thee for his king, and thou, when thou wast sent to do the will of the Lord, hast transgressed it. Therefore he that was saved alive by thee shall die now, and those hidden treasures whereof he spake he shall not show thee, and he that is born of him shall be an offence unto thee. And Samuel came unto Agag with a sword and slew him, and returned unto his house.

Chapter 59

LIX. And the Lord said unto him: Go, anoint him whom I shall tell thee, for the time is fulfilled wherein his kingdom shall come. And. Samuel said: Lo, wilt thou now blot out the kingdom of Saul? And he said: I will blot it out.

2. And Samuel went forth unto Bethel, and sanctified the elders, and Jesse, and his sons. And Eliab the firstborn of Jesse came. And Samuel said: Behold now the holy one, the anointed of the Lord. And the Lord said unto him: Where is thy vision which thine heart hath seen? Art not thou he that saidst unto Saul: I am he that seeth? And how knowest thou not whom thou must anoint? And now let this rebuke suffice thee, and seek out the shepherd, the least of them all, and anoint him.

3. And Samuel said unto Jesse: Hearken, Jesse, send and bring hither thy son from the flock, for him hath God chosen. And Jesse sent and brought David, and Samuel anointed him in the midst of his brethren. And the Lord was with him from that day *forward*.

4. Then David began to sing this psalm, and said: In the ends of the earth will I begin to glorify *him*, and unto everlasting days will I sing praises. Abel at the first when he fed the sheep, his sacrifice was acceptable rather than his brother's. And his brother envied him and slew him. But it is not so with me, for God hath kept me, and hath delivered me unto his angels and his watchers to keep me, for my brethren envied me, and my father and my mother made me of no account, and when the prophet came they called not for me, and when the Lord's anointed was proclaimed they forgat me. But God came near unto me with his right hand, and with his mercy: therefore will I not cease to sing praises all the days of my life.

5. And as David yet spake, behold a fierce lion out of the wood and a she-bear out of the mountain took the bulls of David. And David said: Lo, this shall be a sign unto me for a mighty beginning of my victory in the battle. I will go out after them and deliver that which is carried off and will slay them. And David went out after them and took stones out of the wood and slew them. And God said unto him: Lo, by stones have I delivered thee these beasts in thy sight. And this shall be a sign unto thee that hereafter thou shalt slay with stones the adversary of my people.

Chapter 60

LX. And at that time the spirit of the Lord was taken away from Saul, and an evil spirit oppressed (*lit.* choked) him. And Saul sent and fetched David, and he played a psalm upon his harp in the night. And this is the psalm which he sang unto Saul that the evil spirit might depart from him.

2. There were darkness and silence before the world was, and the silence spake, and the darkness became visible. And then was thy name created, even at the drawing together of that which was stretched out, whereof the upper was called heaven and the lower was called earth. And it was commanded to the upper that it should rain according to its season, and to the lower that it should bring forth food for man that *should be* made. And after that was the tribe of your spirits made.

3. Now therefore, be not injurious, whereas thou art a second creation, but if not, then remember Hell (*lit.* be mindful of Tartarus) wherein thou walkedst. Or is it not enough for thee to hear that by that which resoundeth before thee I sing unto many? Or forgettest thou that out of a rebounding echo in the abyss (*or* chaos) thy creation was born? But that new womb shall rebuke thee, whereof I am born, of whom shall be born after a time of my loins he that shall subdue you. And when David sung praises, the spirit spared Saul.

CHAPTER 61

LXI. And after these things the Philistines came to fight against Israel. And David was returned to the wilderness to feed his sheep, and the Madianites came and would have taken his sheep, and he came down unto them and fought against them and slew of them 15,000 men. This is the first battle that David fought, being in the wilderness.

2. And there came a man out of the camp of the Philistines by name Golia, and he looked upon Saul and upon Israel and said: Art not thou Saul which fleddest before me when I took the ark from you and slew your priests? And now that thou reignest, wilt thou come down unto me like a man and a king and fight against us? If not, I will come unto thee, and will cause thee to be taken captive, and thy people to serve our gods. And when Saul and Israel heard that, they feared greatly. And the Philistine said: According to the number of the days wherein Israel feasted when they received the law in the wilderness, even 40 days, I will reproach them, and after that I will fight with them.

3. And it came to pass when the 40 days were fulfilled, and David was come to see the battle of his brethren, that he heard the words which the Philistine spake, and said: Is this *peradventure* the time whereof God said unto me: I will deliver the adversary of my people into thy hand by stones?

4. And Saul heard these words and sent and took him and said: What was the speech which thou spakest unto the people? And David said: Fear not, O king, for I will go and fight against the Philistine, and God will take away the hatred and reproach from Israel.

5. And David went forth and took 7 stones and wrote upon them the names of his fathers, Abraham, Isaac, and Jacob, Moses and Aaron, and his own name, and the name of the Most Mighty. And God sent Cervihel, the angel that is over strength.

6. And David went forth unto Golia and said unto him: Hear a word before thou diest. Were not the two women of whom thou and I were born sisters? and thy mother was Orpha and my mother was Ruth. And Orpha chose for herself the gods of the Philistines and went after them, but Ruth chose for herself the ways of the Most Mighty and walked in them. And now thou and thy brethren are born of Orpha, and as thou art arisen this day and come to lay Israel waste, behold, I also that am born of thy kindred am come to avenge my people. For thy three brethren also shall fall into my hands after thy death. And then shall ye say unto your mother: He that was born of thy sister hath not spared us.

7. And David put a stone in his sling and smote the Philistine in his forehead, and ran upon him and drew his sword out of the sheath and took his head from him. And Golia said unto him while his life was yet in him: Hasten and slay me and rejoice.

8. And David said unto him: Before thou diest, open thine eyes and behold thy slayer which hath killed thee. And the Philistine looked and saw the angel and said: Thou hast not killed me by thyself, but he that was with thee, whose form is not as the form of a man. And then David took his head from him.

9. And the angel of the Lord lifted up the face of David and no man knew him. And when Saul saw David he asked him who he was, and there was no man that knew him who he was.

Chapter 62

LXII. And after these things Saul envied David and sought to kill him. But David and Jonathan, Saul's son, made a covenant together. And when David saw that Saul sought to kill him, he fled unto Armathem; and *Saul* went out after him.

2. And the spirit abode in Saul, and he prophesied, saying: Why art thou deceived, O Saul, or whom dost thou persecute in vain? The time of thy kingdom is fulfilled. Go unto thy place, for thou shalt die and David shall reign. Shalt not thou and thy son die together? And then shall the kingdom of David appear. And the spirit departed from Saul, and he knew not what he had prophesied.

3. But David came unto Jonathan and said unto him: Come and let us make a covenant before we be parted one from the other. For Saul, thy father, seeketh to slay me without cause. And since he hath perceived that thou lovest me he telleth thee not what he deviseth concerning me.

4. But for this cause he hateth me, because thou lovest me, and lest I should reign in his stead. And whereas I have done him good he requiteth me with evil. And whereas I slew Golia by the word of the Most Mighty, see thou what an end he purposeth for me. For he hath determined concerning my father's house, to destroy it. And would that the judgement of truth might be put in the balance, that the multitude of the prudent might hear the sentence.

5. And now I fear lest he kill me and lose his own life for my sake. For he shall never shed innocent blood without punishment. Wherefore should my soul suffer persecution? For I was the, least among my brethren, feeding the sheep, and wherefore am I in peril of death? For I am righteous and have none iniquity. And wherefore doth thy father hate me? Yet the righteousness of my father shall help me that I fall not into thy father's hands. And seeing I am young and tender of age, it is to no purpose that Saul envieth me.

6. If I had wronged him, I would pray him to forgive me the sin. For if God forgiveth iniquity, how much more thy father who is flesh and blood? I have walked in his house with a perfect heart, yea, I grew up before his face like a swift eagle, I put mine hands unto the harp and blessed him in songs, and he hath devised to slay me, and like a sparrow that fleeth before the face of the hawk, so have I fled before his face.

7. Unto whom have I spoken this, or unto whom have I told the things that I have suffered save unto thee and Melchol thy sister? For as for both of us, let us go together in truth.

8. And it were better, my brother, that I should be slain in battle than that I should fall into the hands of thy father: for in the battle mine eyes were looking on every side that I might defend him from his enemies. O my brother Jonathan, hear my words, and if there be iniquity in me, reprove me.

9. And Jonathan answered and said: Come unto me, my brother David, and I will tell thee thy righteousness. My soul pineth away sore at thy sadness because now we are parted one from another. And this have our sins compelled, that we should be parted from one another. But let us remember one another day and night while we live. And even if death part us, yet I know that our souls will know one another. For thine is the kingdom in this world, and of thee shall be the beginning of the kingdom, and it cometh in its time.

10. And now, like a child that is weaned from its mother, even so shall be our separation. Let the heaven be witness and let the earth be witness of those things which we have spoken together. And let us weep each with the other and Jay up our tears in one vessel and commit the vessel to the earth, and it shall be a testimony unto us.

11. And they bewailed each one the other sore, and kissed one another. But Jonathan feared and said unto David: Let us remember, O my brother, the covenant that is made betwixt us, and the oath which is set in our heart. And if I die before thee and thou indeed reign, as the Lord hath spoken, be not mindful of the anger of my father, but of the covenant which is made

betwixt me and thee. Neither think upon the hatred wherewith my father hateth thee in vain but upon my love wherewith I have loved thee. Neither think upon that wherein my father was unthankful unto thee, but remember the table whereat we have eaten together. Neither keep in mind the envy wherewith my father envied thee evilly, but the faith which I and thou keep. Neither care thou for the lie wherewith Saul hath lied, but for the oaths that we have sworn one to another. And they kissed one another. And after that David departed into the wilderness, and Jonathan went into the city.

Chapter 63

LXIII. At that time the priests that dwelt in Noba were polluting the holy things of the Lord and making the firstfruits a reproach unto the people. And God was wroth and said: Behold, I will wipe out the priests that dwell in Noba, because they walk in the ways of the sons of Heli.

2. And at that time came Doech the Syrian, which was over Saul's mules, unto Saul and said unto him: Knowest thou not that Abimelec the priest taketh counsel with David and hath given him a sword and sent him away in peace? And Saul sent and called Abimelec and said unto him: Thou shalt surely die, because thou hast taken counsel with mine enemy. And Saul slew Abimelec and all his father's house, and there was not so much as one of his tribe delivered save only Abiathar his son. The same came to David and told him all that had befallen him.

3. And God said: Behold, in the year when Saul began to reign, when Jonathan had sinned and he would have put him to death, this people rose up and suffered him not, and now when the priests were slain, even 385 men, they kept silence and said nothing. Therefore, lo, the days shall come quickly that I will deliver them into the hands of their enemies and they shall fall down wounded, they and their king.

4. And unto Doech the Syrian thus said the Lord: Behold, the days shall come quickly that the worm shall come up upon his tongue and shall cause him to pine away, and his dwelling shall be with Jair for ever in the fire that is not quenched.

5. Now all that Saul did, and the rest of his words, and how he pursued after David, are they not written in the book of the kings of Israel?

6. And after these things Samuel died, and all Israel gathered together and mourned him, and buried him.

CHAPTER 64

LXIV. Then Saul took thought, saying: I will surely take away the sorcerers out of the land of Israel. So shall men remember me after my departure. And Saul scattered all the sorcerers out of the land. And God said: Behold, Saul hath taken away the sorcerers out of the land, not because of the fear of me, but that he might make himself a name. Behold, whom he hath scattered, unto them let him resort, and get divination from them, because he hath no prophets.

2. At that time the Philistines said every man to his neighbour: Behold, Samuel the prophet is dead and there is none that prayeth for Israel. David, also, which fought for them, is become Saul's adversary and is not with them. Now, therefore, let us arise and fight mightily against them, and avenge the blood of our fathers. And the Philistines assembled themselves and came *up* to battle.

3. And when Saul saw that Samuel was dead and David was not with him, his hands were loosened. And he inquired of the Lord, and he hearkened not unto him. And he sought prophets, and none appeared unto him. And Saul said unto the people: Let us seek out a diviner and inquire of him that which I have in mind. And the people answered him: Behold, now there is a woman named Sedecla, the daughter of Debin (*or* Adod) the Madianite, which deceived the people of Israel with sorceries: and lo she dwelleth in Endor.

4. And Saul put on vile raiment and went unto her, he and two men with him, by night and said unto her: Raise up unto me Samuel. And she said: I am afraid of the king Saul. And Saul said unto her: Thou shalt not be harmed of Saul in this matter. And Saul said within himself: When I was king in Israel, even though the Gentiles saw me not, yet knew they that I was Saul. And Saul asked the woman, saying: Hast thou seen Saul at any time? And she said: Oftentimes. And Saul went out and wept and said: Lo, now I know that my beauty is changed, and that the glory of my kingdom is passed from me.

5. And it came to pass, when the woman saw Samuel coming up, and beheld Saul with him, that she cried out and said: Behold, *thou art Saul, wherefore hast thou deceived me?* And he said unto her: *Fear not, but tell me what thou sawest*. And she said: Lo, these 40 years have I raised up the dead for the Philistines, but this appearance hath not been seen, neither shall it be seen hereafter.

6. And Saul said unto her: What is his form? And she said: Thou inquirest of me concerning the gods. For, behold, his form is not the form of a man. For he is arrayed in a white robe and hath a mantle upon it, and two angels leading him. And Saul remembered the mantle which Samuel had rent while he lived, and he smote his hands together and cast himself upon the earth.

7. *And Samuel said unto him: Why hast thou disquieted me to bring me up?* I thought that the time was come for me to receive the reward of my deeds. Therefore boast not thyself, O king, neither thou, O woman. For it is not ye that have brought me up, but the precept which God spake unto me while I yet lived, that I should come and tell thee that thou hadst sinned yet the second time in neglecting God. For this cause are my bones disturbed after that I had rendered up my soul, that I should speak unto thee, and that being dead I should be heard as one living.

8. Now therefore *to-morrow shalt thou and thy sons be with me*, when the people are delivered into the hands of the Philistines. And because thy bowels have been moved with jealousy, therefore that that is thine shall be taken from thee. And Saul heard the words of Samuel, and his soul melted and he said: Behold, I depart to die with my sons, if perchance my destruction may be an atonement for mine iniquities. And Saul arose and departed thence.

Chapter 65

LXV. *And the Philistines fought against Israel*. And Saul went out to battle. *And Israel fled before the Philistines*: and when Saul saw that the battle waxed hard exceedingly, he said in his heart: Wherefore strengthenest thou thyself to live, seeing, Samuel hath proclaimed death unto thee and to thy sons?

2. *And Saul said to him that bare his armour: Take thy sword and slay me before the Philistines come and abuse me. And he that bare his armour would not lay hands upon him.*

3. *And he himself bowed upon his sword*, and he could not die. *And he looked behind him and saw* a man running and called unto him and said: Take my sword and slay me. *For my life is yet in me.*

4. And he came to slay him. And Saul said unto him: Before thou kill me, tell me, who art thou? And he said unto him: I am Edab, the son of Agag king of the Amalechites. And Saul said: Behold, now the words of Samuel are come upon me even as he said: He that shall be born of Agag shall be an offence unto thee.

5. But go thou and say unto David: I have slain thine enemy. And thou shalt say unto him: Thus saith Saul: Be not mindful of my hatred, neither of mine unrighteousness. . . .

Printed in Great Britain
by Amazon